"Mam had five sons and after each birth she said
to my father, 'Right Dave, now go and register the
birth. You can choose his first name.
That would only be right, wouldn't it?
I'll choose the second name.'
And they did.

Then Mam called each of us boys, for the rest of
our lives, by our second name.

I was the second born, so my name is Lynn. I'm
not going to tell you my first name because that
would be betraying Mam.
But when I was especially bad,
or good, she called me

'Boyo.'"

The beating heart of this extraordinary novel is its realism, because it is essentially a true love story, with real people, real places, and real events.

It's a story that stretches across the world, across cultures.

It's an engrossing discovery of the extraordinary lengths to which our young Welsh protagonist is prepared to go – up and down the entire country in his bright-red sports car as he pursues his Kiwi love on her quest to win the Miss Zealand Beauty Contest.

It's a rollicking good laugh.

And, at last, we have a passionate love story from a man's point of view – a perfect antidote to "Fifty Shades of Grey".

Tender and sexy, fast-paced and hilarious, this real romp of a story has everyone rooting for our hero right to the irresistible end...

"Boyo makes that too often quoted cliché actually come true – once you start reading or watching, you can't stop till it's finished." - Mike French

What people are saying...

A wild and very funny ride! I learnt a lot about men and romance, and laughed out loud, again and again.
Jane Thomas

An incredibly honest and refreshing snapshot into life in the Sixties in Wales and New Zealand.
Terri-Ann Berry

One of the key strengths of this book is its realism – the fact that it is clearly based on a true story. And what an amazing true story!
Mike French

I loved the mother and the beef bones, Tomo and Shirt-out, Gareth and the letter vandal, in Wales, the ample tap-dancer, Morrie and the panto, the pig hunt, Nancy and the skinning disaster … oh, so many marvellous scenes and situations in New Zealand! Such great pleasure!
Natalia Valentino

About the author...

Lynn John was born and educated in Wales and now lives in New Zealand. He is a writer of screenplays, stage-plays, television series for children and parents, novels, television drama series, short films, language and drama textbooks, travel articles, opera librettos, and a children's television animation series.

He's an opera singer with New Zealand Opera. He trains male voice choirs. He was awarded a Winston Churchill Fellowship to record indigenous music in the Pacific..

BOYO
is based on real events and real people.
The names have been changed.

Sometimes truth is stranger than fiction.

DEDICATION

To Mam

Boyo

A true story of love at opposite ends of the world

A NOVEL BY
LYNN JOHN

Published by
Filament Publishing Ltd
16, Croydon Road, Beddington
Croydon, Surrey CR0 4PA
www.filamentpublishing.com
+44(0)20 8688 2598

Boyo
Lynn John
ISBN 978-1-913623-91-3
© 2022 Lynn John

Printed in the UK and worldwide

Table of Contents

ACT ONE

Wales

Chapter 1
A soft-sand beach

"It's dead."

"No, it isn't. It's just lying still."

"It's dead," said Dewi. "The bloody thing hasn't moved for five minutes. And you'd see it breathing if it was alive. Look – its mouth's shut."

"A snake doesn't breathe by opening its mouth," I said. "It breathes through slits at the side, like a gill."

"That's fish, you silly bugger. This isn't a fish."

"Righto then, fychan, pick it up!"

"Righto then, I will." Dewi licked his lips and bent closer to the snake. "Right then," he repeated. "Find me a stick to lift him up with then."

"But, he's dead. You said so. What do you want a stick for?"

"Snakes are slippery. It's a well-known fact that snakes are slippery. Just get me one, will you, while I watch him."

"Watch him?" I laughed. "Watch him? Where's he going to go if he's dead? To the snake heaven? Slip away when you aren't looking to the secret burial ground where all snakes go to die?"

"Get the bloody stick!" he yelled.

"OK, OK!" I backed off. "Do you want a long one or a short one?"

He ignored me. He was watching the snake intently. "He's only a grass snake anyway," he said to the snake. "He's not an adder.

He's got little triangles on his side, and he's lying in the grass, for God's sake, so he's a grass snake." He moved even closer to it and blew gently on it, closing his eyes after each puff. "He's harmless," he announced.

"Pick it up then."

"Right ... right then," and very slowly he stretched out his hand, finger-tipping his way over the grass towards its head. His face white.

"Wait a minute," I said. "I'll get you a stick."

He sat back on his haunches immediately, "Yeh, don't want to hurt him."

I looked up the hill towards the castle ruin. Nothing. No trees, no shrubs, just dune grass. I turned back down towards the beach. There was a bramble bush halfway down to the cliff's edge. I scrambled down the sheep runs and carefully avoiding the thorns, broke off a two-foot length of dry, brown, blackberry bramble.

Neither Dewi nor the snake had moved. He took the bramble in his right hand and slowly, gently, insinuated the point of the stick between the snake's belly and the grass. No reaction. He paused. His breathing had become loud and laboured. He was sweating. He lowered his right hand to the ground and lifted the point. The snake's body arched in the middle, humping over the stick, the hump growing inch by inch as he lifted it from the ground, and suddenly, it was free, clear of the ground, hanging limply like spaghetti on the end of a fork.

"There you are," breathed Dewi. "Dead as a doornail." He lowered the stick to the ground again and, so quickly that neither of us had time to move, the snake coiled on its tail and slithered forward through the grass towards Dewi. He let out a terrified scream and fell backwards, sprawling awkwardly, with his head facing down the slope towards the beach and the cliff. The snake disappeared under his legs.

"Don't move!" I cried. "The snake's under you."

"Aah!" he screamed, and he rolled over onto his side. No sign of the snake.

"Keep still, you bloody fool!" I yelled at him.

"Aah! Aah! It's biting me! It's biting me!" He tried to get up but only succeeded in thrashing around.

"Keep still!" and I lunged for him, holding his shoulders to the ground, pressing with all my weight. He stopped struggling and looked up at my face, pleading. His head was upside down to mine and I could see his nostrils flaring spasmodically as he dragged in air. "Good … now don't move," I ground out savagely between my teeth.

"It bit me in the arse," he breathed at me. "I felt its teeth. You'll have to suck out the poison."

"There's no way I'm sucking anything out of your arse, fychan! Anyway, it's only a grass snake. You said it was. You'll be alright."

"Don't listen to me!" he cried, "I don't know anything about snakes. I just said it was a grass snake."

"Which side?"

"Which side what?"

"Which side of your arse!"

"This side …" and he started to move his hand down his right thigh.

"Keep still you fool – I think it's still under you." He withdrew his hand quickly. I looked down his right side. No point, I thought, wouldn't see any bites anyway. They'd be too small. And then I saw it. The blackberry bramble. Stuck to his arse. Thorns embedded. And I started to laugh. There we were, poised in a grotesque ballet, and I couldn't stop the laughter welling up in me. I lost strength and sank onto his chest.

"Get off, you silly bugger!" he gasped at me. "What are you doing?"

"It's a bramble," I laughed, "you're lying on a bramble."

"What? What ...?" And he tried to twist his head uphill to see for himself.

*

WE WRAPPED UP the snake in my shirt. We tied knots in the sleeves and the neck, pushed and prodded it into the remaining opening and then Dick Whittingtoned it down the hill to the beach. I wanted to keep it. To preserve it. In a bottle like the one in the glass cabinet in the hall of my primary school. So it had to be my shirt.

We lurched ankle-deep in the soft sand until we came to the fresh water stream where it deepened in a bend before flattening out to meet the on-rushing sea. This was the best place to swim when the tide was coming in – a wrinkle- less, soft-sand beach shelving steeply into deep water and screened on three sides from the prevailing winds by high, perpendicular limestone cliffs. And no one else there. No roads. No access, except by foot over two miles of forest, valley and dunes.

We waded in the gently flowing stream, following its meandering course up the valley. You never knew what you might see. There were trout in this stream in the upper reaches of the valley, and saltwater fish when the tide was running. We passed the valley headland and looked up the length of the valley to our camp.

I could make out two figures near our tent. Bright red top one, green-blue the other. Girls. They had to be girls.

"They came! By God, they came!" exclaimed Dewi. He turned to me, "I told you they'd come."

"You mean Matti and ...'

"Sandra. Yeh, Matti and Sandra. Two right little scrubbers. I wonder if they're gonna stay the night? Hey!" and he stopped. "Sandra's mine, right? I got them here so I get first choice, agreed?"

"What if she ...?"

"No 'What ifs'. You take Matti and I'll have Sandra. No arguments then."

"But what's Matti like. I've never even seen her."

"There she is. She's got the same as any other girl – in the same places. Right? Agreed?"

"OK, OK, agreed."

And we resumed our course, Dewi leading at a fast pace, me following with the bundled snake held high, like a lantern, in front of me.

As we got close to the camp Dewi slowed down to a casual walk and they, having watched us intently from afar, sat down on their bags and began studying the burnt-out fire, the trees, and only very occasionally glancing our way.

"Hi!" said Dewi, and he turned away and walked into the tent.

"Hi!" they both said, heads bowed.

I walked over to the fire and sat down on the log facing them. I placed the stick and its bundle very carefully on the ground next to me and looked directly at them. About eighteen or nineteen. Both on the short side with those hour-glass figures that shorter girls seem to have – jutting bums and breasts. Must be because they've got to get it all in a smaller area. Which one was Matti?

"Hullo, I'm Marc."

"Yes, we know. Dewi told us." Dark one, blue eyes, wide forehead, plump fingers playing with the strap of her carry- all. "I'm Sandra, and this is Matti."

Matti looked up at me and smiled, fleetingly. Olive skin, brown eyes – almost black. Perhaps Dewi made the wrong choice after all.

"You go to University, don't you?" she asked, eyes flicking up at my face and then away again.

"I did, yes. Just finished. I start teaching in September. What do you do?"

"Work in Boots, the Chemist. We both do. The one in High Street. You know it?"

"Yes, I know it."

"Yes," she lowered her eyes again and then seeming to see the bundle for the first time, pointed at it and asked, "What's in the shirt?"

"That's an adder, a viper," said Dewi, emerging from the tent. He had put on a clean T-shirt and had Brylcreamed and combed his hair. It was slicked back. "Caught it on the hill this morning. Attacked me, it did."

"An adder?" exclaimed Sandra, but they're poisonous, aren't they?" and she drew in her feet.

"Yeh, deadly," said Dewi. "They can strike up to five or six feet. No antidote. Got to know what you're doing." He walked over to the bundle and started playing with the knots.

"Don't let it out!" screamed Sandra, rising and backing away.

Dewi jumped, startled by her scream, and stood up again. "No, I won't – don't worry – just checking the knot's tight. Marc wants to keep it, don't you Marc?"

"Yes, bottle it in brine. But we'll have to kill it first, and without damaging it."

"Well, you can do that when I'm not here," said Sandra, picking up her bags.

"'Course he will," said Dewi, and he moved to her side quickly and took one of the bags from her hand. "This is your tent, is it? I'll put it up for you."

"Oh, we're not sure we're staying yet. There's a six o'clock bus back. We only brought the tent, in case."

"'Course you're staying," said Dewi. "Over a mile lugging bags. Wouldn't be worth the effort," and with one movement he emptied the contents of the tent bag onto the ground. "Right! Let's find a nice, flat piece of ground for you," and he crabbed sideways searching with his hands. "Where's the mallet, Marc?" He looked at me appealingly.

"In the canvas bag just inside the tent," I said. "Hold on, I'll get it for you."

"No, no, I'll do it," and he darted into the tent. "Have it up in no time. You get rid of that snake and I'll put the girls' tent up." He emerged brandishing the mallet. "Righto lovelies, where do you want it?" And without waiting for them to answer, he began laying out their tent on the ground, turning the door to face the door of our tent, talking to himself the whole time.

I picked up the stick and carried the bundle to the side of the stream and laid it out on a flat rock, about three feet from the water. I untied the bundle from the stick and jiggled the shirt with my left hand and waited, poised with the stick in my right hand, for the snake's head to emerge. It seemed to be holding on, reluctant to come out, and then suddenly it fell, coiled in a tight ring, onto the stone. I transferred the stick to my left hand and took out my bone-handled knife. I thought I'd kill it with one sharp blow on the head with the heavy handle. But how hard to hit it? Between the eyes. Between its beautiful liquid eyes. Its head looked unreal, unnatural, too symmetrical, manufactured, like an expensive lizard skin belt. I couldn't hit it. I'd ruin it. Can snakes live under water?

I scooped the snake back into the shirt, laid the stick over the opening and walked back to the tent. The girl's tent was almost up. Dewi was digging a ditch around their two-man, two-girl pup tent, while the tent sides heaved with jutting buttocks as the girls tried to lay out their sleeping bags in the confined space. I picked up an empty milk bottle and waved to Dewi. He mimed patting and stroking the straining backside nearest to him and made soundless gorilla grunts.

It filled two-thirds of the bottle. I placed a large, flat pebble on the top and lowered the bottle into the stream. By lifting the edge of the pebble, I filled the bottle with water. And for the first time the snake seemed to take notice, to come alive. It twisted and writhed upwards until its head was in the air space trapped in the top of the bottle. I turned the bottle upside down and immersed it in the stream again. I had my specimen.

We shared the girl's packed sandwiches for lunch, sitting around the burnt-out fire. The specimen bottle was propped in the ashes between us. But Sandra and Matti didn't seem to be interested. They kept looking around the campsite as if searching for something, something that was missing.

"We can't see it," said Sandra.

"See what?' said Dewi.

"Your toilet."

"Our toilet!" laughed Dewi. "Of course you can see it. Right Marc?"

"Right – just look and it's there."

"Where?"

"There!" and Dewi stretched both arms wide to the bushes, hills, stream, dunes. "The trees," he said, "we hang from the branches over the gully. No mess. Natural. Use big leaves."

"Ugh! Revolting!" said Sandra. "You don't expect us to do that, do you? Hang from a tree with everyone watching?"

"Who'll be watching? We'll look the other way, won't we, Marc?"

"But it's open ... there's ... animals and things!" cried Matti.

"Animals?" Dewi and I hugged each other with laughter.

"We'll have to blindfold the sheep, dirty buggers." I gasped.

"I don't think it's funny!" snorted Sandra angrily.

"It's not," said Dewi, contorting his face to seriousness, and then he burst out laughing again, "It's not! Tell you what ... we'll jump in the water and have a swim, splash a lot and make a lot of noise and all the animals will watch us. Then you can do your business!" He hooted to the sky.

"Come on!" I yelled and ran for the stream. We lurched to the water's edge, pulling at our clothes, flinging them high and wide onto the banks and all the time yelling and whooping. And finally, bolshie naked, we jumped and splashed our way across the stream calling the rabbits, the sheep, the squirrels and the birds to watch us, to come and have a play. And they did. Well, the sheep did anyway. But Sandra and Matti didn't. They had disappeared without a trace.

We stayed in the water a long time, hoping they would reappear and be aroused by our nakedness, hoping they would join us. But the fresh water was icy cold, and we got goose-pimples, and we shrivelled, despite the excitement of it. Dewi got more shrivelled than me, and that started an argument as to who had more to start with to get shrivelled. So we got dressed. Wherever they had gone, they were a long time about it.

They came back as if they'd just visited the second left, first door on your right – back-combed, eye-shadowed, brushed and lipsticked. Ready to enjoy themselves. Ready to go out.

"There's a pub back up the road, isn't there?" asked Sandra.

"Yes, 'The Gower Inn'," said Dewi. "Why?"

"We thought you'd like to take us for a drink."

*

WE EMERGED FROM the trees into bright sunlight and turned

to look back up the hill at the two girls. They were crawling sideways down the track, placing each foot carefully on a stone while holding tightly to a tree trunk or exposed root as they shifted their weight, and talking all the time, reassuring one another, giving little 'oohs' and 'aahs' of surprise or fear as a twig snapped or a stone rolled.

"We'll get some scrumpy," said Dewi. "They won't know what hit 'em. You've drunk scrumpy, haven't you?"

"No, but I've heard it's strong."

"Strong? God's guts, it'll burn your tits off. It's cider, bottom of the barrel. Thick. Thick like syrup. Stand a spoon up in it. One glass of that stuff and you're away." He rubbed his hands together in anticipation.

"Expensive?"

"Hell no, not like their lager and limes. Four bottles will do us, so we've got to get the girls back to the tent again before they break us with their fancy drinks."

"How?"

"I don't know? You're the one with all the education. Y o u think of something."

"What about the track, and going back in the dark, and drink?"

"Might work," said Dewi, "but I wouldn't bet on it. Once those two get their bums on a soft seat, they won't want to budge." He raised his voice, "Alright then, are you girls?"

"Yes, but not thanks to you two," said Sandra. She brushed down the front of her skirt.

"I offered you a hand on the other side of the hill, but you didn't want any help."

"I was more worried about your hands than climbing the hill. Everywhere they were." She turned to Matti who seemed to be testing the ground in front of her as if she expected quicksand or lion traps, before stepping out onto the grass.

"Anyway, where's the pub from here?"

"Over the bridge and we hit the road. Pub's about a hundred yards from there."

"Well, come on then," and we walked off Indian file, Dewi and I in the lead, the girls following.

'The Gower Inn' was bursting with people. We could hear the din of the public bar long before we could see it – talking, shouting, laughing, and the clink of bottles and glasses. Dewi stopped outside the main entrance. Heavy beam lintels and doors, white-washed walls. The smell of stale beer was overpowering.

"You'd better wait here while I get a few bottles," he said to the girls.

"Aren't we going in?" asked Sandra.

"I think they've only got a public bar here. Ladies not allowed," said Dewi. He looked at me uneasily.

"They're bound to have a Ladies' Lounge – and I'm sure I can hear women's voices anyway, so ..." and she stepped into the entrance foyer, with Matti close behind.

"Damn," muttered Dewi under his breath.

"Yes, here it is!" cried Sandra. She flung out her arm and stood like a pointer dog, unerringly fixing her quarry, then she disappeared inside, with Matti at her heels.

"You go and get them a drink while I get the scrumpy," said Dewi. "I'll be as quick as I can," and he opened the door of the Public Bar and pushed his way inside.

Sandra and Matti were sitting in the far corner on a plush, upholstered bench seat. They looked up expectantly as I came in and smiled at me.

"What would you like to drink?" I asked.

"Two Babychams, please Marc," said Sandra. "We always drink Babychams, don't we Matti?"

"Yes, we do," said Matti.

I ordered the Babychams and two pints of best bitter. The barman looked at me hard, obviously mentally debating my age and even though I was almost twenty-two and had my National service registration card in my pocket to prove it, I still started sweating. He seemed to make his decision and without saying anything, began drawing the pints. I turned and looked around the bar.

"Hi!" she said. Standing right next to me. Huge blue eyes, thick, chin-cropped blonde hair, smiling mouth. Loris.

I swallowed. "Hullo," I said, and swallowed again. "What are you ...?"

"... doing here?" she finished for me, and hooking her arm in mine, she turned to her companion. "Peter, look who's here." Her voice rang clear, sharp through the room. English voice, confident, cultured. I stiffened and glanced sideways at Sandra and Matti. They were watching.

"Marc, this is Peter, Peter, Marc." She still held my arm possessively. "Are you on your own Marc? Come and join us. We were just ..."

"No, I'm with friends. They're sitting in the corner, and Dewi, my mate, has just gone to get some bottles." I pointed vacantly at the doorway.

"Well, let's meet your friends, eh? We can have a party." She looked directly at Sandra and Matti sitting in the corner of the room, hands clasped together on the table, clutching their handbags. "Where did you say your friends were, Marc?"

And Dewi huffed into the room brandishing four large bottles of dark brown fluid. He headed straight for Matti and Sandra.

The barman cleared his throat behind me. I paid for the drinks and struggled vainly to pick up the four glasses.

"Let me help," said Loris, and she picked up the Babychams and walked across the room to the corner table. She laid the drinks on the table in front of Sandra and Matti and said, "These would have to be for you," and she smiled brightly at them.

"This is ... er ... Loris," I stammered, "and her friend Peter. Dewi, Sandra and Matti. Loris and Peter were at University with me."

"Hullo Loris," said Dewi, all eyes.

"Hi Dewi," she said, sitting down next to him. "But not Loris please – hate it – my friends call me Clit."

Sandra spilt her Babycham on her hands and down onto her skirt.

"Clit, did you say?" asked Dewi. "That's an unusual name. Clit. How did you get ..."

Loris smiled at him and opened her mouth ...

"It's a nickname!" broke in Peter, "she's very stimulating, we always say." And he winked hard at Matti and Sandra. Both girls looked down and started brushing Sandra's skirt with quick, jerky strokes. "Yes, very stimulating. Mind if I sit here?" and he sat down next to Matti. "And what do you two young ladies do for a crust? Model clothes?"

"Oh no," said Matti, giggling, "we work in Boots, the Chemist, in the cosmetic ..."

"You'll never guess what we've been doing this week," said Loris loudly.

"I'm sure we won't," said Sandra.

"Oh, but you'd have loved it, wouldn't she Peter?" She leaned forward. "We've been delving in caves."

"Speleology," said Peter.

"Oh, don't be so boring Peter," said Loris. "Delving in caves sounds much more earthy and exciting." She looked directly into Dewi's eyes, "Into the womb of Mother Nature."

"Into the womb ..." began Dewi.

"Yes, we've been exploring the caves at Dan-Yr- Ogof," said

Peter. "Limestone caves. Go for hundreds of feet. Underground streams even rivers, pools, enormous stalactites, stalagmites, and, they must have there in Neanderthal times."

"How do you know that?" I asked, drawing up a chair next to him.

"You can tell by the rock formations, by the aging process. There's a lot known about limestone ..."

"Oh, don't be so stuffy, Peter," broke in Loris. "He'll bore you all day long with his silly facts, if you let him. Who's going to get me another drink?"

Dewi moved to get up but found Sandra's arm linked in his.

"I will," I said, rising. "What are you drinking?"

"Whisky, thank you. Neat. No water … and I'll come to keep you company." And she picked up her glass, drained the last drops and led me to the bar.

"And what are you doing so far out of town?" she asked me in a confidential whisper as we stood at the bar. She was standing very close to me, so close that she was touching but not touching. I could feel her hips and breasts almost brushing me, but not quite. And I was sure she knew it, was using it, was exulting in it.

"We've got a tent pitched in the valley over the hill, below Craigwen Castle, near the river."

"The four of you?"

"No, no, just Dewi and me. Sandra and Matti turned up today – with their own tent."

"How lovely and how lucky! Peter and I are looking for somewhere to stay tonight." She put her hand on my arm and turned me to her. "We're not together. Peter and me. Peter's not into girls, if you know what I mean, as I'm sure you do. So, you'll put us up, won't you?" Her knee was resting against my leg. "I'm sure you could fit us in, couldn't you?" Her eyes were huge.

"Yes, of course, I'm sure we could."

*

THE JOURNEY BACK took a lot longer than the one coming, what with Dewi's bottles of scrumpy, Loris' and Peter's packs, Sandra and Matti's seeming reluctance to take a step without a steadying male hand, and the frequent stops to relieve ourselves of Babychams, whisky and best bitter.

We dined on one of my camp specials – a soup-stew that had every can in it that you could imagine – stewed meat in sauce, peas, beans, tomato soup – all cooked in one pot over a primus gas stove.

While I washed the plates and the one-pot in the river, Dewi filled everyone's mug with the famed scrumpy and Peter, because it was getting dark, lit his lamp for troglodytes – a carbide flare lamp, which worked on the principle of adding rock to water which emitted a hissing gas and, when touched with a spark or flame, burned with a fierce, spitting, sodium white glare. The shadows of the inhabitants loomed large against the tent walls, flickered, died, then loomed large again. From the outside, it looked like the magic lantern films we used to see at Sunday school, with a pale, anaemic Jesus walking his way up into the clouds. But he wouldn't have had a mug of scrumpy in his hand.

They were already onto the second round by the time I got back into the tent. Peter was tying his caving lamp high up on the central pole while Dewi was trying to pour more scrumpy into Sandra's mug. She was trying to stop him by splaying her fingers across the top of the mug, but Dewi was pouring it between her fingers. Loris was squatting, cross- legged, on my bed, her mug of scrumpy in one hand and holding the snake-filled milk bottle in her other hand up to the flaring light. I sat down beside her.

"Like it?" I asked.

"It's beautiful. So strong. So masculine. Even though it's dead, it looks so alive. And naked."

"Naked?" cut in Sandra, "How can you call a snake naked?"

"Easy," said Loris. "Every animal I've ever seen has been naked. Cows are nude, sheep, snakes, horses – all nude. Come on Sandra, you must have noticed all those dangling bits."

"But they have fur and things, and wool – and birds have feathers," said Sandra, her voice rising, despite herself.

"Feathers!" laughed Loris, "but that's just like hair – you do have hair on your body, Sandra, don't you? And I don't mean on top of your head."

Sandra blushed and turned away.

"Oh, come on, Sandra. Everyone has it – but some of us pretend we don't. Hidden away, right? Secret." She put down her mug and the snake-bottle and lay back on the pillow. "I bet you even shave under your arms," and to emphasise her point, she put her hands behind her head and splayed her elbows wide, revealing tufts of dark blonde hair under her arms.

Sandra reacted as if stuck. "That's vulgar," she said, looking away, "dirty."

"Dirty? Vulgar?" cried Loris, and she leapt to her feet. "We're not animals," said Sandra, and she smiled at Matti who shook her head and smiled back.

"Not animals," laughed Loris, and she took a step closer to the two of them, "of course we're bloody animals! We pee ..." she paused, watching their faces, "we shit, we mate, we drop our brats, we stick our tits in their mouths – tits, you know," she cried, and she popped the buttons of her blouse, snapped the catch of her bra and threw both garments to the floor. "These things!" and she cupped a hand under each breast and aimed them, like torpedoes, at Sandra and Matti. "Tits," she said, quite matter-of-factly.

No one spoke. No one moved. We stared. At the nipples. At the dark brown nipples. Peeping between her fingers in the flickering, cave-lamp light. They shouldn't have been so brown. They should have been pink. Like her lips. Like the inside of her mouth. They looked like they belonged to someone else.

She lowered her hands.

Dewi got slowly to his feet, bottle in hand. "Anyone want some scrumpy?" He was looking straight at her breasts – tits – his head moving up and down slightly in time with her breathing. "Loris? I mean, Clit?" he stammered.

"Yes, thank you Dewi," said Loris. She bent down and picked up her mug. He stretched out the bottle and poured. The glass chattered against the rim of the mug. She lay her hand on top of his and held it steady while he poured. It overflowed. She bent forward and sipped the brimming mug. Dewi's eyes followed. Then she sat down cross-legged, next to me. There was an audible sigh as the watchers simultaneously let out their breath.

She smiled at me. "Silly bitch," she said between her teeth. "Come on, let's go outside," and she rose, taking hold of my hand. I followed her, looking straight ahead, not looking at the faces of the others and showing them that I wasn't looking. She led me into the dark, sure-footed like a cat, as if she knew exactly where we were going. In a gully between two high, soft-rounded dunes – I was seeing breasts everywhere – she stopped, dropped to her knees and knelt in front of me. "And do you think it's dirty, Marc?"

I looked down at her. I could only see her face, bare shoulders and breasts. I pulled my shirt out of my trousers and slowly undid the buttons, watching her all the time. She lifted her buttocks from the sand and pulled her shorts and pants down and off, as one. My hand shook on my belt and I dropped my shorts and pants to the ground. I stepped out of them, because I suddenly felt very silly standing in a puddle of clothes, then moved back in front of her. She lifted both hands and cradled me. She tilted her head back and looked up. Huge now blue-black eyes. I wanted to kiss them. Each one separately. But I also didn't want to move in case she moved. And I waited. And hoped. And prayed. She pulled me down beside her.

She lay back, resting her head on a grass tussock. Her head was encircled in grass almost like a halo. She pulled me on top of her, moved her hand down and taking hold of me guided me between her open legs. I slid down her body to her belly and kissed her gently, over and around her mound, edging nearer and nearer, but without actually touching it. She started to moan. "Inside," she gasped, "I want you inside me."

I moved further down on her and probed gently with my tongue.

"I want you inside!" she insisted.

"No," I said, deep into her hair.

"No? Why? Why not?"

Because I'm a virgin. Because I haven't. Because I won't.

Because I'm not getting caught. Because I've got so many things I want to do and none of them includes babies and ties and commitments. Because I'm free and I'm staying free.

"Because ..." I said out loud, "because I don't know if we should, yet. I'm not sure ..."

Loris jerked her head, and then jerked it again, violently. She gave a yelp of pain, throwing her head from side to side and beating at her hair with both hands.

"What's the matter?" I yelled.

"Stinging!" she panted, hitting her head so forcefully that her hair flew at each blow. "Bites! Stings! Oh God!"

I held her head in my hands and saw them – ants, hundreds of ants, crawling over her bare neck and shoulders. She had been lying in a nest of them. I started to beat at her hair and all the time shouting, "It's ants! Don't worry, it's just ants!"

She staggered to her feet, crying and clawing at the hill of sand behind her, desperately trying to escape.

"The water! Get in the water!" I urged, and half-pushed, half-carried her down to the river.

We lurched to the water's edge and plunged straight into the moving darkness that was the river. I lost my footing on a stone and fell headlong into the water, dragging Loris with me. I surfaced in the shallows, gasping at the exertion and at the cold water impact of it. Loris had both arms wrapped around my legs. With difficulty, I broke her grip and lifted her to her feet. I forced her head down and began furiously ladling water onto her head with cupped hands.

"Help me!" I cried, "it's the only way we'll get rid of them."

But she seemed to freeze, bent double, head and arms hanging forward, crying. I stood behind her and turned her head and shoulders more into the light. The light. The light coming from the open flap of the tent. And in that instant, I saw in my mind's eye a unique tableau – three watchers, blackly silhouetted by a flickering white glare, staring transfixed at two animals, bolshie-nude, coupled together, starkly white against the flowing black water.

Chapter 2
Staccato steps

As I opened the main school front door we were met by shouting and confetti. Well, it seemed like confetti. There were hundreds of little bits of paper scattered over the foyer floor and cascading from the Head's hands. He was standing in the middle of the foyer like an angry, aged bridegroom, and shouting, to no one in particular, "I want him! I want him!"

Our view was partly blocked by a large pair of buttocks. Evans, Deputy headmaster, was down on his hands and knees trying to fit the confetti pieces together as if he were doing a giant jigsaw puzzle. Miss Denzill, Senior Woman, was helping him, buttocks to the Head, perhaps to escape his wrath.

The caretaker, Cess Williams, who was sweeping the bits into tidy little piles, much to the annoyance of the two jigsawers, added his two-pennyworth, "I reckon it's an inside job, Mr Crawshaw."

"Of course it's an inside job, you fool," yelled the Head. "They're inside, aren't they? Or do you think the postman ripped the letters into neat little piles before posting them through the door?"

So it was the mail. The mail of education – which sat every day morning on the education mat inside the education main front door. Today it was confetti.

Dave and I scuttled quickly across the foyer and ducked into the staffroom. The rest of the staff were already there – and they all knew about it. They were laughing and pushing behind the door, wanting to see, wanting to hear. But not to help. No one wanted to help. After all, it was boss's business.

And she was stretching up to a locker in the far corner of the room, side on to me. I could see the whole length of her, straining, reaching on tip-toe. And the noise and commotion around and behind me faded to nothing, and in the hush of my mind I trembled with the quiver of her, and in that quiver I was erect. Instantly. Uncontrollably. In my mind's eye, I saw my lips resting on the soft skin behind her knee, over the tautness of her thigh, lingering there. And then, as if she knew, as if she felt the touch, she turned at full stretch and looked at me. Grey-green eyes that widened and smiled at me. I smiled back and shivered with the pain of it, the agony of it. And then someone, I think Dave, shoved me violently in the small of the back, propelling me into the room. And she wasn't looking any more. She was sitting on a chair, tucking the skirt of her dress, very deliberately, under her. In my staffroom.

Who was she? Where had she come from? Walking into my little world of playing at teaching, without a by-your- leave or an excuse-me? And then giving me – no, coaxing me – no, forcing me – into an iron-hard clanging erection? How dare she have waited so long? Twenty-three years of my life had drifted aimlessly by while she had deliberately, callously, not come, not intruded, not forced her way in. How dare she! Thank God!

I walked staccato steps across the room and sat opposite her. And smiled again. Strategy. She was looking vacantly around the room, looking everywhere, it seemed, but at me. Working hard at it. I got up from my chair and stood directly in front of her, obstructing her view of the rest of the room. I held out my hand. "Hullo, I'm Marc Thomas."

She hesitated and then stood, had to stand. "My name's Carole," she said, "Carole Meadows," and then a whisper of a hand, just brushing mine. Honey-hair, piled high off the neck; soft, almost see-through dress, pink and white check, high-frilled collar to the chin, and two swelling rows of frilled buttons over the breasts. She saw my eyes. She watched me looking. And the throb of it became so intense that I knew I would have to sit down. Perhaps she can see it. Of course she can't. Anyway, she isn't looking there. Perhaps she can see it in my eyes. I sat down on the chair next to her.

"Are you ... are you going to be teaching here?" I stammered, afraid of the question, afraid of the answer.

"Yes," she said – only it came out as "Yis" and I took it as "Yes" because I wanted it to be "Yes". She hesitated then went on, "I'll be here for a while anyway. I'm relieving for a Mrs Maddocks, the clothing teacher. Have I got her name right?"

"Yes, yes – I didn't know she was sick."

"She isn't. She just decided she wasn't coming here any more – or so they told me. Is the school that bad?"

"Bad? You wouldn't believe the things ... well ... no ... no, not really, I wouldn't call it bad really ... more ... interesting. Yes, I'd say interesting – and this my first year – only been teaching here since September – tell me, what's your accent? Are you South African?

"South African?" and her eyes widened beautifully again, "Good heavens no! ... I'm a New Zealander."

"The Head has called an emergency assembly of the whole school," announced Evans D.P. from the doorway, "all staff on duty please!"

"Oh my God!" I breathed.

"What? What's the matter?" she cried, starting to rise from her chair.

"Come with me," I said and I took her hand, and I was able to hold it the length of the staffroom, across the swept foyer, down the corridor to the assembly hall, and only had to release it as I ushered her through the hall doorway. She stopped and backed up slightly at the sight of so many earnest faces, so I had to place my right hand under her elbow and gently press the fingers of my left hand in the hollow of her back, just above the swell of her buttocks – oh it was lurching rock-hard and singing – and help her to the climbing bars on the girls' side of the hall. After a moment's hesitation, I decided I'd better remove my hand that was hovering, wanting to slip down – despite all my instructions for it not to – so I did – but I left the other hand under her elbow, just in case she needed reassurance.

The children were deathly quiet – not because they knew of the despicable deed. They didn't. But because it was An Emergency – we didn't have assemblies on Mondays.

"Her Majesty's mail, Her Royal Highness' Imperial postal service has been defiled ..." began Crawshaw, white and trembling.

"They won't understand a word of that," I whispered into Carole's ear, and I was able to brush her hair with my lips, " ... they probably think the Queen's coming."

"... a vandal ..."

"They'll understand that word."

"... a vandal in our midst." And then he launched into his favourite lecture on school tone, how ninety-nine per cent of the children were good, law-abiding citizens who were now impugned by the actions of the irresponsible one per cent. The children had heard it all before. They shifted, restless.

But then something new. "I am shortly going to leave this stage and go to my office. Mr Evans will dismiss the assembly. I will wait ten minutes for the boy or girl responsible for ripping up the mail to do the decent, the honourable thing and come to my office. If he or she does not ... then ... he or she will suffer the consequences, and – let me assure you – they will be dire consequences indeed."

As the children began to file out Miss Denzill squeezed her way along the side wall towards us.

"Here's one of our more famous dire consequences coming now," I hissed, close, "to get you, no doubt." I gave her elbow a gentle squeeze, "See you at morning break." I floated down the hall towards my little ones.

Crawshaw waited half an hour. No one came. Except Gareth Watson. Gareth was a second year. Tiny, dark, with huge horn-rimmed glasses. He'd achieved fame the previous year by asking Charlie Edwards, the music teacher, if he could play the violin in the school orchestra.

"Can you play the violin?" asked Charlie, surprised.

"I dunno yet," said Gareth, "I haven't tried, have I?"

Gareth had seen the letter vandal, so he told the eager Crawshaw, in the act. Trouble was he didn't know his name, but he was dead sure he'd recognise him again.

So tiny Crawshaw and miniscule Gareth toured the school, classroom by classroom. As they entered each room, all the children were made to stand. Gareth, followed closely by Crawshaw, walked down each aisle of desks peering short-sightedly at every child, even the girls, in fact, according to Winnie Winstone, he seemed to take particular interest in the girls, especially the big busty ones. Miss Croft, Religious Instruction, swore later that he even gave her a queer look.

Tension mounted as the duo, so far unsuccessful, neared the last classes. Mine was the last but one. 2C History that had become 2C English. I had borrowed primer readers from young Harry Davies, Junior English, and 2C were absorbed – looking at the pictures and the very occasional word.

Crawshaw came in.

"Good morning, Mr Thomas."

"Good morning, Mr Crawshaw."

2C sat up. Tomo waved to Gareth. Gareth, hidden behind his glasses, registered nothing. He was on important business.

Crawshaw faced the class. "Stand please 2C."

They leapt to their feet. Tomo, in fact, most of them, beaming. They probably hoped it was one of them so he could be caught, so they could be there when he was caught, so they could see Crawshaw smashing and pulping him. I wouldn't have been surprised if one of them had owned up there and then, innocent or guilty, just out of sheer excitement.

But none of them did, and Gareth identified no one, and he didn't even look too hard at the girls. Not the 2C girls. The pair left for Travis' room. The last room.

But Gareth didn't find the culprit there either. Crawshaw ordered the registers checked to see who had gone missing since the start of the morning. No one had. He could have skipped roll call of course. Gareth suggested starting all over again but Crawshaw dismissed the idea with a "Humph" and sent him back to class.

When the bell rang for morning break I hurried across to the staffroom so that I could be the first there. But Jenkins P.T. had beaten me to it. He was leaning in the doorway, blocking the entrance. Smirking. Smirking so hard that his shoulder kept slipping off the doorjamb causing him to stagger as if he were drunk. I pushed past him and stood over the tea urn, ready, two cups in hand, for her to arrive. Jenkins P.T. was still leaning in the doorway, forcing everyone to stop, hesitate, then push past him. They nudged me and muttered at me but I held my ground. And I saw Carole standing beyond him in the foyer, obviously disconcerted by his stance, unsure, wavering. I put down the cups, crossed to Jenkins P.T., turned him by the shoulders so that he was side-on to the doorway, and smiled Carole through.

Crawshaw busied in behind her, crossed to the fireplace, stood, back to the fire, which was out, placed his hands under his jacket flaps, one hand on each cheek of his backside and rubbed furiously as if the fire were blazing. He coughed for attention. Jenkins P.T. was at his elbow, oil and honey. "You'll be pleased to hear that I've ... that we've caught the letter vandal. Mr Jenkins here ..." and Jenkins P.T. slowly and deliberately cupped his hands over each cheek of his backside and rubbed rhythmically, "... conducted his er ... own inquiries, and it appears that the culprit was ... is, Gareth Watson."

There was instant uproar. People laughing, swearing, repeating the name as if it were magical, telling each other what Gareth had done in their class the other day ... and in the noise and confusion Carole turned her face up to me and mouthed, "Gareth?"

I pressed my lips close to her ear and shouted, "Yes ... the boy who said he'd spotted the one who'd ripped up the letters."

Her eyes widened, "The little one with big glasses ... who went around the school ...?"

"Yes!" I laughed, "the lad himself."

And a few of those near me heard and laughed and repeated the phrase to their neighbours.

"Why?" Carole again.

"Why? Why what?"

"Why did he do it?" she asked.

"Why did he do it?"

She nodded slowly at me.

"I wouldn't have a ..." and I stopped and looked at her.

She wanted to know ... she really wanted to know. "Hold on – I'll find out." And I raised my voice to a bellow above the din, "Excuse me, Mr Crawshaw!"

The noise stopped abruptly as if someone had pulled out the plug. Crawshaw spun around to face me. "Yes?"

"Why ..." and I was conscious that my voice was very loud in the sudden silence, I lowered my tone, "... why did he do it?... Gareth, I mean, why did he ...?"

"Well ..." cut in Crawshaw, "because ..." and he stopped, mouth open, then turned to Jenkins P.T. "... Mr Jenkins?"

And Jenkins P.T. looked at me hard as if I had suddenly turned quite nasty. "Because ..." he started, "... because he's a delinquent little bastard, that's why!" and he shouted the last at me, his eyes little points of light. "Why do you think? Fancy he's a political satirist, eh?" and he grinned in pure glee at his audience, "... one of your 'Young Anarchists' eh? eh?" and over the welling laughter he stepped in closer to me and snapped, "Who cares anyway? We got the little bugger and that's all that matters, isn't it?"

There was a chorus of agreement from those around us.

"Is it?" asked Carole, quiet.

"Is it?" I repeated louder.

But no one was paying any attention any more. It was done. Finished. Solved. And bodies pushed past me to their usual chairs, to the tea urn, to their well-earned morning break.

Chapter 3
Shirt-out

It was a cold, winter grey day. The sky outside was low, heavy and leaden. I peered through the window which overlooked the staff carpark. A thin mist was hanging in the air. I could barely see the road beyond.

Winnie Winstone was sitting huddled over the hissing gas fire. His favourite position. His chair. His spot. He was reading the local paper, checking the town police court reports for Pentrefach graduates. "Only five this week," he announced loudly.

He looked up at me, then at Carole. Carole kept on marking her test papers. What would it be like to run my tongue along those fine hairs on her arm? Make them rise up. Make them curl. Does she feel as I do? Does she want to touch but is too frightened to in case she's rejected and once rejected it's over. And the dream ended.

"One of our better weeks, eh?" continued Winnie. "Pity about Terry Davies though, isn't it?"

When I was a young boy I used to watch the clean young girls, especially the blonde ones, the ones with ribbonned hair and blue eyes and white ankle socks, and I used to wonder if their bodies were really like mine. With holes and things. Sitting on the toilet. No, they couldn't. They wouldn't. They were all soap and perfume and clean knickers. No holes. No orifices. No smells. Smooth, unpunctured bodies, like angels or like those undressed mannequins in women's dress shops that we used to sneak looks at on our way home from school and marvel at their ship-prow breasts and the nothing- between-their-legs.

"Pity, I say Carole, about Terry Davies isn't it? Good boy that one. Up for breaking and entering. In with the wrong crowd I'd say, wouldn't you?"

Carole sighed, pressed finger and thumb into the corners of her eyes and rubbed. She looked across at him and smiled, "We're all in with the wrong crowd, Winnie. I'm in with the wrong crowd."

Oho! She means him of course. I beamed at Winnie, proud of her, proud as if it were me. I must ask her. I can't put it off any longer. I must ask her now. "Carole," I said quietly, Would you ..."

But Winnie was up, walking. Excited, stimulated. He'd succeeded. He'd got our attention and now he was going to exploit it. "I don't know why you spend all that time marking," he said. "You should do what old Llewellyn did. You know – the art bloke before Dave came."

I tried to stop him. "Yes, you've told me about it before, Winnie."

But Winnie was not to be done out of his story. He lived for his reminiscences of past glories and disasters at Pentrefach. "But Carole hasn't heard it." He leaned over the table towards her, "Old Llew was marking papers see. Exam papers. And he collected them all into one pile. All the classes together. One pile. He turned them upside-down and thumbed back the bottom corner of the top paper. He put an "A" on it, then a "B" on the next, then a "C", then a "D", and then an "E". Then an "A" again – and so on, right through the lot." Winnie giggled and sat down again in his chair. "He did it here in the staffroom. We all saw. "Perfect distribution", he said, the old bugger. Anyway, he filled in his reports from these grades and then put in the remarks.

And what remarks! He put "Trying – very trying!" for one girl, and "No talent – should go far, or even further" for another, and for Earl Carson, a boy in the fourth form, he wrote "His Grace has been one right Royal pain." Laugh? I could have died."

"I don't find that particularly funny," said Carole. "What did Crawshaw do?"

"Crawshaw? Decisive, as usual. He made Evans D.P. stick self-adhesive labels over the remarks and poor old Evans had to make up comments and write them in. Llew refused to do it. Said he didn't like his professional integrity being questioned."

"So Crawshaw had him fired."

"Had him fired?... Crawshaw? Never. Too frightened of the scandal. Reflect on his school. No. Llew left of his own accord. Got a job in Cardiff."

Carole returned to her papers and I to my looking and resolving. She could only say no or tell me to go to hell or piss off or ...

"Did you see Shirt-out this morning?" shrilled Winnie. He was losing us.

"Shirt-out?" said Carole.

"Yes, Shirt-out, you know, in 3C, shirt always hanging out the hole in the arse of his pants."

"Why?" asked Carole.

"Why?" echoed Winnie, "what do you mean 'why'?"

"Why does his shirt always hang out of the hole in ... his pants?"

"Because of bloody gravity that's why! Jesus, what kind   of bloody question is that?"

"No need to get abusive Winnie!" I snapped, wanting to hug him, wanting to cuddle him, wanting to plant a knightly kiss on his scaly, fire-breathing nose. "Carole obviously doesn't know Shirt-out, does she?" I leaned confidentially in to her, "Always dressed in rags, broken shoes, no socks, buttonless shirt, summer and winter ... and of course, the pants with the large hole!"

Carole said nothing. She bent to her bag which was on the floor beside her chair, searched inside it with her hand and then drew out a long, thin piece of card or wood. A taper. A cardboard taper that pipe-smokers use to light their pipes. Starting at the top of the taper, she began to slowly, carefully, tear it into two long strips, working the strips evenly. She didn't watch her hands. Her eyes were on Winnie.

"As I was saying," said Winnie, injured, resenting the distraction, resenting my interference, "you should have seen Shirt-out this morning," and he stopped again and sat back in his chair.

Bloody annoying man. Not only does he interrupt my asking Carole, but he has to drag out his damn stories as well. Not content just to tell them. He has to make you ask him to tell them. "Alright Winnie," I said, "why should we have seen him this morning?"

"Well, he's got these women's high-heeled shoes on, hasn't he? His mother's. White high-heels. Well, off-white really. You know, the type women wear to dances."

"What?" I said.

"Tried to pretend he liked them, poor bugger, but the other kids crucified him. Well, the boys did anyway. Whistled at him, touched him up, you know. Wouldn't come out of the toilet last I heard."

And Carole's head went down low over the taper. She tore it quickly, in sharp little jerks. It separated and she made a soft, gasping noise in her throat. She looked up at Winnie and stared at him, then she stood abruptly, picked up her papers and her bag and walked out of the staffroom.

At lunchtime Dave and I were on dinner duty. We lined up the boys and girls in two long lines outside the dining hall. And there at the front of the boys' queue, was Shirt-out. Grinning. Grinning all over his round, little face – and with shining-new, brown, Brogue shoes on his feet. He looked at our faces expectantly.

"Duw, there's swank," said Dave.

Shirt-out looked around at the other boys to make sure they were listening, "Miss Meadows bought them for me sir."

"Miss Meadows?" I repeated.

"Yes, up town in her car she did sir. Cor, she's a smashing driver – took all the corners on two wheels she did sir."

"She never!" said Smytto, standing behind him.

"Bet you!" cried Shirt-out, "bet you she did." And then he turned on Smytto and grabbed him by the lapels, "I was there, see."

"But the shoes ..." I broke in, "where did you get them?"

"Brogues they are sir, 'Last a lifetime' the man said. And then she paid him sir, two pounds seven and six. Just like that. Out of her purse."

"He was hiding in the toilet sir – and he wouldn't come out ..."

"Yes, I knew that Smytto ..."

"... but she went in and got 'im sir!"

"Miss Meadows went into the boys' toilets?" I repeated.

"Yes sir. Walks right in, past all the boys ... you know sir, up against the wall sir, and she asks us where Shirt-out is, sir – when we was peeing sir," and he covered his face with his hands to hide his shock and his glee and his giggles.

"She didn't see nothing though, sir!" shouted Shirt-out, "'cause I comes out as soon as she calls me sir, and then she takes me in her car. Cor, she's a smashing driver she is ..."

Dave stepped to the front. "Alright you lot. Straight lines or we don't move in."

They shuffled straight – the poorest, the hungriest in the front.

The "Free Dinner" children. The ones whose parents could not afford to pay for the cheap school dinners.

The ones for whom the school dinner would be the main, perhaps the only meal for the day. They filed into the long, rectangular dining-hall, girls the left, boys to the right. They stood behind their benches. No one moved or spoke.

The teachers were already seated at the long central table which separated the boys' and girls' areas. Carole was eating her meal but looked up as the children stood in silence behind their seats. Her eyes sought him out, found him, and shone. But Shirt-out didn't even know she was looking. He was straining his eyes sidelong at the serving hatch to see what he could see, to see what he could smell.

Dave made a downward gesture with his hand and the children took their places, unbelievably quietly, and immediately sat up, backs straight, arms folded, heads straining upright. It was important to be first.

Dave pointed to a girls' table then a boys'. The children moved quickly with cloth feet to the serveries at the right-hand side of the hall. They each picked up a plate, fork and spoon and crowded, bodies touching, waiting to be served.

Stew. It was stew today. A favourite of the children. A thick mutton stew with carrots, parsnips, potatoes and peas, and two slices of bread.

While Dave continued to direct the traffic, I crossed to the teachers' table, picked up a dish of stew and forced myself down between Carole and Miss Denzill. Miss Denzill refused to move along the bench and so I ended up lapping her flowing thigh on one side and leaning into Carole on the other. Carole edged along, allowing me to sit down. Miss Denzill glowered and huffed her thighs at me. I ignored her and started to eat my meal. I could feel Carole's leg warm against mine, from her hip to her knee, and I abandoned the questions I had ready about Brogues and Shirt-outs and dates and just let my leg concentrate and absorb as much as possible. But the kitchen staff were very efficient and stew is easy to serve, so by the time the last children had returned laden to their tables, the first children had finished and were sitting bolt upright again. My turn.

I walked across to the servery. I could feel the eyes following me. "Are there any seconds, Mrs Lewis?" I asked

"Yes, plenty Mr Thomas. Send them up."

I looked around for the Free Dinner children. I sent them up one at a time, alternating boys' then girls'. Seconds lasted four tables. Then the pudding – lemon cake smothered in thick, lumpy custard – and the same process began all over again.

Miss Denzill had got wise to me. As I approached with my steaming dish, she rolled up tight to Carole, shutting me out. I eyed Miss Croft, on the other side of Carole, willing her to move apart, just enough for me to slip in between, but I recognised the futility of it. She was nose down in her custard.

So, I sat down directly opposite Carole. And watched her eating. Watched her cutting the cake evenly with the edge of her fork, then lifting it to her mouth, laying it on her curved tongue and drawing it in. Do I do that? Does everybody ...

"Is there something wrong with the cake, Marc?" she asked from across the table.

"What?" I said, startled.

"You're not eating – you're watching my every mouthful as if you thought it was poisoned."

"I am?"

"Yes."

And every pair of eyes at the table fastened onto me.

"It's just that ... I don't particularly like it."

"Why not?" She was relentless.

"It's ... it's usually dry and ... and scented somehow."

"Then let me take you somewhere where we can get the best – something that you will like."

And the table went unbelievably quiet and still.

"... take me somewhere?"

"Yes," she said, so brightly that even the kids would have heard. "I've seen a beautiful Patisserie-type restaurant in town – near the Post Office ... I don't know what it's called ..."

"The Gondola," said Miss Croft.

"It's Italian," said Winnie.

"And expensive," said Harry Davies.

"Well?" she said.

"Well ..." I stammered.

"How about this Saturday? Are you on?"

"Am I on?" I said.

"He's on!" cried Dave, "He's on! What time?"

*

I DIDN'T SEE Carole again till the next morning.

She was crying. She was standing in the middle of the corridor outside the assembly hall, crying quietly to herself, letting the tears roll slowly down her cheeks to her chin and then fall onto her dress.

"What ... what's the matter, Carole?"

She shook her head slowly from side to side.

I stepped in close and lay my hands on her shoulders, "Tell me," I urged.

"Shirt-out's got the high-heeled shoes on again," she whispered. "His mother sold the Brogues."

Chapter 4
"We've got a dog, you see"

"I know you'd like her Mam."

"Would I?"

"Yes, I'm sure you would. She's soft and kind – she's the one who bought the shoes for the boy I told you about. You're bound to like her. She's gentle."

"And pretty?"

"Oh yes – absolutely – takes your breath away ..." and I realised too late that it had rushed out, pell-mell.

"Well, she obviously takes yours away," said Mam to the damp pillow slip she was stretching in her hands. Then she turned and looked at me levelly, "Likes you, does she?"

"Well, I don't ... I'm not sure ..." and I knew my face was beetrooting red. She could always do this to me. Why was I talking to her about Carole at all? For approval? For permission? "... she seems interested anyway."

"Interested," she repeated, sotto voce. "Well, I'd like to meet this beauty of yours. Why don't you bring her home with you one day after school? Is she local?"

"No. She lives in town, in a flat."

"In a flat."

"With ... some friends."

"With friends." She raised her eyebrows at me.

"Two friends. Two New Zealanders travelling with her."

"New Zealanders travelling with her." And her face became stone, hard-set and grey. There was a long silence while she methodically folded the washing into two neat, damp piles. Then she patted the piles with her hands as if they were good little boys for their mam. And she sighed. I knew that sigh.

"She's relieving for a teacher who's left."

Mam lifted one pile of washing and placed it carefully on top of the other.

"She'll probably be here for the rest of the term ... before she goes home ..."

Mam pushed down hard on the monster pile with both hands.

"... to New Zealand."

And the muscles in her forearms swelled and knotted with the pressure as she flattened the damp washing into a rectangular box. Then she sighed again and leaned forward onto the box as if it had drained all her energy, had taken everything out of her.

I stood up. "Let me take that through for you Mam."

"No thank you," she said, pushing herself upright again,

"I've always managed on my own and I suppose I always will." She forced her hands under the pile of washing and heaved it to her chest. She looked over the top of it out of the kitchen window. "You'll be asking her out then soon ... this New Zealander of yours," and she said the name as if it were a fishbone in her throat.

"Yes I have ..." I knew it was a lie, of course, but an oh-so-necessary lie – the thought of trying to explain ..." we're going to the Gondola tomorrow afternoon."

"The Gondola! Well, well, we are out to make an impression, aren't we? Of course, they wouldn't have fancy Italian restaurants with your cassatas and gateaux on trays in New Zealand, now, would they?" She steered a blind path to the door. Then she stopped, turned side-on so she could see me, and smiled, "Well, if you've got that much money to throw away, you can treat me to an iced coffee or gelato or whatever they call it, can't you? I'll drop in and meet your young lady. You won't mind, will you? Just to say hullo, I mean. I won't stop long. Just meet her and get a good look at her – and let her get a good look at me. Now, isn't that lovely to look forward to?"

*

"I COME FROM a little place called Maranganui."

"Mar-an-gan-ui?" I spelt out each syllable, very carefully.

"Yes, that's very good. It's a Maori name."

"What does it mean?"

"I'm sorry ..." and she laughed, "I haven't a clue. Isn't that terrible? – to live in a place all your life and not know what it means."

"Not really. I'd have no idea as to what most Welsh place-names mean – and I didn't speak English till I was five."

"Didn't speak English?"

"Not really – we spoke in Welsh. Then the day I turned five and had to go to school, my mother stopped speaking Welsh to me and would speak only English."

"So English is your second language?"

"No! ... my first language – I can't speak any Welsh now."

"None at all?"

"Not really. Oh, I can pronounce names, understand a few phrases and sing hymns, but when someone talks to me in Welsh, I just smile and nod my head."

"I think that's terrible," she said, "and strange, because that's what's happened to Maoris in New Zealand."

"Do they still speak Maori?"

"Some do. Ben did. Ben was a Maori I ... used to go out with. We were at teachers' training college together. He was quiet and shy at College and I didn't find out he could speak Maori till I stayed with him on his marae once – that's a meeting house that they gather in – and sleep in sometimes. And what a difference! He stood there in front of everyone and made a speech in Maori, brandishing a stave in his hand, and calling out the names of his ancestors – it was very moving ... I'm sorry," she stopped and laughed self-consciously, "I'm going on a bit."

"No, no, you're not. I want to hear. Keep talking." A waitress hovered near, carrying a three-tiered cake-stand. "Would you like something else?"

Carole didn't answer. She didn't seem to register that I'd asked a question.

"Would you like something more to eat?" I repeated. Her eyes came into focus, "No ... no thanks," she smiled, "I've had enough."

I smiled back at her and waited, but she said nothing more. "It doesn't look as if Mam's going to turn up," I said. "We may as well go, if you're ready." I stood up.

"Are you sure? I think we should wait a little longer, don't you? Just in case?"

I sat down again and signalled the waitress to refill my coffee cup. I leaned back against the wall. "Did you go with him – with Ben, for long?"

"Oh no – just a few months really – and probably only that long out of sheer bloody-mindedness. My father ... my father doesn't like Maoris. He thinks of them as some kind of sub-species. He does! Talks about thick lips and flat noses ... and even about their smell. Their smell for God's sake! Can you believe it?" She looked up at me sharply and I smiled and shook my head.

"He used to call Ben "The Maori". Not to his face, of course. To my face. Never Ben. Always "The Maori". And the very thought that we just might be ..." and she had a pipe- lighter in her hand. I hadn't seen her get it. She dug a groove with her fingernail into the top and started to pull the sides apart, "... that his lily-white, blue-eyed daughter might be ..." and she broke the taper, snapped it, part way down the stem. She stopped and looked at the frayed end.

I stretched out my hand and closed it on hers.

She looked up at me and smiled brightly, "We just finished ..." and she laughed and laid the taper pieces on the table, "... and he took a teaching job in Wanganui and I came here." She pushed the two pieces of paper together with the tips of her fingernails, levered one on top of the other and then lifted them carefully and placed them, still together, in the ashtray.

"Why ...?" I stopped.

"Why what?"

"Why do you tear those things?"

"What things?"

"The pipe-lighters."

"Oh those! No reason. Someone suggested ... I just find it soothes me. Really. They're nothing."

I stood up involuntarily as I saw Mam shouldering her way through the main door. She was heavily laden, bags hanging from both hands. She stopped just inside the door, rested the weight of the bags on the floor and looked around, obviously searching for us.

She was dressed in one of those tea-cosies that Welsh mothers wear – thick woollen coats that button at the throat and bell out to the calves – shapeless, ageless, sexless – but keeping the tea warm. And for one fatal moment I hesitated. I almost sat down again, almost buried my head in my arms, willing it away, willing it not to happen. For that tea-cosy coat and the bags told me everything. Carole was no match. I was no match.

Then she saw me and smiled. A radiant smile, a smile from me to you. She bent to her bags again and surged towards us down the narrow aisles between the tables, miraculously missing the customers and the waitresses, the cake stands and steaming coffee decanters, until she stopped in front of us, Carole standing tall to her right, I to her left. She looked at Carole from the top of her head to her peeping toes, then she looked again from the toes up. The bags were still hanging pendulously from each hand, just off the floor, but she seemed oblivious of their bulging weight. She had eyes only for Carole. Then she spoke, to Carole, very privately, as if only she and Carole were present, "Marc said you were pretty. Well, my dear, he did you an injustice. You are beautiful."

She lowered the bags to the floor where she stood and pushed in beside me, "And so fair!" she cried. "You're obviously not from Wales, are you ferch? Not one of us, no, not with that skin and that hair, oh no, and especially sitting with this dark one here," and she hooked her tea-cosy arm through mine, "... with his black hair and his brown eyes and voice like a ton of coke." She pulled down hard on my arm, forcing me to face her smile. Her face was flushed red, with the excitement and the exertion, but her smile looked strained, brittle, with an edge to it. She faced Carole again, "And when is it then, ferch, that you go back? Back home, I mean, to New Zealand?"

"I'm not sure," said Carole, small voice, "I may stay for a while – certainly to the end of the term – and then I may travel a bit ... haven't really decided ..."

"Got something special for you Marc," Mam broke in. I glanced across at Carole, saw the hurt, wanted to put it right, wanted to wipe it away as if it had never been, but it was done. "Bones I've got for you," she went on. "For soup. Big beef bones, the way you like them. Only two and six they were. There's a bargain. Look!" and she bent to the nearer bag and hoisted it in the air. It was a paper carrier bag with 'Llew Jones, Butcher and

Poulterer' printed on the side. It was streaked and blood-soaked, especially near the bottom where the blood must have eddied and pooled. And then whether by accident or design I'll never know, the bottom of the bag burst and a waterfall of viscid blood and mammoth bones cascaded to the floor. The blood sprayed and splattered in fat raindrops onto the tiles, tablecloths, and the closest customers, while the bones careened and skittered over the floor – knuckle-bones, pelvic bones, thigh bones, ball and socket bones, sliding head over bloody heels under tables, legs and feet, down the aisle.

Mam got slowly down onto her knees, as if she were going to pray, then she dropped on all fours. She lifted her head to the speckled lady at the table opposite, who was peering over her spectacles, studying a large, meat-encrusted hip joint which was leaning against her handbag. "We've got a dog, you see," said Mam, and she began to crawl after the bones. But as she approached a particularly savoury-looking pelvis and tried to pick it up, it slipped in a bloody smear through her fingers and sneaked away. An elderly man in a grey overcoat with a fur-lined collar put out his foot and blocked its flight. "He loves bones," said Mam gratefully. She trapped the bone against his foot and levered it into her lap. "Thank you," she said. For some reason she was speaking in a peculiar accent. In an English accent. A refined, public school English accent. And in a bizarre sort of way, it seemed appropriate.

Carole moved out of her seat. I thought she was going to leave, walk out, disassociate herself from the mayhem and slaughter that was all around her. But I was wrong. She picked up a serviette from the table and bent to the meat-encrusted hip joint. She manoeuvred it onto the serviette with her fingertips and then lifted it, hammock style, into the air. She swung it across to Mam and dropped it alongside the savoury pelvis in Mam's lap. And she was laughing, in little gasps, little sighing gasps as if she had a painful rupture and was frightened of hurting herself further. "They'll make lovely soup," she said to Mam in a bright voice, "lovely beef soup – Marc'll love it – once you get the fluff and the dirt off."

Chapter 5
The tin boot

Dad was bathing his foot. He was sitting on the edge of a chair in front of the living room fire, his foot in a basin of water. He always did it there. In all the years I'd seen him wash his foot, he had never done it in the bathroom. His foot had a heel and part of the arch of the instep. Then it stopped abruptly like a broken wedge, with blue scars, inflamed. The rest of the arch, the pad, the toes were gone.

He patted the tender areas, gently, with a warm cloth, then looked up and saw us standing in the doorway. He grinned at Carole in that way he had – all teeth to the gums. He cradled his foot in both hands, slipping his fingers forward over the wedge and the scars, and lowered it back into the water. "Come in then!" he cried, and he levered himself upright, one foot in the basin, and wiped his hands thoroughly on a towel. He held out his hand to her. Carole crossed to him and took it. He closed both hands on hers and looked at her. "Now, there's lovely," he said, straight into her eyes, "you can come and hold my hand any time you like. Sit down here and tell me about yourself," and he eased himself down again into the chair. Carole sat on his left, up close. Neither of them paid me the least attention. They were like old friends. Dad lifted his foot out of the water and dried it with a towel. And while she talked of New Zealand and trees and mud pools and crayfish, he wrapped fresh bandage around his foot, over the padding, around the heel, under and then over again. He pulled on his sock and shoe. The shoe was creased permanently across the middle.

"I was in India for five years," he said when she'd finished, "in the cavalry. You know, it used to rain frogs in the monsoon season. You couldn't walk outside without stepping on them. Little green things with big black eyes. Burst with wet plops under your foot. Just had to ignore them. Stained your boots though. And through the laces. Had to wash your socks and clean your boots every time you came in. That's the army for you. Was your father ever in the army?"

"No. When the war came, they found he had collapsed arches in his feet …" and her eyes went involuntarily to the creased shoe, then she went on quickly "… wouldn't be able to march, they said, so they sent him on mapping parties in the bush up north instead."

"Don't tell me!" cried dad, "and he had to walk everywhere, right?"

"Up hills, up rivers, up gullies, over cliffs – he says there isn't an inch of Northland that he hasn't walked over – and with a pack on his back."

"That's the army for you."

"He's always talking about it, moaning about how hard it was. But, between you and me, I'm sure he had the time of his life – no kids, no mum, no worries – just fishing and hunting and drinking, especially drinking."

"That's the bloody army for you!" cackled Dad, and Carole joined him and they laughed till they had tears in their eyes.

We made coffee and took it into the front room. Special. Carole sat on the floor, stretched her legs out in front of her and leaned back against the settee. "I like your father very much," she said. "He reminds me a lot of my dad."

"What does your father do now?"

"Real Estate – sells houses and farms mainly – but tell me ... how did your father hurt ... injure his foot?"

I leant forward so that I could smell the tang of her hair. I stretched out my hand and stroked it in long sweeps to her shoulders. "Happened over twenty years ago, so Mam says, when I was three months old. Dad won't talk about it. Refuses to. Just clams up, and if Mam starts talking about it, he goes out."

Carole reached up and held my hand. She didn't pull it away. She didn't caress it. She just held it, held it still in her hair, on her neck.

"He was a plater in the local tinplate works," I went on, "and he dipped the sheets in vats of molten tin to coat them – you know – the tins you buy in the shops. Well, a workmate asked him to change shifts for a night, as a favour. Tending the furnace. And Dad hadn't done it before. Sometime in the night ..."

"It was two o'clock in the morning," said Mam, quiet, almost a whisper, in the doorway. She had little Helen on her hip, tucked in a shawl, asleep. I withdrew my hand from Carole's hair. Mam stepped further into the room and pushed the door closed behind her. "They always tap the furnace four hours after the shift starts..."

"They poke a hole in the casing," I said, "and the molten tin pours out into a trough and down into moulds below. It's white hot. Dad had to skim off the impurities from the surface with a long-handled ladle. There was no rail to the catwalk and he slipped. His foot went into the trough and he ..."

"Don't tell me anymore," breathed Carole, and she turned her head away to look out of the window.

"Oh, but you must hear the rest!" cried Mam, "it's the best part. They carried him home – his workmates I mean – to his bed. To my bed. Lay there like a ghost. His boot coated in tin to the heel. And when the doctor cut the boot away from his foot, what do you think?" cried Mam.

Carole stood up and walked to the window, turning her back on her.

Mam crossed the room and stood behind her. "His foot was whole. Black, smoking but whole. The toes were there, the nails. Everything. But all black and empty inside."

"Please Mrs Thomas," said Carole, her back still turned away, facing out, "... please don't. I hate hearing ... I don't want to know."

"You don't want to know?"

"Mam," I cut in, "don't go on please. She doesn't want to hear any more so why keep going? Anyway, there's nothing more to tell."

"Oh, but there is," whispered Mam, "there is. Do you know Carole, what the Company did the next day, do you?"

"Mam, stop it!"

"They sent a workman around to our house for the tin boot!" and she was shouting.

Carole turned slowly from the window and stared at her.

Mam's head was jutting forward, her lips trembling, "It was valuable, you see. The tin. And it would be just lying there, they said. It was worth a lot of money, they said."

And Carole continued to stare at Mam's face until Mam's gaze began to waver. She looked from Carole to me and then to the sleeping Helen. And she began to sing a wordless song to her three-year-old, swaying back and fore in time to her singing. Then she left.

"I'm sorry Carole," I said. "I had no idea that was going to happen."

Carole walked slowly to the door and pressed it firmly shut. She turned to face me. "Your mother's afraid of me."

"Mam afraid ...?"

"Oh yes! She's terrified of me. Otherwise, why that performance?... and the one at the restaurant? Why the aggression? Why the need to hurt?"

I crossed quickly to her, "She didn't really mean to hurt you, Carole ..."

"Of course she did!" she cried. "She's trying to frighten me off. She's telling me I'm a stranger. I'm not wanted. Surely you can see that?"

"She's worried ..."

"She's more than worried – she's scared to death that I'm going to take her little boy away from her. She's convinced herself that I'm going to wiggle my bum at you and you'll come running with your tongue hanging out and before she knows it, I'll have you chained up 12,000 miles away in New Zealand."

"And are you?"

"Am I what?" she snapped, sharp, irritated.

"Going to wiggle your bum at me?"

"Wiggle my ..." She stared at me for seconds and then she started to laugh, and I hung my tongue out over my lower lip and panted like a St Bernard, and she threw her arms around my neck and laughed into my shoulder. I held still and willed her to keep laughing or crying as long as she stayed – but then she bent her head back and looked me in the face. "I understand her," she said softly. "I understand what she's going through – people I love are on the other side of the world. They're asleep when I'm awake. It's spring in New Zealand now while here ..." her eyes filled with tears "... there's an emptiness ..." She stopped and looked at me for a long time – then suddenly her face broke into a grin, "So put your tongue away little boy and I promise not to wiggle my bum ... and now I'd like another cup of coffee, I think," and she turned and opened the door, crossed the passage and went into the living room. I followed close behind.

Mam was sitting in Dad's chair, nursing Helen. Carole stood over her. "Would you like a cup of coffee, Mrs Thomas?" she asked.

"No thank you, Carole," said Mam, her eyes on the little head on her shoulder.

"Sure?"

"Sure. I don't like coffee. Seems to react on me."

"Oh, go on, Mrs Thomas – it'll do you the world of good. Settle your nerves." She brushed past me and went into the kitchen. "Won't take a minute – and you'll love it the way I make it – I know you will."

Chapter 6
Ordernowladiesangenlemen!

Carole was drunk. Not your dribbling drunk. Not your staggering, falling in the gutter drunk. Just happily drunk. Tickled pink drunk. Finding every little thing uproariously funny drunk. And she'd seemed hell-bent on getting that way right from the start of the evening. She had refused to play Housie, saying she didn't understand what they were talking about. She had insisted on my getting two drinks for her each time I went up to the bar as everyone knows a pint of beer lasts much longer than a gin and lemon, doesn't it?

She kept talking out loud and laughing during the Housie calls, had been hissed and shushed at every time – and I had been twice 'spoken to' officially by the floor manager and asked to keep my 'good lady' in order.

Which became increasingly difficult to do as she had acquired a friend. A sixty-year-old friend, in a pink air-cell-baby's-cot-blanket dress, black fishnet stockings and pink satin petticoat. A friend who leaned on the back of my chair and crooned, breathing gin into my eyes and ears, who let her upper denture drop in her mouth at the end of each croon line and clacked, who had the whitest scalp I have ever seen – you could see it plain as day through the sparse, black-dyed hair. Carole seemed to think she was lovely. She kept feeding her gin and lemons and asking for old-time favourites like 'Jealousy' and 'If I can help somebody as I pass along'. And her friend would launch into the first line of each request with unnerving energy and gusto but then, when the words ran out, as they did at the end of each first line, she'd fall back into her croon, the same croon, a mixture of 'Memories' and 'Moon River'. Carole wanted me to sing with her – but I assured her I didn't have her friend's repertoire.

"Ordernowladiesangenlemen! Ordernowplease!" thundered the M.C. over the speaker system. He must have had the microphone in his mouth. Every breath, lick and swallow was coming across like elephant bowel movements. "The Committee and I hope everyone has enjoyed theirselves so far this evening, but now we come to the main event of the night, Ladiesangenlemen. We have a live band for you ..." and Dewi gave me the thumbs-up sign from across the table. 'A dance,' he'd said, 'a good old-fashioned dance,' he'd said – no mention of Housie or clacking dentures. "... so, if we could have the bestoforder please, while the Committee ladies clear away the Housie gear."

And the roly-poly-pudding of a woman who had been sitting at the end of our table marking six Housie cards at a time and eating salmon sandwiches out of a paper carrier bag clamped between her pumpkin knees, rolled to her feet and dropped all the spent cards into the now empty carrier bag.

We were the first onto the floor. Before the band had finished setting up. Carole smiled at me and rested her hands lightly on my shoulders. Ready.

It was a foxtrot. I placed my hand on her hip, moved out to regulation arm's length and concentrated on gliding. Carole swung her hips in time to the music and then suddenly pushed herself away and began rock'n'rolling on her own, swinging around me in tight circles, gripping my hand and springboarding herself away. I held my hand rigid and tried to look 'hip'. Which is about all the rock'n'roll I can do. But it was enough for Carole.

She gyrated and spun, changed hands constantly, circled me and loved it. The Committee was bound to be pleased.

The first number ended and Carole stepped in close and rested her hands on my shoulders again. Her face had a fine sheen of sweat, right up into the hairline. With the second number I dropped back into my foxtrot routine, holding Carole in close. She melted into me, slipping her leg between mine to the steps, pressing her thighs in tight so that she couldn't avoid rubbing against me. I swelled up immediately and twisted my hips to the side so that she wouldn't feel, wouldn't know. And we tangoed to a foxtrotting rock'n'roll.

I focused my mind on it, willing it away. And it grew with each willing. I concentrated on clacking dentures, sandwiches in a paper carrier bag, Christmas presents, Mam, ice-cream cornets – no, not ice-cream cornets – and it pulsed and throbbed rhythmically. Out of control. Its own master, separate from me, from my brain.

And while I was concentrating, eyes closed, Carole stepped around my out-thrust tangoing leg and closed on me. My eyes flew open in surprise – in time to see her face. Her lips parted and she gasped in air. Then she slowly raised her eyes to mine and held them. And she stayed. She bloody-well, God-Almighty stayed. She rolled around it, wrapping it, pressing it, pushing it but not once losing touch with it. I felt my cheeks and neck burn. Can she see me blush? I looked down into her eyes in the half-light of the room. The pupils were dark and distended, the whites brilliant. But I could read nothing. Perhaps I should apologise, say sorry and tuck it around the corner. And she'll know I'm no rabbit or dog on heat. No, that's bitches. Perhaps she pressed against it by accident and can't pull away now for fear of hurting me or embarrassing me. Perhaps she likes it. Loves it. Perhaps she's been dreaming of it all along. Do girls dream of it the way

I do? Swimming, inhaling, swallowing, wallowing, drowning in the musk of it? Perhaps she doesn't even know what it is. Thinks its my hip bone or my wallet or a fat Housie pencil. But she gasped when her belly touched it and she looked at me. That way. She bloody well knows, alright. Make no mistake about it. So, what is she thinking?

Carole twisted and pirouetted, whirled and rotated. Until one in the morning. Without another touch of it. A performance of great skill and dexterity, I thought. Dangerously close at times – almost brushing by God – but then, at the last second, she'd spin and swing away across the floor. Without even a glance at it. Much to my relief, of course. It had time to think of other things. To lie down. Doze. Curl up and forget about legs and thighs and things. Go to sleep.

She's amazing. So considerate. So thoughtful. I mean, most girls wouldn't even have known what to do, what it needed – and even if they had, they wouldn't have bothered, wouldn't have cared. Girls don't have these problems. Periods yes, birth pains yes, but lover's balls? Not a single woman – nor a married woman come to that – has ever suffered from erectus on the one hand and soft-boiled goolies on the other. Goolies move all the time – tumbling over one another, rolling, never still, seething like simmering dumplings. If ever a woman did, she'd never turn a poor boy on again. They seem to be able to pick it up or drop it at will. Like changing underpants. That's why most prostitutes are girls. The man pops in, pops off, and is done for. The woman lies down, does or doesn't pop off, then leaps up again ready for the next one. That's what you were thinking, wasn't it Carole? Wanted to spare me the pain, the agony, the embarrassment of it, right? Right!

Wrong! Who am I bloody kidding? This is your way of telling me, isn't it? Polite. Refined. Offended perhaps – but don't show it. Disgusted even – but don't say anything – because to say something is to acknowledge it, right? 'Excuse me Marc, but I think you've got a hard on.' 'Have I? Good heavens! Didn't notice. Thanks for telling me. Sorry about that. Never mind, soon fixed. I'll just send it outside. Now Rover, how many times have I told you ...?'

She talked all the way home in the car. Flat stick. About nothing. I pulled into the kerb outside her flat and stopped. I switched off the engine, leant across and cupped her face in my hands and kissed her gently on the lips. Pillow soft. And she slid her lips up over my face and kissed my eyes. She ran her tongue along the hairline of my forehead down to my neck and then suddenly kissed me full on the mouth, forcing her tongue in hard, roughly, and before I'd time to react, she pulled away, head cocked on one side, looking at me. "Come in," she said, "I hate fumbles in the car." And she was gone.

She didn't put any lights on. We felt our way up the stairs in the pitch dark, holding on to one another tightly, bumping into things and laughing into one another just like little kids. She closed the door of her room behind us and switched on the light.

It took my breath away. It was a room from a Victorian doll's house. Not large, just enough for a bed, a dressing table, a rug and a fireplace. But it was perfect – white walls and ceiling, frilled bedspread, bed cushions, lampshade and curtains all in the same pink and white. There was a long-haired, I guessed goatskin, rug on the floor. And everything beautifully fresh and clean and tidy. Everything matching. Everything where it should be – down to the magazines on the coffee table.

"You didn't ..." I started.

"Of course I did."

"Even the painting?"

"Especially the painting," she laughed. "It was all brown

wallpaper. Even the ceiling. Fancy having wallpaper on the ceiling. I painted over it. Sit down please – it'll have to be the bed – or the floor – there's nowhere else."

I sat on the bed.

"Would you like coffee or something?"

"No, not really – but don't let me stop you."

"I've drunk enough already, as, I'm sure, your mother would quickly agree," and she sat down on the bed next to me. "Do you like cards?" she asked.

"Cards?"

"Yes, playing cards – Kings, Queens and things – you know. Let's have a game."

"Now?"

"Yes now."

"We've never played cards before."

"So? I want to play. Is that so strange?"

"No ... no, not strange. That'll be fine."

"Good," she said, "won't be a minute," and she disappeared out the door. I heard sounds of movement somewhere in the flat – the shutting of cupboard doors or drawers, and she was back, brandishing a brand-new pack of cards, still in its wrapping. She sat cross-legged on the goatskin on the floor, facing me. "Right!" she said, "now what will we play?" and before I could say a word, she said, "what about Strip Jack Naked?"

I looked at her. She raised her head from the cards and looked at me. She smiled. I said nothing and sat down, cross-legged on the floor. Opposite her.

"You deal," she said quietly.

I unwrapped the cards and shuffled them. She watched me closely.

"You do know how to play the game?" I asked.

"Sort of ... anyway, you can explain it to me as we go along."

I fumbled the deal and boxed the cards. She was humming to herself.

We played the first game very slowly as I had to tell her what a picture card was and how many cards she had to play after each one. She lost.

"And I take something off now, don't I?" she said.

I said nothing. I stared at her and said nothing. She stood up, unzipped her skirt and let it fall to the ground. She folded it, lay it on the dressing table, and sat down again. She had on very small, plain white underpants. She was sitting with both legs to one side but then seemed to change her mind and sat cross-legged again.

"It can be anything," I said. "You can take off your shoes or stockings if you like."

"Oh, what does it matter? It's all meant to come off in the end anyway, isn't it?" She looked straight at me.

I re-dealt the cards.

She lost again. This time off came her shoes. I think she thought herself slightly ridiculous with shoes on but no skirt.

I lost, and off came my jacket. I lost again, my shoes. I lost three more times in a row and as I pulled down my trousers I started to sweat. Carole's eyes followed my pants down. They stopped level with my straining underpants. I sat down quickly. She was still almost fully clothed apart from shoes and skirt. I decided to cheat. I make no excuses. It seemed the right thing to do. The gentlemanly thing to do. I mean, we couldn't have me bolshie naked and her still with her clothes on, could we? So, at the next deal I made sure the picture cards were mostly in the bottom half of the deck and asked her to cut. I gave her the top half.

Each time she lost she stood up very deliberately and removed a garment, looking at my face, my eyes, the whole time. I kept my eyes level with her knees. She took off her suspender belt and stockings, and her thin white blouse. She was wearing a half cup, lace bra. Her breasts were full, heavy- looking. I could see the nipples through the lace. Dark pink. Almost red. Russet-red.

The next game was very close, despite my cheating. I nearly lost. I held my breath. She hesitated for just a second, and then, without standing up this time, reached behind her back and snapped open the catch of her bra. The click sounded like a gunshot in the small, suddenly hot room. She let her arms fall. The bra hung there sagging at the front. She was breathing quite heavily. She shrugged her shoulders and the bra fell into her lap. Her breasts hung forward, pendulous, then she straightened up, breathed in deeply so that they seemed to swell and move towards me of their own accord. She looked me directly in the eyes. Her breasts were beautiful, satin, curved, the skin glistening slightly with sweat ... and those nipples, those rude-red, impossibly long nipples.

My breathing had changed too. I looked at the cards in my hands. We were both down to just pants. She didn't move. She kept perfectly still and forced me to look up again at her breasts, and then at her face. She nodded.

I dealt the cards. No cheating this time. Let fate decide.

She played seriously now, flipping her cards over quickly, giving little "oohs" each time she won a trick. She played faster, throwing her cards down almost violently. I was down to my last few cards. She played a Joker. Easy. Six cards. I turned my cards over quickly, expecting each one to be the saving Jack or Queen. But there was nothing. Nothing but rag cards.

I stood up. I was suddenly very self-conscious. I mean, it was going to be there ... right in front of her eyes. Inches away. With one swift movement, I pulled down my underpants, made three bottom-swaying steps to the side, swinging the pants in my hand, and sang, "Da, da, data...da, da, da, da..."

✳

AND WE LAY together on the narrow bed and caressed one another, and explored, and kissed, and nuzzled, and stroked. I moved on top of her.

"Wait," she said. Quiet voice.

I stopped and looked down at her.

"What are you doing?" she said.

"I thought ..." and I suddenly didn't know what to say.

"You thought we'd make love," she said, voice unchanged. "Properly."

"Yes," I said. "Am I wrong? We've been kissing one another ..."

"Kissing isn't the same."

"This kind of kissing is! In fact, in some ways, me kissing you there and you kissing me is ... in some ways it's more intimate, more in your face ..." and I laughed. I couldn't help it.

"It's not the same!' she said, more insistently.

I rolled off her and lay on my back, then immediately sat up and stared down at her again.

"For once ..." I said, "for once in my life I wanted ... to be inside. I wanted to be inside you – for us to be – this sounds silly and corny, I know – for us to be like one person, joined – so I wouldn't be able to tell where you began and I ended."

"For once?" she repeated. She sat up and leaned back against the wall. "You haven't, have you?" she said. Statement. Not a question.

"Haven't?"

"Haven't," she said.

"No, not really. Not inside anyway."

"Not ever?"

"No."

"At the age of twenty-three or four..."

"I'm twenty-three."

"At the ripe old age of twenty-three, Marc Thomas is telling me he's still a virgin."

"That's right."

"Why?"

"Because I wanted to wait."

"Wait for what? And don't say the right girl, or I'll throw up – I won't believe you – I won't believe the kind of rubbish that girls who can't get laid come up with."

"Well, it's true – partly true anyway."

"Partly true? That's bullshit, Marc. Don't bullshit me."

"I'm not bullshitting you. It's one of the reasons."

"What are the other reasons?"

"You know the reasons!" I cried, and I knew my voice was getting louder but there was nothing I could do to stop it, "babies, getting pregnant, trapped, caught – all those bloody things – being free to go where I wanted, when I wanted! You know!"

"And now you don't. Now you want to be inside me."

"Yes, I do – because I love you, Carole," I said, without knowing I was going to say it until I'd said it.

She stared at me. She stared at me as if I'd said something unintelligible. Foreign. Perplexing.

"I've loved you ever since I first saw you," I said.

She placed her fingertips on my mouth, "Hush," she breathed, "hush."

I waited, but she said nothing more. She just sat there. Facing me. Nude. Her breasts rising and falling, slowly, steadily, her belly just touching the back of my hand.

I leaned forward and kissed her. I kissed her full on the lips. There was no response. No softening, no warmth, not even a pulling away. Nothing. As if I hadn't kissed her at all.

"Why did you buy the cards, Carole?" I said.

"The cards?"

"Yes, the playing cards. You bought them, fresh. For tonight, right?"

"Yes."

"Why?"

"Because you're shy."

I gasped out loud. Couldn't stop myself. Every time I start to get on keel, she tips me over. "Me? Shy?" I protested. "I'm not shy!"

"Oh, about some things you're not – easy things like singing or speaking to a crowd ... or acting the fool – but important things ... you wouldn't have touched me tonight unless you were absolutely sure I wanted you to – would you?"

She waited for a second for me to answer, and when I didn't, then added, "I know I'm right. So I decided to make you."

"But only so much – and no more."

"That's right," she said.

I didn't know what to say again. The most beautiful girl I had ever seen, had ever dreamed of, had tricked me with a pack of cards – to take all my clothes off – so that I'd have no choice but to make love to her. But not to make love to her. Not to enter her anyway. Everything else – stripping, fondling, kissing, licking, sucking – but no intercourse, thank you, none of this inside stuff. Oh no.

She was bizarre, unreal, frightening.

But then, maybe it was me. Maybe I was the bizarre one, the frightening one.

Chapter 7
... like a shorn, spring lamb

For four weeks. Until that Monday night.

As soon as I stepped into her room, she took my hand in both of hers, and led me to the bed. She turned to face me. She raised my hand to her lips and kissed each finger separately, slowly, as if it were a ritual of deep significance. Then she placed my hand on her breasts. She pressed it into the hollow between her breasts and looked at my mouth. I leant forward to kiss her but she shook her head quickly. "I want to tell you something," she said.

I moved the fingers of my held hand to touch her breast fully.

"Don't move please," she said, "I need to say this to you now, immediately." She drew in a deep breath and then blurted, "I love you ..."

"Carole ..."

"No! No!" she cut in quickly, almost roughly. "Wait!" And she looked down at my hand. "I love you so much ... that I'm going home."

I instinctively pulled my hand away but she hung on, pressing my fingers deeper into her breast. I bunched my fingers into a ball and pulled hard. She came with my fist until she fell against me. And still she held on.

"Home?" I said, more to myself than to her.

She nodded.

"Why? Why for Christ's sake?"

"Because I must."

"Because you must? What kind of answer is that for Christ's sake?" My stomach went cold – "You're married!"

She looked up sharply, "No, I'm not married."

"Then why ... why must you go?" I cried. "Is it the school – that God-forsaken school ... or Mam ... is it Mam?" I gripped her by the shoulders, "... is Mam driving you ...?"

"No – of course it isn't your mother. I can handle your mother better than you think ... and it isn't school either."

"Then what is it?"

"It's you."

How could it be me? How could it not be me? What better reason than me?

"Me?" I said out loud.

She lay her hand on my cheek and started stroking it. "Yes you ... I can't cope with you. I just can't."

"Of course you can! Cope with me? There's nothing to cope with! Forget the sex thing – making love and all that – it doesn't matter. It can wait. I can wait. I'll wait till it's right. I love you ... do you understand that? I love you – I'll do anything for you!"

"And that's why I can't!" and she began to cry. She stood up and turned away from me. Just like she did to Mam that day.

"I don't understand," I said to her back.

"You don't know how sorry I am, Marc."

"I simply don't understand. Everything you've said is a reason for staying – not leaving! You've got to give me better reason than that."

"If you didn't care ... so much ..." she said, still not looking at me, "... if you just used me ... picked me up when you wanted – and didn't come back till next time ..."

"That's crazy!" I screamed, "I'd never do that to you!"

"I know!" she cried, and she turned to face me, "and that's why! If you did – I could cope with it – with you. I could go on seeing you, loving you ... but you don't do that. You want much more."

"Yes ... that's right ... I want you."

"I know you do," she whispered, and then so quiet that I could barely hear her, she added, "... and that's too much."

Too much. I stood up and looked at her. For a long time. Too much. I waited for her to say something more, something different. But she said nothing.

Too much.

I opened the door. "When?"

"As soon as school finishes on Friday."

"This Friday?"

"I fly out Saturday evening."

∗

"WHERE 'EW GOING to then, sir?"

"I'm not going, Tomo. Miss Meadows is."

"Where 'ew going to then, Miss?"

"New Zealand, Tomo," she replied.

"Where's that to then?"

"Other side of the world, Tomo. Near Australia."

"Where's that then?"

I stopped walking and looked down at Tomo, at his wide, flat face, vacant eyes, uneven tufted crew-cut, cut like the shaven heads of those French women collaborators after the War – and realised that he was in earnest, his face waiting to be struck with wonder and awe at the world's mysteries. "A long, long way from here, Tomo," I said and looked at Carole. She smiled at me then dropped her head to look at the ground.

"Further than Bournemouth sir? My auntie goes to Bournemouth every year and mam says it costs a fortune sir."

"Yes, further than Bournemouth, Tomo," I said quickly, and before he could ask another question I pointed at the boys' toilet. "Will you do me a favour, Tomo?"

"Yes sir!"

"Go into the boys' toilet for me will you and check everything's OK? No smoking or fighting?"

"Yes sir!" shouted Tomo and he took off like a rabbit.

"Wait a minute Tomo!" I called after him, and he stopped dead in his tracks then spun around to look at me, jumping up and down on the spot in excitement. "Don't do anything if there is someone smoking or fighting. Just come and tell me and I'll deal with it. OK?"

"Yes sir!" and he bolted for the toilet before I could stop him again.

"You won't ..."

"No, I won't," she said quickly.

"I'm asking."

"I know you are." She touched my arm lightly and then walked on in silence.

"We could try. I'll be less ..."

"I can't!" she cried, her voice suddenly loud and shrill. She stepped away from me into the blackness of a shelter doorway. "How ...?" she exclaimed, then she stopped, closed her eyes for a few seconds and then opened them and asked, calmly, "... how long has this thing been here?"

"The shelter?"

She nodded.

"Carole ... why are you asking me about a shelter?"

She didn't move. She stared into the blackness of the doorway as if I hadn't spoken.

"With one day to go before you leave me, you are standing here asking me about a concrete shelter ..."

"How long?" she repeated, and she poked her head around the doorway. I hesitated, then followed. It was pitch black and smelt of stale, stagnant water.

"Ever since the War," I said. "Since the air raids."

"But that was over twenty years ago!"

"I know that, now you know that, but the Education Authority doesn't seem to. Perhaps they intend converting it into a home for retired pit ponies or school teachers or ..."

"Did you hear about Peggy Simpson?" she asked.

"In the fourth form?"

"Yes. She's been giving biology lessons in here to all the fourth form boys who were interested."

"Little Peggy?"

"Little Peggy. Over a hundred and twenty boys. In the lunch hour usually. One boy, sometimes two, each lunchtime – except when she was sick."

"How do you know all this?"

"Miss Denzill via the senior netball team."

"Did Peggy admit it?"

"Admit it? Said she enjoyed it. Suggested Miss Denzill try it."

"And what about the danger ... getting pregnant?"

"Oh, she had it all worked out. Used one of her mother's caps, she said. An old one."

"Carole," I said quietly.

She turned to look at me.

"Why are you telling me this?"

She continued to stare at me for a few seconds, as if she were considering my question, and then said, "In here! Can you imagine it! Can You?"

I heard someone come panting heavily behind me. Tomo.

Mission completed.

"Anything?"

"Nothing sir," said Tomo, disappointed. But then he brightened, put his hand up in the air as if he were in class and lunged at me in excitement. "Can I do the girls' now sir?" and he froze, waiting for my answer.

"No, you can't, Tomo. Go away and play now," and he gambolled away like a shorn, spring lamb. Only there were no fields of grass – only grey tarmac, no bird-filled hedges – only spiked railings, no trees nodding with blossom or fruit – only drainpipes crowned with barbed wire to stop the children climbing onto the roof to pinch the lead.

ACT TWO

Maranganui

Chapter 8
Vegetables for eight

I discarded the peeling and dropped the potato into the basin of water on the kitchen table. The basin was brimming full – I was peeling vegetables for eight – carrots, parsnips and potatoes. Sunday roast dinner, at lunchtime, in the Thomas household.

Three months, four days and seventeen hours after she'd flown out. And for every minute, every second of those three months, four days and seventeen hours, Mam had been beside herself. With silent joy. With a deep, quiet happiness. Not showing it, of course. When she thought no one was looking, she'd withdraw to a place of contentment, behind her eyes. She said nothing. Never mentioned Carole's name once, never mentioned her going, never asked if she'd written, if I'd written ... nothing. Like a book she'd just finished – very interesting – enjoyed that! Now, what'll I make for tea?

My mind went back to the Sunday morning of my sixteenth birthday. Mam was going to cook a special tea to celebrate it, but that was for the evening, before Chapel. Sunday was Chapel. No discussion. No alternatives. Not even considered. We went to Chapel Sunday morning, Sunday afternoon and Sunday evening. That the way it was. Mam's way.

And we'd walked in formation past the wrought-iron railings of the Anglican Church. At least ten cars inside the grounds.

Wealthy English with their lah-di-dah accents, wide-brimmed flowery hats and minister in a long white nightshirt. We watched them out of the corner of our eyes. Mam stared straight ahead and sniffed. She was walking quickly, making a swishing, rasping noise with each step as her nylons rubbed at her calves. Sniffing, swishing, rasping them away.

But the bells were beautiful. We were right under the tower and the notes showered down on us, overlapping, rising, falling. They sounded so happy, so glad. Their laughter echoing down the streets. Empty streets. Closed for Sunday. Except for Joe Garibaldis. Joe's café was open every day of the week including Sunday. "Godless Roman Catholics" Mam called them. As we got nearer the café and further away from the bell tower we could hear the juke-box and the laughter. On a Sunday. We passed the open door and I could smell the coffee, latin, sensuous, full-lipped coffee. But there were only two local teenage boys standing and drinking. Leather jackets, long side-boards, smoking cigarettes and drinking cappuccino coffee.

We stepped into the Chapel foyer. It was cold. No matter what the weather outside, Chapel was always cold. Our heels clacked on the tile floor. Mam turned left and climbed the stairs. Two girls in front of us went downstairs left, and we filed through the boys' door downstairs right. Bible classes strictly segregated, for purity of thought of course. I pushed into the pew beside Trevor. He kept his eyes forward on our teacher, Emrys Hughes, but gave me a two-finger greeting with his right hand, masked by his cupped left hand.

Mr Lewis rang the bell for Quarterly Meeting. Each class moved to the centre of the chapel below the Deacon's chairs. We sat in families. Each family to a row. Our family filled a centre row, both sides. Mam in the middle, her boys flanking her. She took out a packet of sweets. Hard boils. No wrapping paper to rustle or drop. She passed one to each of us.

Mr Lewis called a little one up to the Deacon's chairs.

Merlys Hanney climbed down from her mother's lap and walked up the aisle. Her ribbons bobbed above the pew tops. The morning session of Quarterly Meeting was for the smallest ones, the toddlers. Theirs to shine, sing, recite, lisp, look shy, and be publicly loved and cuddled. Mr Lewis bent down and, with sounds of great exertion and effort, lifted little Merlys up onto the Deacon's chair in front of him, facing us. He held her safe with his arm around her waist.

"And here's Merlys. Now hasn't she got a beautiful dress on?" He fluffed out the flounces at her shoulders. "What colour is your dress, Merlys fach?" he stage-whispered to her.

"Yellow," she said, straight into his eyes.

"It's yellow," he said to the congregation. "And look at her shoes. They've got buckles!"

Merlys lifted her foot to show us.

"I haven't got any buckles," Mr Lewis said sadly, and Merlys looked over the edge of the chair at his feet and shook her head.

"And what are you going to do for us Merlys fach? Sing? Recite?"

Merlys said nothing. She looked at Mr Lewis, her eyes big, and then she turned and looked at her mother below. Her mother was making huge words with her mouth. Merlys looked at Mr Lewis again, and said nothing.

"I know a song," he said, "'Jesus Loves Me'. But my old voice has got cobwebs on it. Will you help me with it, Merlys? Will you sing it with me?"

Merlys solemnly nodded.

"There's a good girl," he said to her, and then to the congregation, "Merlys has decided to sing 'Jesus Loves Me' and she wants me to help her a little bit, so quiet now for Merlys."

And they sang. Mr Lewis held the tune, in a soft palate voice, singing with his lips, and Merlys followed him, coming in strongly on the last words of each line. And the congregation mouthed their encouragement, finally breaking into full voice, soprano, alto, tenor, bass, and organ, on the last tumultuous chorus.

"Beautiful Merlys, beautiful. Thank you for singing to us," and Mr Lewis reached into his waistcoat pocket, took out a jube, and popped it into Merlys' mouth.

And after Chapel, that same fateful Sunday, I'd hurried home to do one of my regular Sunday jobs – delivering the weekend newspapers to special people in our street. It was a perk, because it saved them from going out in the weather to the newsagent, and it meant a sixteen-year-old boy, from a family of five boys and one girl, could earn a little spending money.

As I neared my last delivery, the rain started to come down in sheets. I tucked the paper inside my jacket, turned up the collar, and ran for Mrs Perkins' place.

The house stood on its own in a jungle of a garden. Stone wall fence, a few sticky shrubs, weeds, and tall grass. Mr Perkins was a bus conductor and worked all the shifts he could get, for the overtime. No children, just long grass, weeds, and Mrs Perkins. I hurried down the path, turned the corner of the house and knocked on the door.

"Come in," woman's voice, muffled.

I lifted the latch and opened the door a foot or so. It let straight into the kitchen. Mrs Perkins was leaning over the sink, washing her face and neck. She had turned her dressing gown under at the front exposing her throat in a deep V. Her skin glistened soap and bubbles. I stepped back outside the door.

"Sorry, I didn't realise ..." I started.

"Oh, don't be silly fach," she laughed, "come inside. You'll get wet standing there."

I stepped inside.

"Here, pass me that towel, will you." She indicated a bath towel on the kitchen table behind her.

I crossed to the table.

"… and close the door behind you. I'll catch my death of cold."

Confused, I turned around again and closed the door, all the time trying not to look at her.

She laughed, almost gurgled, still bent over the sink, her right arm outstretched for the towel. I placed it in her hand. She turned to face me and began dabbing her skin dry. Her hair was jet black and made her skin appear translucent, gave it a white marble sheen, except for a slight pink tinge on her neck where she had been rubbing too vigorously with the towel.

"You look wet boy. Take your jacket off and dry it by the fire. I won't be a minute." She shook her head, making her hair fly like a skirt. She patted the wet ends.

I stood looking at her, not moving. She stopped rubbing and looked at me between her towelled hands and then said, very quietly, "Are you shy, Marc?"

I shook my head.

"I think you are. A great big boy like you afraid to take his jacket off. Here, let me help you." And before I could move, she hooked her thumbs under my lapels and lifted my jacket to my shoulders. Instinctively, my hands leapt upwards and closed on hers. She stopped. Her eyes lifted to my face. I could smell her wet hair and the soap on her skin. Then she pulled down on my lapels, bringing my head down to hers. She opened her mouth and kissed me, moving her wet tongue along my lips, between my teeth and then under and over my tongue. I felt her body closing with mine. She pressed herself against me, wrapping both legs around my right leg. I could feel the heat of her. I was lost. Lost in her legs, her thighs, her belly.

I was trying to swallow. I couldn't function. It was happening to someone else. I was looking down from above, at me, it must have been me, but I couldn't see anything. I could only feel.

She released my mouth and, tipping her head back, looked at me direct in the eyes. Unwavering. "Come on, boy," she murmured, "what are you worried about? Your Mam's not here."

Mam! O Duw, Mam!

She pulled away slightly, withdrew one arm from my lapel and pulled at the knot of the belt that held her gown closed. She teased at it with her fingertips, not looking at what she was doing, her eyes still on my face. Then she gave the knot a sharp tug and the ends separated. My throat swelled up, blocking my breathing. The two sides of the gown fell apart, drifted apart. She was naked. A single, large bead of water from her washing had rolled down the valley between her breasts and was sitting, precariously, on the swell of her belly. It hesitated, rose with her breathing, and then, with the fall, lost its hold and rolled down, down, down, disappearing into her ...

"Your paper!" I cried, and I thrust the newspaper into her hands. I stepped around her and ran for the door.

"Wait!" she gasped.

"Dinner'll be ready," I shouted, as I stumbled out into the rain.

"Wait! I haven't paid you ... for the paper!"

*

I MEAN, THE stuff of dreams – a grown-up, mature, married, naked woman – with a bead of water running down between her breasts, resting on the swell of her belly and then ... who knew exactly what she wanted! With me, for God's sake! The stuff of every sixteen-year-old boy's dreams. Well, nearly every sixteen-year-old boy, I suppose. And I'd replayed the scene so many times in my mind since that day.

What a pathetic little boy I was then! What a pathetic little man I am now!

*

WHY? WHY DID Carole have to leave me? I was ready. I was able. I was most emphatically willing. What is she not telling me? How could it be me? "I can't cope with you," she'd said. Can't cope with me? "You want much more," she'd said. Too right. Too bloody right!

*

MAM WAS BAKING at the other end of the table as I was peeling a carrot. Well, she was more sending up clouds of flour and slamming dough down onto the table, for dumplings, for her Dai, for her girl, for her boys. Happy as a toddler in a sandpit.

I dropped the peeled carrot into the basin of water, lay down my knife, wiped my hands dry with a tea-towel, and turned to face her. "Mam," I said quietly.

"Yes, fychan," she said, without looking up from the dough.

"I'm leaving for New Zealand in three weeks."

She froze.

"I went up to London by train, there and back in one day, during the school holidays, and went to New Zealand House."

She had not moved an inch.

"And I applied for a teaching job in a high school. In Maranganui."

Not a hair.

"Teaching History and maybe some English."

Not even a glance.

"I rang them on Friday. Got the job."

Mam slowly unfroze. She brushed her hands together and a cascade of flour floated towards the kitchen window. She stepped to the side of the table and moved towards me. She picked up the basin of peeled vegetables and water in front of me and tipped it over my head.

She didn't speak to me for a week. In fact, she ignored me completely, as if I wasn't there, as if I'd already gone. Then early on a Wednesday morning, after breakfast, she suddenly seemed to recognise me. She smiled at me and said, "I need to get my hair done at 'Mair's'. Will you drive me there please?"

I swallowed. 'Mair's' was only one hundred yards down the road. Mam walked there. Always, "Of course," I said, "I'll get the car out and wait for you out front."

I opened the car door for her and she got in. I closed the door and walked around to the driver's side and got in. I switched on the engine.

Mam stretched her hand out and patted my hand on the gear lever. "Diolch, fychan," she said, and sat back, comfy, for the one hundred yards.

I pulled in at the kerb outside 'Mair's' and switched off the engine but Mam was already half out her door. She stood on the kerb, bent her head back into the car, said, "Wait here!" and disappeared inside.

I waited.

And a squeal of voices escalated out of 'Mair's' front door. Older voices and younger voices. All female. All talking at the same time. Then 'Mair's' front door suddenly burst open and Mam came out, dragging someone by the arm behind her.

Mam opened the car door, pulled the someone forward and pushed her into the car. Mam held the door open and stuck her head in. "Make a date!" she said. She slammed the door shut and was gone.

Well, what do you say? She was beautiful. No other word to describe her. About twenty, dark auburn hair, slim but with breasts jutting out under her uniform-cum-apron, huge, dark hazel-brown eyes, full lips. The full package really. And she was staring at me in embarrassment, her lips trembling – with fear or uncertainty or even excitement! Who knows? She lowered her eyes and stared at her hands that were clasped in front of her.

"She's a bugger, isn't she?" I said with a laugh.

"Yes ..." she said, "er ... no, I wouldn't call your mother that ..."

"What would you call her then?"

"She talks about you often – whenever she comes in really."

"Does she? Look, I'm sorry – I'm Marc – and your name is ...?"

"Linda."

"Hi Linda. You're a beautiful young woman and must have a horde of male admirers, but shall we take her up on her suggestion?"

She stared at me again. "Her suggestion?"

"'Make a date', Mam said. Would you like to go out with me sometime maybe?"

"Yes, I'd like that."

"There is something I must tell you up front – and this may be jumping the gun, of course, because we have no idea if we will be able to stand the sight of one another after one night – but I'm off to New Zealand in a few weeks, so it ... so we couldn't ..."

"That's alright," she said, "I know. Your mother told me."

"Did she? Well, how about this Saturday? Are you free?"

"Yes, I'm free."

"Great, I'll pick you up at seven, say ..."

"I live in Llansamlet, 14 Croeso Road."

"I know the area ... but do me a favour, please, when you go back in."

"A favour?"

"Yes. Mam will ask you what happened as soon as you get inside and I'd really like you to say to her, 'No, sorry, Mrs Thomas, it can't work.' 'Can't work?' she'll say. 'No,' tell her, 'he's gay.'"

She gasped. "I can't say that!"

"Please ... please do this one thing for me – oh, by the way, I'm not ... not gay – but she deserves it. Please say you'll do it ..."

You could have heard the scream from our house, a hundred yards away.

*

THERE MUST BE someone else. There has to be. A man. Another man she's not telling me about. Why else would she have scuttled off? All the time saying she loved me, as I love her, as she waved goodbye, as she boarded the plane. Who is the bastard?

*

LINDA WAS, IS, a lovely girl. We had a few weeks of fun, of laughter, of sharing, of some intimacy, of loving. I know what Mam wanted out of it. I don't know what Linda really wanted out of it. Perhaps more. Wouldn't that be ironic? In which case it was not fair on her. And for that, I was sorry.

Chapter 9
A tent with two poles and no pegs

I stepped down off the bus into an open shelter. It was deserted. Twelve thousand miles to an empty bus shelter. Now that takes real organisation. The driver unloaded my bags and I dragged them into the shelter. The bus pulled away immediately. I watched it till it reached a corner then it disappeared into the blackness of the night. And I waited. There were four shops across the road from me, but they were all closed. A street lamp shone at either end to show where they started and stopped. I sat on my large case.

And then I saw the lights of an approaching car. It must be coming for me. It had to be coming for me. I mean, why else would it be out tonight? It could be going to a dance, I suppose, in a wooden hall with blokes on one side and sheilas on the other – I'd bought a book of New Zealand short stories in Auckland when I'd landed so I knew about these things. But it stopped in front of me. No sheilas, just two men. The Principal, McNeil, introduced himself and then he introduced Thick Glasses – I didn't catch his name. He was wearing these huge lighthouse glasses – either too much reading, playing with himself or he was actually Japanese, despite the heavy Kiwi accent.

And then I saw a tent billowing down the street towards me, out of the black, a tent with two poles and no pegs. The flaps blew back and forth as it floated along. It stopped in front of me and smiled. I smiled back.

"This is Haydn," said Thick Glasses. "Haydn's a fellow countryman of yours."

I waited for Haydn to speak – to open his mouth and instantly transport me back to the land of lilt and song – but he turned to the Principal at my side and said in a disappointingly Anglicised Welsh accent, "Tea was late and I had to do the washing-up." Deep voice. Then he laughed. A high, surprising, tinsel-bright laugh.

And I wished I was back in the dark safety of the speeding bus. I had enjoyed the last few hours of the yet-to-come, watching the nightmare trees and boulders flashing pale and white in the headlights. The world had been out there, in the dark, unknown. And now it's here. Now I've got to meet people. Pretend and be interesting. Present myself for inspection.

My bags were put in the boot. I still clutched my fishing rod in my hand. God, how pathetic I must look.

Where is Carole?

*

HAYDN WAS PERCHED bird-like on the back seat of the car. I could see him out of the corner of my eye. He seemed to be staring at the back of my neck. I turned to face him, "How long have you been in New Zealand, Haydn?"

"Nearly a year now." Again, that strangely deep resonant voice in so small a man.

The car veered sharply into a wide dual carriage-way. The dividing strips were grassed and ornamented with trees and shrubs.

"The town looks very neat and attractive," I ventured.

"Wait until you see it in the daylight." This from Thick Glasses, whose name turned out to be Don.

Half an hour later I was hunched, sticky and perspiring, over a steaming spotted dick. A favourite of mine, but I was full. The two 'girls' who had prepared the meal were seated opposite me, watching each mouthful I ate as if it were a test. Of them or me? I struggled on.

Thick Glasses cleared his throat, "You're unlucky with the weather. It's rained for a solid week."

"One of the reasons I came here," I lied, "was to get away from the rain. All the brochures make New Zealand out to be a kind of Tahiti with air-conditioning."

"Sixty-eight inches last year and going up all the time. It's the trees, you know."

Bloody obvious. All the Arabs have to do is plant trees in the Sahara and they'll have to swim for it. "The trees?"

Don gave a little whimper of delight and rushed into a long and detailed explanation of the meteorological history of the town, complete with annual mean temperatures, precipitations, pre-planting and post-planting, each tit-bit preceded by a long "aah" as he considered his next statement and to prevent anyone from interrupting him. At one point Pearl, the plump one, did try to speak but Don was in complete charge of the situation, and simply raised his voice and spoke quickly over the top of her until she gave up, and then after a long "aah" he carried on.

A computer. A computer with hair and padding to keep out the rust. A rough do-it-yourself, Kiwi-style, home-made fact-bank with two glass-framed monitors, rapidly blinking to signal it was working, and a clicking mechanical voice.

Where is Carole? Why isn't she here? Why am I sitting here looking at these two dogs instead. Did I call them girls before? Sheila had to be twenty-six, bleached hair, no bust. Like a beach-whitened stick. Pearl is at least forty – and with the biggest breasts

I have ever seen – the type of tits pubertal boys draw on walls. And despite myself, I kept looking at them. Not consciously – it was just that wherever I looked, they were there. Heaving. Pearl's eyes widened innocently with each breath.

Sheila clattered the dishes together and cleared away the remains of the meal. And once the meal was over the gathering quickly broke up. Haydn, who had eaten earlier and had said very little all evening, phoned for a taxi to take me to the hotel where I was to spend that first night. I thanked Sheila and Pearl profusely for the meal and, greatly relieved, hurried out to the waiting taxi complete with bags and fishing rod.

Haydn accompanied me to the car, "I'll call for you tomorrow morning and take you to the hostel."

"Thanks, I'd like to get settled." I closed the door of the car. The driver turned and looked at me. "The Maranganui Hotel please."

"Which one?" he asked, "the old or the new?"

Two of them? In this small town? "I'm afraid my booking just says The Maranganui Hotel, Maranganui."

"It'll be the old one," Haydn called out. "The Education Department wouldn't pay six pounds a night for a Taff." He giggled.

The driver pulled off.

Six pounds a night! The dearest hotel I'd ever been in had cost me thirty-five shillings, bed and breakfast, and that had had a lift. How old was the old one?

The taxi stopped outside a comparatively new, single-storeyed building. It suddenly struck me that every building I'd seen in the town had possessed only one storey, and, even more surprising, was made of wood. I looked at the hotel frontage. There was a two-foot-high concrete base then horizontally laid planks. My eyes followed them up. There was something strange about the roof. It was thin. It undulated. Not slate, not tile, not wood.

The driver had carried in my bags and was coming out.

"What's the roof made of?" I asked.

He looked at me as if I'd asked him the colour of his underpants. "That'll be two and nine, please," he said.

I gave him three shillings, hoping to bribe him into answering my question. "I'm not trying to be funny," I said, "but I've never seen that type of roof before."

"It's corrugated iron, mate."

∗

WHEN I SAW the telephone in my room, I knew I'd have to ring her. Perhaps she's sick. Perhaps she didn't want us to meet in a public situation. I thumbed through the phone book for Meadows. There was only one. And as I looked at her name, her number, in her phonebook, in her town, I had a strange sensation. All that way. And she was at the end of this little line. I picked up the receiver. Then placed it back in its cradle. After twelve thousand miles, by God, I'm going to see her. Face to face. And her eyes, her mouth, her hands, her body will tell me what I need to know.

I slept fitfully until six o'clock in the morning when I was woken by a cheery little man with a grey stubble of a beard, no teeth but armed with a cup of tea and a newspaper. He opened my door, yelled "Gidday" at me from the bottom of the bed and then splashed the tea and slapped the paper onto the table next to my head. He exited, leaving my door wide open, to torment the occupant of the room next door. I peered through the fog at the steaming tea. There were islands of sodden biscuit floating in the saucer. I closed my eyes and went back to sleep. Two hours later I was woken again by a female voice which said, from somewhere distant and high above me, that there was only half an hour before breakfast finished. I willed myself to wakefulness and groped out of bed.

At nine fifty I checked out of the hotel. Haydn had rung through while I was having breakfast to say he would pick me up at ten, so I left my luggage in the hotel lobby and strolled outside to see what I could see. Yes, there was the grass and shrub-divided dual carriage-way I had glimpsed last night. A tracery of tracks weaved between each shrub, beaten presumably by the phantom shoppers eager to get from one side of the street to the other. Just the one street of shops. With neat, round pot holes in the road, half-filled with brown rain water; shockingly white concrete kerbing but no drains, the water presumably ran on and on; concrete strip footpaths in front of the shops, three feet wide, raised two or three inches above the bare, puddled ground on either side. The footpaths stopped at the end of the street where the shops stopped. And the shops themselves – straight out of a Hollywood mock-up of Dodge city, complete with single storey buildings, all of varying heights, highly ornamental false, upper storey frontages, propped up from behind with timber posts and long, low verandahs reaching out over the sidewalk to the street. All it needed was a sheriff's office, a few hitching posts and honky-tonk music coming from the hotel saloon.

I sat down on a low brick wall and waited. The street was deserted. No traffic. No pedestrians except for two men leaning against a wall opposite, at the taxi stand. They were both Maoris. This was a guess of course. They were big men, powerful men, dressed identically – long, thick, woollen tartan shirts, worn outside their shorts, khaki shorts almost to the knee, long, thick, woollen socks and black hob-nailed boots. In winter. Shorts in winter. On the street. Maori Baden Powells. Brown-skinned, Scottish-descended scoutmasters. And I remembered that summer's day long ago, when an army officer had marched up our street in full regalia complete with swagger stick, red cap, bristling moustaches and khaki shorts. All the little boys in the street had, of one accord, lined up behind him, marching in step, calling out their "left, right, left, right", throwing hand grenades and dying impressively where they fell. With true British stiff upper lip, he had ignored the assault and marched on, beef red, to the top of the street.

Our taxi stopped abruptly outside a green house, well set back from the road. It had a bright red roof and uncut lawns. Haydn helped me unload and then carry my luggage up the long drive. He carried my fishing rod – it seemed to amuse him. We stopped outside the front door. He leaned the rod against the wall and began to search through his pockets, methodically, starting at the breast pocket of his jacket, to the sides, to the trousers.

"It's here somewhere," he said to himself, absorbed in his search.

"Do you mean the key?" I asked.

"Of course I mean the key. What the hell else would I be looking for?"

"Why don't you ring the bell?" I countered.

"It doesn't work."

"Is there anybody inside?"

"Yes," he said, pulling the lining out of his jacket pockets to make sure the key was not hiding. "Should be. Douglas and Cliff were both home when I left to get you."

"So why not knock?" I suggested.

"I'm sure it's here somewhere," he said and he began his search from the top again.

I put down my bags and reached to knock on the door.

"No!" he exclaimed, "don't do that!"

"Why not?"

"I'll ... I'll tap on Douglas' window. He'll let us in," and he stepped off the porch and picked his way carefully through what had once been a flower bed to a front window. The curtains were closed. "Damn!" he said, "he's probably praying. Be the devil's own job to get him to hear – unless he thinks it's God knocking," and he giggled. "He goes into a trance." He rapped again, harder, and shouted through the centre window join, "Dougla-a-as!"

The curtain moved. The right corner was lifted and a pale, thin face appeared in the glass.

"I've lost my key!" shouted Haydn at the face.

The face nodded.

"Open up! Let us in!"

The face nodded again and then disappeared, only to reappear as the curtains were pulled apart at the centre. He opened his window.

"Lost your key, have you?" Soft, sibilant, tenor voice. "I'll lend you mine," and the face disappeared again into the room.

"Why doesn't he just open the door?" I asked.

"Oh no, couldn't do that," said Haydn, "no, no, not while he's praying. Lucky to get him to open the window, let alone the door."

A thin delicate hand emerged from the window, a long- boned, parchment-white hand holding a key.

We stepped into the hall. It was dark and musty, smelling of damp – and my stomach fluttered involuntarily in panic.

"In here," said Haydn, and he pushed open a door at the far end of the hall. I entered a small bedroom. It had two single beds, one made up, the other bare springs and rolled mattress. Between the beds was a small, once-varnished chest of drawers. A high-quality amplifier and turntable sat on its top. Haydn edged between the end of the beds and the wall. There was barely enough room.

"You can hang your things in the wardrobe," he pointed at a door in the side wall. "I've got you some coat hangers."

"Thanks," I grunted and unrolled the mattress along the length of the bed.

"Got sheets? I can lend you my spare ones if you need them. They're on the line and I could soon iron them dry."

"No, that's alright. They told me to bring some." I opened my case and lifted them out, still in their J.T.Morgan Ltd. wrapping.

We had green eggs and Beethoven for lunch. Haydn beat six eggs into a froth and cooked them in a frying pan until they turned green. We carried our omelettes into the bedroom. As there were no chairs, I sat on my bed, mug of tea wedged between my feet, plate balanced on my knees. I was not mentally or physically prepared for what happened next. Haydn put a record onto the turntable and switched on the amplifier. The two-foot six-inch speakers could not fit anywhere standing up in the room so Haydn had lain them on their backs under the beds. The Choral Symphony hit me, full volume, in my exposed crutch and groin. Scalding tea spilt over my feet and the bed, and I only saved my green eggs by trapping them between the plate and my chest.

"Damn!" yelled Haydn, "you'll get the speaker wet!" and placing his plate and mug on the floor, he bent double under my bed and began heaving the speaker out of the way.

A face appeared in the doorway. A large, square face with drooping macho moustache and fair, almost yellow, tight-curled hair. Its mouth opened and closed but I couldn't hear a word – the Choral Symphony was reaching a climax. "Turn it down!" I yelled at Haydn's flagellating backside. It didn't listen. I released a hand from the green eggs and stretched across to the amplifier. There were about twenty knobs on it. The fourth one got it. It switched from record player to radio. From pounding Beethoven to screaming Rock, and then, merciful silence. Silence except for macho man. He was staring at Haydn's backside and mouthing words, strange, unintelligible words out of the corner of his mouth, and then a word I understood, two words, "poof ... Pommie poof."

At the sound of his voice Haydn froze, bum jutting between the beds. No one moved. We waited. He and Cliff obviously had a special relationship – and I didn't want to interfere – but my feet were stinging wet, and green egg was oozing between my fingers. "Hullo," I laughed, "I'm Marc. I've just arrived – and you're ...?"

He snorted, turned on his heel and went out the door, slamming it shut behind him.

I flushed red, part humiliation, part anger. "Who was that ignorant sod?" I yelled.

"That ..." said Haydn, his voice reverberating under the bed, "... was Cliff." He pulled himself to a sitting position and, looking me straight in the eyes, said, "You'll like him. He's a good joker, is Cliff. Yes ..." and his face took on a strange smile, "... a good joker – we get on famously do Cliff and I – so I'm sure you will," and he continued to stare and smile at me, almost willing me to respond. I said nothing.

Cliff and Don were already seated at the table as Haydn and I entered the dining room. They were dressed for dinner – Don in jumper to the chin, Cliff in looped rugby jersey. I stood behind a chair and looked expectantly at Cliff. He ignored me. He sat, knife and fork in hand, staring at the formica table in front of him. I nodded to Don who smiled back, and then I turned again to face Cliff. He wasn't going to look. He wasn't going to acknowledge me so he wouldn't have to be polite to me. Bugger you, mate. I'll make you. I looked through the serving hatch and saw Douglas dishing up potatoes onto the plates. He was flicking them out of the saucepan with his fingers, skidding them onto a plate, nudging them where he wanted them, and then flicking again.

I walked into the kitchen. "Hullo Douglas!" I extended my right hand towards him, "my name's Marc. We haven't been formally introduced."

He jumped back, startled. He looked at my hand and began licking his fingers, his flicking fingers. And slowly, without taking his eyes off my hand, he extended his to meet mine. I gripped it heartily. It was soft, wet and slippery. Like a fish. Like a fresh scaled fish that hasn't had time to stiffen. I pumped his arm. "Pleased to meet you. Can't wait to taste your cooking. I'm starving. Here ..." I dropped his hand and picked up a plate "... let me help you take them through," and I carried the plate through to the dining room and placed it in front of Haydn. I did the same for Don, then placed one in front of my chair and returned to the kitchen. "Just yours to come, Douglas," I said cheerfully.

"No, there's one more ..." he stammered "... for Cliff."

"Cliff? Who's Cliff?" I shouted.

"He's ... he's in there!" whispered Douglas, pointing at the wall.

"No, no," I laughed, "there's no Cliff ... unless ... unless he's that peculiar fella sitting between Don and Haydn." I raised my voice even higher, "Is that Cliff?"

Douglas nodded his head.

"Are you sure now, Douglas – sure we're talking about the same bloke?"

"Yes!" cried Douglas, nodding his head at me furiously now, willing me to stop, willing me to shut up.

"Well, you should know, I suppose," I picked up a plate, "seems a bit funny to me." I turned and walked into the dining room. I stopped at Cliff's elbow. "Sorry ... but are you Cliff?"

Haydn was laughing and choking in little gasps, head over his plate. Don was staring at Cliff. Douglas crept quietly into the room, just inside the door, watching.

Cliff looked at the three of them in turn, then turned to look at

Haydn again, to stare at Haydn. But Haydn kept his jerking head over his plate. Finally, Cliff turned to face me, "Funny bugger, eh?" and he reached up to take the plate.

I quickly shifted the plate to my left hand and grasped his outstretched fingers, "Hullo, I'm Marc," I smiled at him, "you must be Cliff," and I gripped his hand hard, pressing my fingers into the base of his knuckles and praying just as hard that he'd be too surprised to retaliate. His eyes widened and the pressure on my hand suddenly increased but then, just as suddenly, he let his hand go limp.

"Yeh, gidday," he said quietly to the formica table, "now can we get on with our tea if you're quite finished with all the poncing around?"

"Sure Cliff, sure," I said, and placed his plate in front of him.

We all sat down. Cliff picked up his knife and fork again and began to cut the fat off one of his fried chops, when Douglas rose from the table, arms extended, eyes closed, and breathed, "Dear Lord!"

"Jesus!" spat Cliff, "I thought at least we'd be spared this tonight!" and he threw down his knife and fork.

"... we thank Thee Lord for all Thy help and succour throughout this day," continued Douglas and he clasped his hands together in front of him. Involuntarily, I started to do the same, but became acutely aware of the others and dropped my hands to the table. "Especially Lord," he went on, "do we thank Thee for Thy guiding hand in the preparation of this meal, and ask Thy blessing for what is to come."

"By God, we'll need it!" cried Cliff, "with your cooking. Look at this!" He prodded the chop he had cut. "Burnt on the outside and raw in the middle. It's about time you got your God on a Gordon Blue course, eh? eh?" and he poked Don with his elbow.

Douglas winced, eyes still closed, hands still together, and then he intoned, "Amen," and dropped into his chair.

The rest of the meal was eaten in silence. It was badly cooked. Besides the raw, burnt chops, the potatoes were unsalted and the frozen peas had been boiled into minute wizened green pellets. Don was the last to finish. He seemed to take a very long time to finish each mouthful. He saw me watching him.

"Twenty-two times," he said.

"Twenty-two times what?" I asked.

"Each mouthful. You're supposed to chew each mouthful twenty-two times before swallowing. For your digestion. Read it in the Reader's Digest."

"Why twenty-two?" I asked. "Why not twenty-three or fifteen? What about the size ..."

"Twenty-two," he broke in. "Proven statistically."

"How can they ...?"

"Proven," he said. "Got machines to chew it small. Small enough to pass through a mesh. The mesh is so fine ..."

"Peaches anyone?" cut in Haydn, making big eyes at me, and nodding in Don's direction.

"The mesh is so fine that ..."

"Give Don some tinned peaches, Marc please," said Haydn "... so he can chew them twenty-two times eh?"

*

IT WAS HAYDN'S turn to wash the dishes, Cliff to dry. It was on the roster. Cliff's duty roster on the kitchen wall. I picked up a tea towel and helped dry.

Haydn filled the sink with hot water, tipped in a liberal sprinkling of detergent and started washing the dishes with unusually quick, feverish, almost violent movements. He was singing to himself, deep, bass, out of tune, singing one line over and over, "Let us now praise famous men."

Cliff was standing close to him, huge, hovering, in his red, black and gold jersey. Like a giant wasp. He inspected every washed item carefully, minutely, until he found what he seemed to be looking for and pounced, on a plate, held it up disdainfully under Haydn's nose and with his lips almost touching Haydn's cheek, whispered "Dirty!" and dropped the plate back into the water. Haydn flinched, but then began his breathy, out-of-tune singing again. And we came to the cutlery. Haydn wiped each piece separately before dropping it into the dish-rack. Cliff stood back and watched him, then he leant forward and put a restraining hand on Haydn's shoulder. A heavy, powerful, restraining hand to stop him.

And suddenly I knew that this had all happened before, that it always happened, that Haydn had been waiting for it to happen.

Haydn seemed to get smaller under his touch. He didn't turn. He waited. Slowly Cliff reached with his free hand and spread the washed cutlery in the rack. He picked up the dessert spoons and one by one he laid them carefully upside down on the rack, pausing after each placement to look at Haydn. "Turn them over," he said, a thin smile on his lips, "they drain better that way. Didn't your mummy teach you cleanliness and good habits when you were a little boy?" He increased the pressure of his grip on Haydn's shoulder, twisting and forcing him to turn and face the rows of serried spoons. Haydn's body buckled. The colour drained from his face.

"Here Haydn, I'll finish," I said, and I pushed him away from the sink, breaking Cliff's grip. "You make us some coffee. I'll do the rest. You've done enough anyway." I dipped my hand into the sink and picked up a fistful of cutlery. I turned to face Cliff. "You'd like some coffee, wouldn't you Cliff?" and I threw the fistful down on the rack. Some bounced and spilled onto the floor. One finished face down. It was draining lovely.

Chapter 10
Far from home

I made the taxi stop at the farm gate and let me out. I paid the driver and waited until the car's lights rushed red around the bend in the road and I was left in the dark. There was a quarter moon – just enough to see the cattle-stop. I stepped and jumped across it and then slowly picked my way up the drive. It was scored with deep wheel ruts and even deeper, black potholes. I walked on the central raised grass mound between the ruts. The lights were on in the house. Thank God for that. Didn't think of checking before sending the taxi off.

My feet are wet. Soaking. Through to my socks. Perhaps I should take them off. That'd be an entry. "Excuse me, I've just arrived from Wales. Can I dry my socks?"

I reached the front door and stopped. I didn't want to knock. It's better not knowing. Once I knock, it's on. Or off. Perhaps I could lie down here on the porch and they'll find me in the morning, frozen stiff, like The Little Match Girl. And they'll cry and say what a waste, and Carole will hug my lifeless form to her and breathe into me to try, vainly, to revive me. She'll put her warm lips on mine and blow her warm life into me. Reluctantly, I knocked on the door.

No one answered, so I knocked again more loudly. The porch light came on, and she opened the door.

And despite myself, I stepped back.

"Hullo," she said.

Kiss her. Pick her up. Rub bellies. Have it off right here on the porch. In wet socks. "Hullo," I said.

And we both breathed.

"Well, you're here then."

"Yes, arrived last night."

"Last night? You should have phoned."

"Right," I laughed, "should have – didn't think of it."

She laughed with me.

"Who is it, Carole?" Thin, high-pitched voice from inside.

"It's Marc, mum. Marc Thomas."

"Well, bring him in, girl – and close the door. You're letting all the cold air in."

As I stepped into the lounge, Carole's mother rose out of her chair and fluttered across to me, took hold of my arm and pulled me to the chair opposite hers, near the fire. She was tiny – about four foot ten or eleven – neat, slim, pert as a sparrow, her movements quick and fussy. "Well," she said, "let's have a look at you."

And while she looked and talked, I looked at Carole. She was standing behind her mother's chair watching me. Her eyes were brilliant, the dark centres catching and reflecting the flames of the fire. Then they flicked from me to her mother, back to me, and I realised that Mrs Meadows had asked me something.

"I'm sorry ..." I stumbled

"I was saying you're bound to want a cup of tea coming all that way, wasn't I, Carole?"

We had tea and fruit loaf out of a biscuit tin. Coronation biscuit tin. Mam had one.

"I'm afraid father isn't here at the moment," said Mrs Meadows, or Nancy as she insisted I call her, "and he's been so looking forward to meeting you," she smiled and nibbled at her fruit loaf, "but it's the same old thing every Saturday, I'm afraid – week in, week out!" and the more she talked, the more upset she became. "Golf comes first as far as Morrie goes – nothing else matters! I swear I could die in the morning and he'd still be out there with his damned clubs in the afternoon!"

Carole smiled at me, "He's a bit late, I'm ..."

"A bit late!" cried Nancy, "a bit late? He should have been home hours ago! Not that I should be surprised of course – the day he came home on time – when he said – when he promised – that would be the day I'd be surprised!" and she took a large bite of fruit loaf. "He'll be drinking, mark my words, drinking himself stupid, even more stupid than he normally is," and she started spitting fruit loaf into her empty teacup. Then she humphed and muttered her way into the kitchen, pulled open the door of the oven, then slammed it shut.

I smiled at Carole.

"How's your mother?" she asked, and she sat on the floor against Nancy's chair. She glanced up at me then looked into the fire.

"She's fine," I lied. How do I say the truth? That she's sick with fear, foreboding. That she cries herself to sleep. That she considers me dead. "Little Helen takes up all her time. It's lovely for her and dad having a baby so late."

"I suppose it is," she agreed. And there was a silence. Nancy was hitting something in the kitchen. The something snapped and then crashed into a tin of some kind.

"I hate seeing good food go to waste," said Nancy as she resumed her seat, "especially when I'm the one who has to cook it ... I don't know what makes me more mad – having to throw his dinner in the bin or having him reeling in, stinking drunk. He never ..." She stopped in mid-sentence. A car's headlights had flashed across the windows and then we heard a sudden rush up the drive. Nancy rose from her chair and smoothed down the front of her dress.

"That'll be father," said Carole.

There was a clatter and a rattle and the sound of something heavy being dropped in the porch. He came in at a rush.

"Sorry Nancy, didn't realise it was late." Hoarse voice, pleading. Heavy smoker. He dived at her, lips pursed, trying to kiss her on the cheek. She grimaced and pulled away, pushing hard at his chest.

"Late? It's eight o'clock, Morrie. You left for golf at nine this morning." Words like bullets.

"Got held up. Had a slow four in front of us."

"For eleven hours? Held up would be right. Against the bar. I can smell it. You're shika again, aren't you?"

"Oh Nancy, give a man a fair go!"

"A fair go? You've had a fair go. You have a fair go every time I let you out of my sight. You can hardly stand up."

"Oh balls!"

Carole smiled at me.

Nancy folded her arms and looked at him. Her lips were pressed together in a thin hard line.

Carole rose and went to her mother's side. I sat where I was and looked at my feet.

"Dad," said Carole tentatively, "this is Marc."

I stood up.

"If that's the way you're going to talk ..." spat Nancy, head jutting forward, "... in front of me, in front of ... visitors, then all I can suggest is that you turn around and get back out to your boozy mates at the golf club."

"You made me say it!" he cried.

I sat down again.

"I made you say it?" she repeated. Then she turned to me in marvellous disbelief, eyes wide, head shaking slowly from side to side, "I'm very sorry, Marc, I didn't realise ... I made him say it," and without looking at Morrie again, she went out into the kitchen and put the kettle on the stove.

Morrie crossed to the settee opposite me, sighed loudly, and sat down and closed his eyes.

Carole introduced me to him again. I didn't stand this time. He opened his eyes to look at me, nodded, and then closed them again. He went to sleep.

We had another cup of tea. The three of us. Then Carole and I went out onto the porch.

She stood close, holding the rail in both hands and looking out into the dark. I could smell her smell. Hers. Different from anyone else. Must go back to animal origins. In a cave. Sniffing out in the dark. The way cats and dogs do. Licking. She's looking at me now in that strange way of hers – with that little smile at the corners of her mouth.   Do you want to kiss me, Carole? Go on, be a bugger. Give me a sloppy French kiss. Blow in my ear. Go on. "You haven't changed at all," I said.

"Of course I haven't changed," she laughed. "It's only been four months."

Only? What do you mean "only"? He's only got cancer. Only cancer?... oh well, that's alright then, isn't it? "Yes, only four months," I said. "I haven't changed."

"No," she said quickly, "you look exactly the same."

"I didn't mean my hair," I said, "or wrinkles or dandruff. I meant ... I haven't changed."

She looked up at my face and, for a moment, for the first time since I'd arrived, held my gaze. "I got such a shock the day I heard ... the day they said you were coming. Why didn't you let me know?"

"I thought I'd surprise you."

"Well, you certainly did that. Dave McNeil ... he's the Principal..."

"Yes, I've met him."

"Dave told the staff in the last week of term that you were arriving. I was just sitting there – in a staff meeting – and out came your name – from Dave's mouth. I was on my feet – I don't remember getting up – and everyone was looking at me – so I sat down again."

"And now everyone knows."

"No, no one knows," she said quietly.

"No one?"

"No one – except mum and dad – and they won't be saying anything."

"Why?"

"Why what?"

"Why won't they be saying anything?"

She just looked at me.

"You must have asked them not to," I said. "Why the secrecy?"

"It's not secrecy!" she exclaimed, "... it's just that it's ... it's complicated."

"Complicated?" and I knew my voice was rising but I couldn't stop it. "What do you mean 'complicated'?"

"There's others ... others to consider ..."

And I was suddenly very alone and very far from home.

"... if I'd known you were coming, I'd have written and told you ..." she said, and she turned half away from me, "... there's someone else ... there has been all along."

✳

I STEPPED OFF the porch into the dark of the driveway. The gorge welled up in my throat and I swallowed to keep it down. What does she mean "all along"? "All along" when she was getting me to strip? "All along" when she was buying the bloody cards? "All along" when she was kissing me down ... I staggered blind as my foot hit a pothole. I righted myself and kept walking. She was shouting something behind me. "All along" with him, for Christ's sake! How is it possible for anyone to be so witless, so simple, so bloody wet!

"Dad'll drive you home!" she called at my back.

Dad'll drive me home. Dad ... and I started to laugh – quietly at first, but then it rose in me like a choking fit ... "Sleepytime Dad?" I gasped to myself, "... you mean fall down pissed as a newt Dad? Drunk as a fart Dad ...?"

"At least let me call you a taxi!"

"Don't worry!" I yelled without turning. "I'll walk. I want to walk. I've been wanting to walk all along!" I reached the gate.

"Marc!" she cried.

I turned right towards the lights of the town.

Chapter 11
Can you dance?

Three little boys were gliding Indian file in front of us, in the iced gutter, bare-foot, sliding and shrieking their way to school. There had been a hard frost overnight. Haydn and I were heavily clothed and well muffled for the long walk to school. The little ones stopped and stared at us as we passed.

"Gidday!" they yelled, their breaths forming little white clouds.

"Gidday!" answered Haydn.

They smiled encouragingly at me. "Hullo," I said, and they forgot us immediately and went splashing, blue-footed, red-toed on their way.

"Do you always walk?" I asked Haydn, "It's a hell of a long way."

"Not much choice, is there? I can't afford a car. I get a taxi sometimes when it's raining."

"What about Cliff? Doesn't he ever offer you a lift in his car?"

"Cliff? ... offer me a lift? He wouldn't give me a sheep dropping if he thought I wanted one. Anyway," he muttered, head down avoiding the icy ruts, "... I'd never ask."

We walked on in silence until we'd climbed to the top of the hill. "He'll pass us soon. I swear he times it just as I'm nearing the gates."

We came to the crossroads and waited with a number of College students for the road to clear. Cliff pulled up in his car, roared in first gear across the intersection, then pulled into the kerb at the far side. He got out of his car and stood waiting, hands on hips, on the kerb opposite us.

I stepped off the kerb but Haydn grabbed my arm and held me. "Don't cross," he hissed. "Stay here and watch this."

I stepped back off the road. The others crossed. And as the students passed in front of Cliff, he inspected them from head to toe. He pulled two boys to one side.

"Where are your caps?" He prodded each in the chest.

"In my bag sir." Tall thin boy. Bad acne.

"Well, get it out!" he roared. He turned to the other. "And you?"

"It's at home sir. I forgot it."

"Well, get back home and get it."

"But I'll be late, sir."

"That's your problem – and don't answer me back or I'll tan your backside for you."

Acne couldn't find his cap. Cliff reached for his bag and tipped the contents onto the ground. He picked up the cap and placed it carefully, deferentially, on the boy's head.

My day was all Music and English. No history at all. Because the Head of Social Studies liked to teach the history himself. English, because anyone can teach English, can't they? Music, because I'm Welsh and can sing and who else was there anyway? So Haydn and I took double-sized classes together, sixty to seventy boys and girls at a time for singing. Haydn played the piano and I coaxed, bullied, bellowed them into singing. Hymns mainly. Welsh hymns especially. 'Bread of Heaven' and 'Aberystwyth'. Real culture.

I saw her for the first time at school as I walked into the staffroom at the end of the day. She was just coming out of the workroom and she stopped and looked at me. And I looked through and past her, and then turned abruptly and went into the kitchen. That'll show her! That'll teach her! 'Someone else'! Well, here's someone else who's someone else! I poured a little milk into a cup. By Christ! I've come twelve thousand miles ... twelve thousand miles – for what? To snub her in the staffroom? To be petty and childish? To prove I'm someone ... I dropped the cup in the sink and darted back into the room. She'd gone.

It was nearly a week before I saw her again. She didn't come to the staffroom during the day. Stayed in her room. "Always used to come," said Haydn when I asked. "Probably making something special for the pantomime," he offered, "or maybe she's not feeling well."

I was late to class after lunch and when I entered a girl was standing in the middle of the room, her skirt around her ankles. She was well-developed – one of those big-boned, awkward, thirteen-year-old girls who develop years earlier than their contemporaries, and with straining bust and jutting bum look like burgeoning Eve alongside their flat-chested, boy-bottomed girlfriends; and who, for one brief moment in their lives, confound their plainness, and are alluring. And she knew it, and wanted everyone else to know it. Everything about her, her stance, the angle of her shoulders, the sidelong look, the provocative jut of the pelvis, everything said, "Look at my breasts, look at my hips. Look – I'm a woman."

And everyone was certainly looking – Haydn from behind the piano, me from the door, the girls, and the boys, at her dimpled legs and at her panties, her cream, silk, tight panties.

"Pick up your skirt, Sheryl," I said, looking at a spot high up on the wall over her right shoulder.

"But it's broke, Mr Thomas, the elastic's ..."

"Pick it up, Sheryl," I repeated, more loudly.

"It was an accident, Mr Thomas," broke in Haydn. "She stood

up and it sort of ... fell down."

"Don't know how it happened, Mr Thomas," continued Sheryl. She hadn't moved. The skirt was still around her ankles. "It just sort of ..."

"Pick it up!"

"Yes, Mr Thomas," she gasped, and bending low, she stepped out of the skirt, lifted it high in her right hand and walked towards me with it held out in front of her.

"Put it on, girl!" I snapped, resisting the impulse to get behind the piano with Haydn. The girl was as brazen as brass.

She stopped, seemingly surprised at the suggestion. "But it's broke, Mr Thomas."

"Put it on and hold it together with your hand," I said, almost pleaded.

She considered that. Then slowly, with exaggerated care as if the whole skirt were about to disintegrate in her hands, she pulled it up over her thighs and stood, weight on one foot, holding it together at the front.

"Now go and get it fixed."

"Where sir? Can I go home sir? I don't live far. My mother will fix it."

"Yes, I suppose you'd better ..." Carole. Let her go to Carole. Take her to Carole! Carry her to Carole, skirt, jutting bum, silk panties and all! "No, no ... on second thoughts, you can't walk all the way home dressed like that – you'll have to go to Miss Meadows, I'm afraid, in the Clothing Room." I turned to Haydn, "Someone had better go with her unfortunately, Mr Morgan. Would you like to escort Sheryl and her skirt to the Clothing Room while I stay and look after the class?" and I'll break both your legs and feed them up your anus if you say yes.

"Oh no, Mr Thomas," beamed Haydn, coming out from behind the piano, "the class won't be any trouble to me. I'll just play them something on the piano while you go with Sheryl," and to show me how happy he was to look after them, he immediately sat down again at the piano and began playing. "Roaming in the Gloaming" it was, "with my lassie by my side."

I turned and nodded to Sheryl. She smiled up at me, wide-eyed, all innocence, clutching her skirt.

We walked side by side through the school. There were few people about, much to my relief and to Sheryl's obvious dismay. She slowed down every time we came alongside a bank of windows, willing heads to turn, to wonder, to marvel, but I crossed to the inside, walking between her and the windows, and snapping my fingers at her to keep her to heel. Carole was sitting on a chair in the middle of the room.

She was hand-sewing a design onto a piece of cloth. The girls were clustered around her. It looked so peaceful, so idyllic, English cottage, and Carole, in matching pinafore and dress, so pure and clean, was all bluebells and homebaking, fresh milk and farm eggs. Was this the woman who stripped me with a pack of cards? I stood tongue-tied. She waited patiently, then smiled a little smile of encouragement, which made me worse.

"It's my skirt, Miss," said Sheryl, "the elastic's broke."

I nodded in agreement, confirming it. Carole rose from her chair, placed the sewing on it, and came towards me.

"Thank you, Mr Thomas, I'll fix it." She paused and looked at me expectantly.

I opened my mouth to tell her how lovely she looked, how my crutch had turned to water. I closed it again.

"You can leave her with me," she said, and waited.

I nodded.

"I'll send her back when it's done."

I smiled at her and backed out of the room. I stood in the corridor and looked at her door. I hadn't said a word. Not a single word.

About half way through the last lesson on Friday afternoon, when the class, Haydn, and I were pleading to be fed till we wanted no more, a dark, heavily built figure entered the back of the double room, took a seat in the back row, boys' side, and joined in our singing. A rich nasal, annoyingly flat, bass voice, booming out in near harmony.

And at the end of the song, he clapped lustily, calling out for "More" and "Another".

"Who is that?" I whispered to Haydn.

"Arch Reynolds," said Haydn, "Head of Science – and now Singing," and he giggled, head down behind the piano. "Was a Japanese prisoner of war in Malaya for two years."

Arch stayed with us for the rest of the lesson. Apart from their initial surprise when he started singing, the children accepted his presence and in fact sang all the better because of it. When the bell went, he sauntered down to the front of the class, grinning from ear to ear. "I enjoyed that," he said, and he thrust out his hand to me. "Name's Arch but you can call me Archibald for short." He pumped vigorously. There were deep burn marks, I guessed chemical burn marks, on the back of his hand. "Just appointed you Assistant Stage Manager for the Panto," he beamed.

"Assistant Stage Manager."

"Yes, you've got the voice for it."

"Panto?"

"Yes, can you dance?"

"Dance? – no, not at all!"

"Good. Don't need any dancing."

"Assistant Stage Manager?"

"We've been through all that!"

"Who's the Stage Manager?"

"Haydn – unfortunately he's a bit of a dancer."

Haydn nodded and grinned at me.

"I'm the Producer," said Arch, "and as you know, I can sing. We'll make a great team. Let's go and have a cup of coffee and talk duets and sets and things."

And over coffee he introduced me to the last quarter of the school Panto team: Pearl Spence, wardrobe mistress, property mistress and owner of the two enormous tits which I'd already met, and who, it now transpired, was twice married and twice divorced. She looked as if she'd eaten both husbands and was still hungry. They were steam-rollering me. Pearl had her arm hooked in mine, pressing home her points about set colours needing to fit together, to join, to become one flesh as it were.

I grasped at straws, "But I've only just arrived. I don't really know anyone."

"What better way of meeting people than working with them, closely," breathed Pearl, trapping my arm in the valley between the two of them. "Almost everybody on the staff's doing something – Dave McNeil does front of house, Molly and Kaye make the props – even Douglas has a part ..."

"Carole?"

"Oh yes! Carole's in the Panto. One of the stars you might say – not that anyone would say that of course – we don't go in for stars here – but ... we couldn't be without her! She's the Princess. Lovely as a picture – can't sing a note of course but you can't have everything, can you?" and she rubbed my elbow hard across her right breast, "Elsie Morris sings for her from behind the sets while she mimes." She stopped rubbing and looked at me sharply, "Well? Are you in or not?"

"Oh yes," I said softly, "I'm in."

Chapter 12
Like a burst sausage

"... a local woman's house burnt down three nights ago. You probably know her – Mrs Moloney – but no, you wouldn't, would you, seeing as you're not long in the country?"

Her voice was harsh and rasping. I transferred the phone to my other ear.

"Anyway, I thought ... I had the idea we'd give a concert for her, to raise some money, I mean – because she's got nothing. She's two children and ... it all went – all their clothes, everything. So we decided we'd raise money through a concert and we thought that you might sing. You do sing, don't you?"

"Well, I have ..."

"Yes, we'd heard that. That's good then."

"When is the concert?"

"Next Saturday at the Presbyterian Hall. You know the one? Opposite the Moorend shops?"

"No ... I don't actually ... but how did you know ... who told you I could sing?"

"Oh Nancy! Yes ... Nancy Meadows. Said you'd love to do it – and you've got such a lovely voice, she said, so I ..."

"Nancy! Well then ... can't disappoint Nancy, can I? Moorend shops you say. I'll find it – Nancy would know, wouldn't she? ... of course she would – perhaps you could give her a special invite ... yes, she'd love it ... and her husband Morrie, right? And I think

they've got a daughter, haven't they?... Yes, I thought they did –
well, the more the merrier, right? Poor Mrs Moloney. Now, what
would you like me to sing?"

"Oh anything, anything you like, er ... you're Welsh, aren't
you?"

"Yes."

"Well, there you are then. Anything to draw the crowds in."

"How many others will be performing?"

"Oh lots! Crowds!   Lots of talent here in Maranganui. You'd
be surprised."

"And what time would it start, Mrs Saunders?"

"Oh, about 7.30."

"Fine! – I'll see you then ..." and I almost missed it "... er – just
a second, Mrs Saunders ... seeing as Nancy Meadows suggested
me to you, perhaps the polite thing would be if I were to give her
a call – on your behalf of course ... look, I'd be only too happy to
do it."

Carole answered the phone. I couldn't believe it. I held my
breath – thinking what to say – what stunning thing to say –
what surprising, delightful, brilliant thing to captivate her with,
startle her, make her laugh, make her eyes shine ...

"Yes?" she repeated.

She's going to hang up! Say something you bloody fool! –
anything! "Hi!" I said, "it's me." Now, there's brilliance for you.

"I thought it was," she replied.

"I almost did it again – didn't I?"

"Did what?"

"The dumb act – you know – like the other day when I brought
that girl to you ..."

"Sheryl."

"Yes, Sheryl – with the broken skirt ... you must have thought
me a right idiot – I didn't say a single word to you."

"Well, I did wonder ..."

"And I almost did it again now, didn't I? – Not speaking, I mean – I never used to be like that, did I?"

"In Wales, you mean?"

"Yes."

"No, you certainly weren't ... perhaps you've changed."

"No! I haven't!" and I'd blurted it before I could stop myself. And I was glad. I was happy. I was ... but why did she suggest that? Does she think I've changed? Or did she want me to tell her that I hadn't? Or was she telling me that she'd changed! "No, I haven't changed," I repeated, calmly, "... at all."

"Well, that's good to know – you had me worried there for a while – anyway, to what do I owe the pleasure of this call?"

"Now ... this may seem funny – especially seeing what we've just been talking about, but ... actually, I wasn't ringing you – I was ringing your mother."

"My mother?"

"Yes – not that I don't want to talk to you. I'm loving talking to you. I desperately want to go on talking to you – I can ring your mother back later ..."

"Now that's plain silly – I'll get her for you," and she put down the receiver.

Oh, well done! Brilliantly handled! Absolutely superb – the finesse, the ingenuity, the stupidity!

"Hullo?" Tiny voice.

"Mrs Meadows – it's Marc Thomas here."

"Yes – Carole told me it was you."

Of course she would have, you bloody fool! Get your brain into gear or you'll blow this too. "Right! And I want to thank you Mrs ... sorry, Nancy, isn't it ...?

"Yes, I much prefer Nancy."

"Thank you, Nancy for suggesting me for the charity concert.

It was very thoughtful of you."

"Oh, as soon as I heard about that poor woman and the fundraising – I thought of you – I mean – you're from overseas after all, aren't you? – I knew you'd be only too pleased."

"Mrs Saunders was so grateful for your suggestion Nancy, she made me promise to ring you straightaway and insist that you, Morrie and Carole, all attend the concert as special guests."

"Special guests?" Tinier voice.

And I knew I had her. "Oh yes, insisted on it – the three of you. And I thought – this is only a suggestion of course – but I thought I should turn up at the same time as you – so we could go in as a party as it were ... what do you think?"

"Oh yes – I think that's a very good idea."

"Excellent! So it's just a question of my working out how to get there on time ..."

"Don't you have a car?"

"No, no – not yet anyway – but that's no problem – I thought I'd walk – or get a taxi if it's wet ..."

"Of course you won't! We'll come and pick you up."

"No, please! – I wouldn't dream of it ..."

"Morrie can stay home from golf for once in his life – that way we can be sure he'll be sober – and we'll pick you up at ... what time does it start?"

"Seven thirty."

"Right – we'll pick you up at seven o'clock, and we'll be sure of getting good seats."

"That's very nice of you, Nancy."

"Not at all! Wouldn't miss a dress-up occasion like this for anything – I mean – they come so rarely around here anyway – and, I should be thanking you for getting us invited – as special guests!"

*

THERE WERE ABOUT twenty-five people in the hall. Seats had been set out for two hundred or more. Most of the twenty-five were congregated at the back. At the front, there was a small stage fringed with faded brown curtains, and on the floor to the right, an upright piano. The main lights were on.

It was obvious that someone had slightly misjudged the situation. We were overdressed. Haydn and I were in dark suits, Morrie in sports jacket and rugby tie, and only half pissed, while Carole and her mother were in cocktail dresses and handbags. The others in the hall, apart from one man, dressed in dicky-bow and tails, were, at best, described as casually dressed, including a few in the ubiquitous bush shirts, called Swandris, I'd discovered, shorts, socks, and boots.

Carole made slight hesitant moves to the door as if she wanted to leave but I confidently ushered our party to seats in the middle of the hall and ducked in beside Carole just before Haydn, unthinking sod, sat down. We waited. Nothing happened for a long time. Mam would be passing hard boils along the row by now, I thought. Haydn fidgeted with the music he had to play, turning it over and over. I smiled at Carole. She smiled at her mother. Her mother smiled at me. Morrie sighed a deep, long sigh.

Eventually a small woman, her hair piled in tresses and wearing a full-length, deep green gown, came out of the stage side door and crossed to the front. "Good evening, ladies and gentlemen."

The audience gradually quietened down. Two small boys who had been running around, in and out of the back seats, were hissed at by their mother and sat down.

My rasping telephone friend, Mrs Saunders, because that was

who she obviously was, welcomed everyone, talked at length about the poor family on whose behalf we were all gathered together, invited us to a supper after the concert was finished, and then introduced the first item.

A Scottish dancer. A Highland Scottish dancer. A large, red-headed, big-bosomed, middle-aged, Highland Scottish dancer. She stood in the middle of the stage, hands curved above her head, right foot toe-pointing forward. There was a shuddering gasp then a long droning wheeze off-stage, followed immediately by the high-pitched wailing of the bagpipes, and our dancer wheeled and gyrated across the stage to the obvious delight of the audience who showed their appreciation by hand-clapping in time to the dance. By the end of her second piece she was visibly perspiring, her enormous bosom heaving with the exertion. She bowed low, arms wide to the audience. The crowd clapped loudly and a few small boys sent her loud piercing whistles.

My heart had sunk when we'd entered the hall, risen momentarily during the dancing, and sunk again at the whistles.

A Margaret Crosbie, soprano, was next. She had chosen Mozart's "Ave Maria" and Haydn was accompanying her. He was very nervous. I was almost as nervous as he, for I knew that he was not properly prepared for the music despite the fact that he'd soaked his hands in hot water for half an hour before the concert in order to make them supple.

Margaret sang well. She had a full, rich, bell-like tone and I was enjoying it. However, the trouble started at the end of the first page. Haydn had to turn over quickly. He grabbed at the sheets, fumbled them and missed the turn. Margaret, a real trouper, carried on, hoping he would quickly correct his error and catch up. Haydn got redder and redder as he got further and further behind. In panic, instead of stopping and selecting a suitable re-entry point, he tried to improvise an accompaniment.

Margaret flinched but kept on singing. The audience was deathly quiet, instinctively realising something significant was happening. Margaret sang on to the last high note and held it. She held it hoping that Haydn would seize his chance and allow them to finish together. But Haydn was beyond such subtleties by this time. Realising that she had finished, he sought to end his agony quickly, and improvised three completely inappropriate but ending-sounding chords, smiled palely at Margaret and lightly took her arm as they resumed their seats. The audience applauded enthusiastically, Morrie leading them. He was on his feet, his hands above his head, clapping and laughing. Clapping and laughing long after everyone else had stopped, long after Haydn had sat down. I think he wanted an encore.

I smiled across at Haydn and whispered through my smile, "You do that to me and I'll break your bloody back, boy bach," then sat back, moving my right leg so that it rested, full length, against Carole's, and held my breath. She must have noticed – but she gave no sign, nothing – except that she didn't shift her leg away. Now that's a sign, I said to myself and released my breath.

Meanwhile a trombonist had taken the stage. Dicky-bow, coat and tails. We were guessing he was a trombonist because he was holding a trombone case still unopened in his hands. Centre-stage, facing the audience, he painstakingly released the catches on his case, lovingly removed the instrument and while the audience watched attentively, assembled the parts. When he had finished, he looked up at his audience for the first time. He was a big man, with a florid, pock-marked face. He looked like a farmer.

"I'd like to play Handel's 'Largo' in 'G'," he announced quietly, and the words hardly out of his mouth, he put the trombone to his lips and blew. He played in fits and starts, each phrase played as a separate entity, pausing at the end of each line, taking a long slow breath and then beginning the next.

He was obviously not happy with his performance or rather with his trombone. Suddenly he stopped, disconnected the mouthpiece and blew down it sharply. A fine spray of spittle rained down on the luckily empty front rows. He resumed his playing, still unhappy, and at the end of the piece calmly dismantled his instrument, tapped the main stock against his knee, dislodging some more spittle, in larger drop sizes this time, onto the stage, packed his instrument into the case at his feet, made a brief bow to the audience and, case in hand, went off. The audience clapped sympathetically.

I was next. Our mistress of ceremonies announced me as 'a visitor from Wales'. A visitor. Was she clairvoyant? Did she have premonitions of what was about to happen?

Carole whispered, "Good luck!" to me, and rested her fingertips on my knee. I didn't move. I made an instant decision not to move while her fingers were there. She must have known, because she immediately lifted them and tapped me as if it were a signal to go. I went.

Haydn walked to the piano and sat down. I passed near to him, punched his arm, gently, and crossed to the front of the hall. I stood on the hall floor on the same level as the audience as I did not want to be associated with the disaster that had just taken place on the stage.

My song was one I had learnt painstakingly with my singing teacher in Wales – Handel's "Hear me, ye winds and waves!" A bit on the heavy side, perhaps, but at least I knew it well.

Haydn played the opening bars, tentatively at first, but then more confidently. I relaxed. The song, appropriately, was a despairing prayer for the release of death, and I closed my eyes momentarily in order to attain the necessary passion and sadness that the song demanded. The audience was quiet and, as I started to enjoy the sheer beauty of Handel's music, I opened my eyes, held my head high and started to sing. At the end of the first line, I glanced down and saw a small boy standing two feet in front of me. He was no more than three or four years old. He was staring straight up into my face and his nose was running. Two long rivulets of snot were hanging from his nose. The rivulets had joined at the bottom to form a long, pendulous, natural, shining necklace.

I faltered. The audience was no longer listening to my singing, all eyes and attention were focussed on the rivulets. Haydn glanced across at me, beaming. I looked up quickly and saw Carole's face. Inscrutable. I closed my eyes momentarily, swallowed hard, concentrated on the accompaniment and began to sing again, trying hard to convince the audience that my momentary silence had been part of the song. My little friend, obviously having lost interest, walked slowly to the side of the hall, rivulets swinging slowly in rhythm with his walk. All eyes, including mine, followed him.

Mercifully I got to the end of the song. I moved quickly, yet trying not to appear to hurry, back to my seat. Morrie was shaking. I stared at him. His face was impassive but his body was shaking. I looked at the ceiling, said 'Dear Mam!' quietly to myself, and glanced at Carole. She was smiling full face at me. "Lovely," she breathed. Oh God, I thought. I dared not look at her mother.

Morrie was still shaking. I could feel it in my chair. Little explosions of air were popping from his nostrils. His face was stone. His eyes were glazed. But he kept popping down his nose. Like The Little Red Engine.

And still the agony was to go on. The Scottish dancer was back but this time as a tap dancer. She was dressed in a pink, skin-tight sequinned costume which cut deeply into her bulging thighs.

The bodice was very tight and flattened her breasts, spreading them sideways under her armpits. On her feet she wore red tap-dancing shoes decorated with fluffy pink bobbles. She looked like a burst, uncooked sausage.

An unseen assistant put on a record and she began. She began one of those forward-running-but-going-nowhere foot-banging tap dances that were the rage of Hollywood in the Forties and Fifties. At each foot bang she quivered dangerously. Each tremor rippled up her thighs, belly, breasts, armpits and cheeks and then down again. Her body was a river of involuntary movement.

Morrie was leaning forward, staring at her. Her routine required so many steps to the left and so many to the right but the stage was so small that she periodically disappeared into the wings, still tapping, only to reappear seconds later, smiling and undulating. Each time she disappeared Morrie cried out "More! More! More!" And when she reappeared, as she inevitably did, he clapped and cheered uproariously. He was a born leader. Within seconds, most of the children at the back of the hall, led by my little friend with the shining necklace, had run down the aisle and were gathered around him – like Jesus outside Jerusalem. And to his cries and cheering they added wolf whistles, foot-stamping and the occasional punch.

I didn't want any supper. Neither did Haydn. But Morrie insisted we stay – he was hungry he said and besides, he was sure I'd want to stay to talk to my fellow 'artistes' he said. Swap experiences and that. You know – showbiz stuff! There he'd been, all his life, he said, thinking that 'artistes' were a bunch of girls – when all the time they were such talented people who could lead you into a magic world of winds and waves, bagpipes and belly-dancing. He stepped in close to me, confidential, "I'd really like to learn to play one of those spraying things that that joker had – you know, the bent pipe thing that he kept spitting out of

… what's it called now…?"

And I could have kissed the insensitive, red-necked, bigoted, beautiful little shit, full on the lips – for there Carole was, standing next to me, brushing against me, laying her hand on mine, smiling up at me and squeezing my arm as she told me to take no notice, as she argued passionately with him, as she defended me to the hilt. I didn't have to say a word. It was all worth it – the spittle, the rivulets, the armpits and the fluffy pink bobbles. It was more than I had dreamed it could be. I smiled at him. I nodded in agreement, urging him on, willing him to excess.

And Cliff, my Cliff, our Cliff from the men's hostel, walked down the hall towards us. He stopped in front of me and held out his hand to Carole. "Ready?" he asked.

I don't know if Carole said anything. I don't know if she looked at me. All I could see was Cliff's face, inches from mine. He was chewing. Not gum. Just chewing. A matchstick or something. And they left.

Chapter 13
Like a pair of silk knickers

It was late by the time we got home. I'd had to ring for a taxi at a nearby house – there was no phone in the hall. Morrie had insisted he'd drive us, Haydn had accepted, and I'd refused. Point-blank. And to my relief, Haydn hadn't argued. He'd remained silent while we waited for the taxi in the dark outside the hall and then during the trip home. Some kind of sixth sense. We walked up our drive. The lights were on in the house. I stopped and looked at them, working out which windows they came from. His were on. "Thank God!" I breathed.

Haydn stopped alongside me. "You didn't know, did you?" he said, matter of fact.

"No, I didn't." And I started to move on up the drive.

He gripped me by the elbow, "The funny thing is ..." and he giggled in that strange way he had, "... he still doesn't know."

I turned and looked at him. The lights from the house were reflecting off his glasses and I couldn't see his eyes. "Doesn't know what?" I asked.

"About you and Carole ... in Wales."

"How the hell did you ...?"

"Oh, come on, fychan!" and his giggle turned to a full-blooded laugh, "... anyone with half a brain would have worked it out by now – the way you look at one another, the questions you ask, her trip to Britain, to Wales, you rushing out ... yes ..." and he laughed again, "half a brain ... and that'd be why Cliff hasn't figured it out yet." He cackled, then his tone suddenly changed, "What are you going to do?"

I walked up the drive and opened the front door. His room was the second on the right up the hall. The door was closed. I turned the handle and pushed it open. It hit and quivered against the wall behind. He wasn't there. I quickly checked the lounge, kitchen, dining room and bathroom. He wasn't home. I stood in the dark of the hall and closed my eyes tight, screwing them up so tight that lights flashed and pulsed behind the lids – shutting out the images that came flooding, forcing themselves into my brain. And when I was calm again, I stepped back into the light of his room.

He had a double bed. Set against the far wall, in the middle of the room. Perfectly made – bedspread evenly touching the floor on three sides, top turned back almost a third of its length, matching sheets and pillows. And curtains. The curtains were the same material and colour as the sheets. I looked up at the ceiling and knew before I looked. Everything was fresh, clean and matching. I sat down on the end of the bed, rucking the cover. I pulled up my feet and rucked it a little more. He had two wardrobes, two free-standing double wardrobes, a chest of drawers, with fitted mirror, two straight-backed chairs and an armchair – all in a palace of a bedroom, in a huge, interior-designed, colour-coordinated bridal suite of a bedroom. For two. And I knew which two.

Haydn was in our cupboard of a room, in bed, reading.

I stood over him until he looked up at me. "Why does Cliff have a room three times the size of this room when you and I are crammed in here together like sardines?"

He stared at me.

"... and would I be right in assuming that all the furniture in his room belongs to the Education Department – provided with the hostel?"

He didn't answer, so I waited.

"Yes ..." he stammered, "... the furniture all belongs to the hostel, to the Department – except ..." he added quickly, "... for the bed. Cliff bought that himself."

"And the room? Why does he have a room that size all to himself?"

"Because ..." and he paused, as if he were considering the matter for the first time, "... because he's Cliff!"

"Because he's Cliff," I repeated, "... because he's Cliff!" And the anger, the fury, suddenly welled up in my brain ... and flooded it.

"I'll be wanting a hand later," I said, and closed the door behind me.

The wardrobes were almost empty. He had four white shirts and a tie-rack hanging in one, and a charcoal grey suit, two jackets and three pairs of slacks in the other. But the wardrobe floors were covered – in shoes, neat, polished, sitting in perfect paired rows, in the first; and cardboard boxes, with lids, labelled, in the second. The boxes contained certificates, trophies, and photographs. Hundreds of photographs. The same photographs. Cliff's stern, unsmiling face glared fiercely out at me, from mascot to junior grade rugby to senior men's rugby to rugby coach. His expression didn't change. Man and boy.

Then one box with no label. It was tied with string like a parcel. I sat on the floor and carefully undid the knots.

Photographs. All of Carole – at the beach, posing with one knee jutting forward, at parties, at dances, dressed in Cinderella hoops and petticoats, and one mouth-watering shot in netball uniform, aged about twenty, in black boots, black stockings, black gym slip, white long-sleeved shirt, red tie and red girdle – I slipped it into my pocket – and then underneath, in a separate envelope –

as if there was something private or maybe not quite right about it – a collection of photographs of a young girl, a young girl at high school, from Carole's first day in white blouse and flat chest, to every class she'd attended, every team she'd played for. With dates. In strict order. How did he get them? More important, why did he get them? Ten years of photographs. In an envelope, in a shoebox, in the bottom of his wardrobe.

I lay everything on the floor near the window beyond the bed. I tipped the wardrobe next to the door onto its side and manoeuvred it onto a large mat. I opened the door and pulled the mat and wardrobe out of the room, down the hall and stopped clear of Haydn's door.

He didn't want me to do it. He did want me to do it, but he was scared shitless. After all, Cliff could come home any second. He could walk in on us mid move. Then where would we be? We couldn't carry it all ourselves anyway, could we? We'd need ... God! ... he would go berserk! I didn't know him ... he'd scream and smash ...

When he'd finished, we stripped both beds and carried the frames into our new room. Then the chest of drawers and our other belongings. We had got Cliff's wardrobe in place in our old room and were steering the double bed on its side through the doorway when I became aware of watchers. Two watchers. In doorways and pyjamas. I said "Hi!", and Don and Douglas said, "Hi!", but they didn't offer to help. Probably had enough furniture. Haydn put Cliff's things in the wardrobe while I swapped curtains. Ours were too narrow for the new window. There was nearly a foot gap in the centre. But we didn't complain. You couldn't open his very far in his new room but they matched his bed of course. So he couldn't complain.

And we were done. I sat on my bed, fully clothed, and waited. I was wrong of course. I had no right. What I had done was unreasonbable, unjustifiable. But, on the other hand, I was also totally right, perfectly reasonable, absolutely justified.

Haydn got into bed, pulled the blankets up high, then got out again, put on his dressing gown and sat on the bed. It seemed the right thing to do.

At 12.32am Cliff arrived home. We heard his key turn in the lock, the latch pull back, the door swing open and then close. Six strides, then the bedroom door swung open. He stepped into the room and stopped. He looked straight at me. His face didn't change – except his eyes seemed to get smaller. His head snapped to Haydn and held, then to the curtains. Without a word, he backed out of the room and walked down the hall. Haydn made a little moaning sound, started to get out of bed, then got back in again. We heard the sound of a door open and then silence.

"It's my fight," I breathed to Haydn. "Stay out of it."

There was a roar from the other end of the house, and then the roar came rushing towards us. I braced myself. My heart was thumping in my chest.

He went straight for Haydn. He seized him by the throat and bunched his pyjamas hard into his face. "Right, you little ponce!" he spat, "I'll give you ten seconds to get your arse out of my room or by God I'll ..." and he yanked Haydn off the bed onto the floor.

"Hey!" I yelled and leapt out of bed, "it's me! – not him! Leave him be!"

He ignored me completely and straddled Haydn's body on the floor, knees either side of his head. He bent his face close to Haydn's, raised his bunched fist and screamed, "Do you hear me, eh? Do you hear?"

I grabbed him by the shoulder and tried to lift him to his feet. He twisted into the bed, forcing me to release my grip or break my arm. I rammed my foot under his arching backside and heaved him over Haydn's head. He crashed against the wall, landing on his back and shoulders.

I was shaking. My hands, my arms were shaking uncontrollably. I stepped over Haydn and gripped the desk top with both hands. "I did it!" I cried. "It was my decision – I moved you out, and I moved us in!" And the shaking grew worse. My legs seemed to have lost their knees.

His eyes didn't leave me. He twisted and turned his body – his breath coming in short, sharp grunts with the exertion – until he was crouching on the balls of his feet. And all the time his eyes didn't waver. He said nothing. He just watched. Then he surged upwards and hit me in the chest with his lowered head. I staggered backwards and fell. I couldn't breathe. He was coming for me and I couldn't breathe. I looked up at him. He was moving flat-footed, the way a boxer does, his head jutting forward, his neck sunk between his shoulders. I scrambled to my feet, backing away towards the doorway. My hand touched the desk. I grasped blindly for something, anything that would help me. My fingers closed on something hard. I stabbed it forward in front of me. It was a 'Time' magazine, still rolled up in its postal wrapping.

And he grinned. His face lit up in a wide grin. He was enjoying himself, he was telling me. This was going to be fun. I backed into the hall. He followed and lunged playfully towards me. I jabbed him in the face with the magazine. It struck him right on the end of his nose. He snorted, stopped, a startled look on his face. Then he brushed his nose with the back of his hand and came forward again. I jabbed again. Direct hit. He roared and then charged. I backed down the hall, jabbing him in the face at every step. His nose began to bleed and each jab spread the blood over his face and shirt. My stomach heaved with panic. He kept coming and I kept jabbing to keep him away, to make him stop. The blood was spurting in gouts from his nose. It was in his mouth. It was in his eyes.

And Douglas, blessed Douglas, at that very moment, stepped out of his room into the hall, right between us. I lunged forward and pushed him hard into Cliff and then, in the same motion, propelled the two of them through the open doorway into Douglas' room. They fell and sprawled together on the floor, all arms and legs. I yanked the door closed and held on to the handle with both hands, my feet braced against the door jamb.

The room through the door was all swearing and shouting, and then just swearing. The handle suddenly twisted in my hands. I concentrated all my strength, all my energy, into my hands and held on. It twisted again savagely. And again, and again. But then it stopped. I waited. Knowing it would come again. It would be sudden and it would be all out. The sweat was in my eyes, part blinding me, so I closed them tight and waited for him. And when it came it surprised me and almost caught me. He threw himself against the door itself. He crashed against the timber and it shook and groaned above me. I thought he was coming through and almost let go. But then came the violent wrench on the door handle. Devious bastard. I twisted back and held him – and gave a little laugh, I couldn't stop myself. I took the strain again, ready for the next assault. It didn't come. He could be climbing out of the window of course. I turned my head to face the front door, expecting him to burst through at any second. But nothing happened. I hung on in the silence and prayed and hoped and promised.

And it was over. For some inexplicable reason, it was over. I waited for about ten minutes and then let go of the handle. It didn't move. Why? Why had he given in? Fear? Pride? Maybe that was it. He'd lost so much already – going on could only make it worse … the shame … the humiliation. I would have got madder – crazy even.

I went to our new room. Haydn was sitting up in bed. His face was lead grey. He was trying very hard not to cry. Grown men don't cry, do they? I nodded at him. His lips trembled and then he smiled, a soft, shy, child smile – like the girl who used to sit behind me in primary school. And I understood. I understood why Cliff needed to hurt ... needed to prove masculinity ... needed ... I smiled back at Haydn. I changed and got into bed. And as I lay there in the dark, through the rest of the night, I thought of my new room, my new wardrobe and my new armchair ... and shut out each image of Cliff with Carole that rose up, that burst in, and failed of course.

∗

I LINED UP my class in a column facing the door and as soon as the lunch bell started to ring, I emptied them out of the room. Like a tap.

I had to catch her before she left. In the event, I had to wait in her porch. I held back, just out of sight, until the last straggler agonised over her lunchbox in the doorway of her room and then finally left. I stepped inside and locked the door behind me.

She didn't seem surprised. She was sitting at her table in front of the blackboard working with some material. She looked up, gave me a brief smile, then looked down at her material again. Expecting me. After last night, she knew I'd come. Has Cliff seen her? Has she seen Cliff?

"Why didn't you tell me?"

"I did."

"You didn't tell me it was Cliff!" I cried and I crossed to her table.

She looked up at me and said, "You didn't give me a chance ... you rushed away that night like a great wounded puppy ... then you cut me ... in the staffroom ... and last night it didn't seem ... it just didn't seem the right place."

"You still haven't said his name."

She put the material she was pinning onto the table. "Cliff!" she said, and she clasped her hands in front of her, "now are you satisfied?"

"Satisfied? Satisfied?" I shouted, "Why in God's name should I be satisfied?"

"Keep your voice down!" she hissed.

"Tell me why!"

"Why what?"

"Why him! Why Cliff for God's sake! He's just an animal ... a loud-mouthed, ignorant ..."

"He's not an animal!"

"He damn well is!" I screamed. "He's uncouth ... he's a bully ... you have nothing in common with him ... he's years older than you ... how can you bear to let him touch you, Carole? How can you bear it?"

"And not you, you mean? You can't stand the thought, can you..."

"Right! Dead right!"

"... of him touching me because ..." and she faltered and looked down at her hands.

"Because I love you," I said quietly.

"And don't you think he does?" she cried.

"He may," I said, "... he may ... but I'm not interested in that. I'm not interested in him. I'm only interested in you."

She looked up at me for a long time – never taking her eyes from mine. Then she stood, moved from behind the table and brushed past me. I thought she was going to walk out on me, and I started to move towards her, then stopped. She was crossing to the window. She lay her hands on the ledge and looked out. At the end wall of the Engineering block. She stared at it as if it were new, as if it hadn't been there the last time she'd looked, as if I wasn't there.

"You've known him since you were a young girl, haven't you?"

She said nothing.

"And you've been going out with him for at least ... what would it be?... six, seven years?"

"Six."

"Why?"

And my "Why?" hung in the air between us. I could see it. I could hear it over and over and over.

Carole didn't move. She stared at the wall.

"Why have you ... why did you go with him ...?"

"Because I was young!" she cried. And she turned to look at me, "... because I didn't know any different! ... I was sixteen and I was flattered." She took a step towards me. "He used to pick me up in his car – do you know what that felt like? and drive me to school, and then when school was over he'd drive me home. He took over – took over my life totally. He just swallowed me up! No matter what I did from then on, he was there. He broke up any friendships I had ... he drove off the boy I was seeing ..."

"How? How did he do it? Did he threaten ..."

"No, that's wrong – he didn't do it," she said, "I did it." And she smiled. "It was easy ... it was flattering ... I had a twenty-three-year-old high school teacher who told me he loved me ... who gave me presents ... who treated me like a grown-up ..." and she laughed, "and there was I, sitting at school next to boys with half-broken voices, hairy legs and shorts!"

"But what about when you went away – to Teachers' College?"

"Oh, he drove me to College ... he came and picked me up and took me out at weekends ... he rang me and wrote to me ..."

"And Ben?"

"Ben?... now that was beautifully done ..." and she was calm again. She was telling me a story and she was lost in it. "He must have found out about Ben somehow – I don't know how – probably one of my girlfriends – girls do that – anyway, he told my father ... he worked on my father ... Dad thought – still thinks – that Cliff's wonderful... everything a man should be – you know ... hunter ... tough ... rugby ... one of the boys ... so that finished that."

And right in the centre of me a little worm of worry started to grow, and the more she talked the more it began to eat at me. 'There's someone else' she'd said that night I arrived, 'there has been all along'. Why was she still with him? Why was she with him last night, for Christ's sake? She left me to go with him – to be with him – till after midnight. What were they doing till after midnight? It was only last night, for Christ's sake! She could talk to me about it now, analyse it, explain how it started – even laugh about it – but she was still there! She was still with him. He had a hold on her – a hold that she couldn't break ... or that she didn't want to break. Now there's the truth.

Face it, boyo. It has to be. You are here. He's here. And she's choosing to be with him. Because she loves him? Ask her. Ask her now – find out once and for all. No! For Christ's sake! What if she says "Yes"? What do you do then? Don't ask. Don't push her into saying something that isn't true, that you don't want to hear – and once said, becomes a fact. Accept the situation. And then undermine it. Spoil it. Replace it. By stealth and cunning. By patience. By scheming. By laughing and lying and cheating if need be ... no confrontations, no arguments, no threats. Just be there. Always. Close to her – soft, warm, comfortable, protective – like a pair of knickers – God, now there's a thought! – like a pair of silk knickers! Fancy being ... stop, stop, for God's sake, before you say something really stupid. Think cunning. Think devious.

"Can I see your dress?" I said.

She stared at me, "... my dress?"

"Yes – your pantomime one ... you know ... as the Princess. Is it finished?"

"Why yes ... and there are two by the way."

"Well, how about trying them on for me?"

"Now? Here?"

"Yes! You're not shy, are you? – I'll go and get a pack of cards if you like."

"You go to hell!" she said, and she laughed, her eyes bright and shining and full of life. "You can see them on Opening Night."

And she unlocked the door.

I smiled at her. She smiled back. 'Like a pair of silk knickers' – now wasn't that a beautiful thought – and left.

Chapter 14
The pantomime

It had been a warm day, still and cloudless, with the air that clear and sharp that it never was in Wales. I crossed the road and entered the college grounds. There were a dozen cars parked near the assembly hall. All but one had a sheet of newspaper pinned to the windscreen by the wipers. Despite the heat, the locals were expecting a late frost.

There was a hubbub of noise coming from the rear of the hall. I crossed the courtyard. The lights were on in the music room. I stepped into the garden and, like a prowler, peered in at the windows. The room was awash with number 9's, number 5's, mascara, carmine and puffs of pink face powder; mandarins, beggars, scimitar-wielding soldiers, a gigantic genii and hordes of pantalooned damsels, big beefy ones, tiny flat-chested ones, one with a moustache, all ready, two hours before curtain up, for the big night. The players were being tended, creamed, dabbed at, painted and powdered by five eager, enthusiastic, amateur make-up artists, mothers on the P.T.A.

A girl from my fifth form English class saw me. She waved excitedly and that began a rush of pantaloons to the window. Pink arms, pink necks, shining, unnatural, red-brown American Indian faces, ruby lips, crimson and black eyes, rouged cheeks. Hideous. Hideous and happy.

I went to the side door to the hall and was immediately

confronted by a gaggle of swarthy, grinning harem guards, all disguised as Charlie Chan. I escaped backstage.

Haydn was already there. He was playing with the switchboard, zooming the dimmer switches up and down, flicking the floods in and out, simulating a one-man, silent fireworks display.

"Enjoying yourself?"

"Shshsh. I'm concentrating." He hunched further over the switchboard. "Now, watch this. My climax. My piece-de-resistance!" And he threw all the switches to off, leaving only the eerie, unearthly, glowing purple of the ultra-violet lights. His body was invisible except for his white jumper which hung suspended in the air as if on a clothesline.

I clapped. "It makes me very humble to be in the presence of real talent."

"I know, I know," he said quietly, "and who'd believe that a few years ago I was only a genius?" He flicked the stage lights on.

I could see our "Invention" in the wings, partly obscured by the side curtains. "Come on, we'd better set it up before the others arrive."

The pantomime was "Aladdin and his Lamp", but Arch wanted it to come as a surprise to the audience, despite the fact that it was described on the programme and plastered on posters all over town as such.

It was to open on a "picture-book" scene. A mother and little girl sat front stage reading from a book of fairy tales while behind them scenes from the tales were presented in tableau form on a revolving stage. The college had no revolving stage, so Haydn and I had made one. We had built a ten-foot-wide, circular platform, set on three large castors. On top of the platform, three six-foot flats were butted together in the centre to form three mini-stages. Arch's idea was that the platform would be revolved to fit into the storyteller's reading, thus presenting three little tableau scenes, ending with, surprise, surprise, "Aladdin and his Lamp".

That was the theory. In order to achieve two controlled part-revolutions, Haydn and I had fitted a wide-grooved rim to the underside of the platform. A thick hemp rope was wound around the platform in the groove and the two ends stretched along the ground into the wings on either side. I had to brace my feet against a block of wood nailed to the floor in one wing and pull strongly and evenly, while in the other wing, Haydn, similarly braced, had to pull against me, and slowly the stage would revolve.

It had worked perfectly at every rehearsal and was particularly impressive at audience eye-level which, being below stage level, meant that the rope could not be seen.

We manoeuvred it centre-stage, then I lay on my stomach and fed the rope around the rim. There was a snigger from the orchestra pit. I turned my head and inhaled three fingers of whisky. Morrie. Resting his chin on the edge of the stage, not three feet away from me, leering. It could only be described as a leer. Professional job. Expensive. His mouth had just the right angle, the right tilt.

"Won't work," he said.

"Hullo Morrie!" I cried, and I smiled a big welcome.

"Got all the makings of a first-class cock-up," he laughed.

He was obviously very pleased with himself.

I laughed with him. "You'd be right there, Morrie," I said, "we've just been lucky so far, eh?"

"Greasing bastard," whispered Haydn from the far side of the platform.

"Jesus!" breathed Morrie, "wish I was down here in the orchestra pit," and he ducked down low and squinted up. "Imagine what a man could see from down here! Them dancing, lifting their legs, bending over – my God, it'd be more than a man could bear!" and he grinned at me.

I grinned back.

"Think of it ..." and he leaned towards me, "... think of that big Hori in the chorus – think of the arse she'd have on her!"

And I tried to let him see I was thinking about it. But Haydn started pulling on the rope and spoilt it all. Morrie climbed onto the stage and went to his post. On the curtains. The stage curtains. Opening and closing them. Had a different job each year, Pearl said. And buggered it up each year, Pearl said. Anything from blown lights to falling sets to wet paint, to stuffed amplifiers. Morrie had improved them all. So Arch had set him on curtains this year.

He unhooked the curtain cords from the specially designed cord trestle he had built in the wings. They snarled. I held the stepladder while he climbed it. I'm so nice to him it's making me ill. I can smell whisky on his shoes. Every time I've met him – at his home, at the 'concert', at the dress rehearsal and now – he's been boozed. And yet, he doesn't stagger, his speech isn't slurred, and he stays awake.

He climbed down the ladder, let the cords swing free, closed the curtains, and then joined his mate, Nev Utting, our amiable genii, who was disappearing into the changing room.

By 7.30pm, everything was ready backstage. Morrie had returned happy, straightened the skies, trimmed the side curtains and for ten minutes practised opening and closing the front curtains. He was trying to do it in one continuous pull but he kept getting the open cord tangled with the close cord and, as the audience was starting to fill the hall, Haydn ordered him to stop.

Haydn called everyone together for a last-minute pep talk. Just as he finished going over the order of the scene changes, there was a scraping and a bumping on the stairs and Douglas came through the side curtains followed by his rickshaw. Douglas and his rickshaw were due on stage in scene four, the market scene. He was scripted to pull his rickshaw from stage left to stage right while calling out his one line, "Anyone wantee rickshaw ride?" Local colour.

At every rehearsal Douglas and his rickshaw had been in the wings before the first scene, ready, and remained to everyone's dismay and frustration, until the last scene. He rolled the rickshaw over people's toes, blocked entrances and exits and always managed to get the thing on during a love scene or deep inside the inaccessible Aladdin's Cave.

With a shriek, Haydn leapt at the rickshaw and began kicking it. Douglas, fearing for his rickshaw's life, lurched backwards into the wings, crashed against the wall and, turning in truly Oriental rickshaw boy style, scrambled down the stairs.

Meanwhile, Morrie was back on the curtain cords. Ignoring the fact that the hall was by now nearly full, he gave a few investigative jerks and the curtains gaped and closed, gaped and closed, like an enormous, green velvet flasher.

"For Christ's sake, get us started, Haydn," I hissed.

Haydn swallowed what he had been about to yell at Morrie and instead sent him down to call the opening actors on stage.

The house lights went out but the stage lights came up, the actors in the "picture book" scene poised, and Morrie executed the fastest one pull curtain draw seen in Maranganui, or anywhere else for that matter. Which was unfortunate for Ngaire Wilson. She had composed herself, picture book in hand, ready for her opening line, when the swishing curtain hit her side-on, sweeping the book from her grasp. But the curtain slammed home on the end staunchion with such force that it bounced back, recoiling ten feet onto the stage. Which was fortunate for Ngaire Wilson. Hidden behind the curtain, she retrieved her picture book and by the time Morrie had jerked the curtain into its rightful place, she was composed again, smiling down at her angelic offspring as if nothing had happened.

I heard a groan from the wings across stage. Haydn.

"Once upon a time, in a far-off land," began Ngaire, "there lived a beautiful princess named Snow White ..."

"Shit!" Clear and distinct. Haydn again.

Going on a bit, no point in abusing Morrie now. It's done. I sat on the floor, facing the stage, placed my feet carefully against the block and pulled the rope taut. Wait for it. Wait for the cue.

"... white horse with her handsome prince, she waved goodbye to her faithful dwarfs."

Now! I leant back on the rope and slowly began hauling it in. But it was coming too quickly. It was loose. The platform wasn't turning. Where was Haydn?

Suddenly it jerked taut.

"Thank God," I gasped. I pulled steadily again. The platform started to turn, more quickly than in rehearsal, but it was turning.

There was a frantic scuffling behind the back drop – someone running across stage. Morrie, wild-eyed, breathless. "Stop! Stop you bloody fool. The rickshaw knocked out Haydn's block hold. You're pulling him onto the stage."

I stared at him. His mottled face was inches from mine. All I could think of was his breath. It was pure Highland malt.

"Let go!" he cried. "Quick!"

I let go.

And the platform took off. It careened like a rudderless sailing ship across the stage, struck the back drop, crushing it against the wall, and spun into the wings, beaching half on, half off the reef of the stage.

And for once Morrie did the right thing. He catapulted the front curtains together.

The audience clapped.

I stared at the wreck. The picture book characters were still on board. On their knees. On their backs. But still on board. And I began to laugh. I lay back full length on the floor, feet still on the block, and closed my eyes. Perhaps we could turn it into "Robinson Crusoe" now, with Douglas paddling his bloody rickshaw onto the island as a Chinese Man Friday. Only knowing Douglas, it would be Man Sunday and then we'd have a service.

But by the middle of the first scene everything had returned to normal and we were still doing Aladdin. After all, we had all those pantaloons and Charlie Chan harem guards to employ.

Carole was due on at the end of this scene so I took up the best vantage point I could to see her. Morrie was up his ladder having a smoke. He cupped the cigarette in his hand and every time he drew on it, his hand lit up like a lantern. I stood on the bottom step of the reverse leg of his ladder and leant out over Elsie, but I got only two fleeting glimpses of Carole. For most of the scene she was surrounded by a beefy army of what the programme called "Ladies of the Harem". But finally, she and Aladdin were alone on stage together.

She was dressed in a sumptuous, vaguely Oriental costume, designed to suggest wealth and exotic seductiveness and yet, despite the bare midriff, the jewels, the silks and the brocade, all I could see was her standing there in white blouse, suspender belt, stockings and white panties, and skirt around her ankles. With Elsie's help, she 'sang' her duet. I clapped long and loud – long after everyone else had stopped – and got what I was after – a full frontal, held for just a moment, as she left the stage.

"What did I say eh? What did I say?" hissed Morrie, above me, leaning over the front of the ladder.

I nodded vigorously at him.

He climbed down and put his lips to my ear, "You and your Taffy mate really ballsed it up, didn't you?" He laughed into my ear. I hated it. I hated the touch of him on my skin. His wet lips. The rasp of his stubble. "I told Nev what was going to happen, and it did, didn't it?" He couldn't believe it himself. I was sure he was going to kiss me.

I pulled my ear out of his reach and wiped it with my sleeve. "I want to thank you, Morrie, for getting across to me so quickly to warn me about the block hold."

"And then to let it go sudden the way you did! Of all the damn fool things to do that one takes the biscuit."

"I must have panicked, Morrie. I thought you were yelling at me to let it go, and I did. Without thinking. Trouble is I'm not used to the accents yet."

"I've always said immigrants should have a language test before they let you in the country. Stands to reason, doesn't it?"

"Too right, Morrie. Thank God you closed the curtains when you did, I say."

"Well, someone's got to keep their head."

And then I noticed her – standing behind me to the left – watching the acting from side stage. Watching me. In the dark. I could sense it. I could feel her exploring me, touching me. I turned slowly to face her. She was looking directly at me. Not smiling, not speaking, just ... looking. The hair on the back of my neck curled stiff and my loins lifted. With just a look. I stepped towards her – and she turned and hurried down the steps to the music room without even a glance back.

Haydn's head appeared around the backdrop. "Marc! Morrie!" he hissed, and he made huge come-to-me motions with his hands, and then he disappeared behind the backdrop again. We followed him into the men's changing room. In the middle of the room was Nev, our amiable genii. On the floor. On his back. Sloshed to the eyeballs. "I can't lift him, he's too heavy," Haydn complained. So the three of us tried, but we couldn't raise his enormous bulk off the floor. The most we could do was to lift him to a sit-up position. We lay him down again.

"Do you think we should give him the kiss of life?" asked Haydn.

"You do, and he'll kill you later if he finds out," swore Morrie. "Look, all he needs is a stiff brandy and he'll be right – I was ... talking to him not ten minutes ago – I'll see if I can find one," and he hurried out.

I rolled Nev – the way you would a log – over to the wash basin and splashed cold water onto his face and neck. And ruined his make-up. He didn't move. Morrie returned with Arch and most of the cast but no brandy, so I left them to it.

Carole was back, in her watching place in the wings. I hurried towards her – and saw him. Cliff. Behind her. Hand on her shoulder. I hesitated, then turned away. What the hell is he doing here? This is mine! He has no right ... I turned back to face her, and smiled. And I kept on smiling as I skirted the rickshaw – Douglas had got it back on stage in the confusion – and stopped in front of her.

"Right panic back there!" I laughed.

"Something about Nev Utting, isn't it?" she said, all concern.

"Yes, he's sozzled. Out cold on the floor."

"Heh! Heh! Heh!" cackled Cliff behind her. "Good old Nev Utting!"

"Cliff ...?" I said, "well, well, didn't see you there. Never thought we'd get you backstage among all the poofs ... anyway Carole," and I turned to face her and went on quickly before he could speak, "... Nev won't be going on stage tonight."

"Are you sure?" she asked. "Some of those ... older ones can take a fair amount of drink."

"Too bloody true!" broke in Cliff. "These are Kiwi jokers you're dealing with here – none of your poncing cocktail drinkers these.

He'll be as right as rain after a lie down, you just wait and see."

"Excuse me Marc," Arch, from nowhere, at my elbow. "Could I talk to you for a second?" And his face shone. "I've got a little favour to ask ... well, a fairly big favour actually."

I waited. He said nothing. I shook my head. "No, I couldn't."

"Of course you could."

"I couldn't."

"You could."

"They'd recognise me."

"They won't. You'll be behind the gauze and only the ultra-violet lighting will be on."

"He's bigger than me."

"Only wider – and we can pin it where it's too big."

And Cliff did a snigger – a Morrie snigger.

"I don't know the lines."

"You can read the script, behind the gauze."

And I'd got him. "I won't be able to see the script in the ultra-violet lighting!"

"No problem. He only says 'Yes, O Master' and 'At your command, O Master.'"

"But my voice is different!" I was getting desperate.

"Your voice is the deepest we've got, and with your Welsh accent, you sound like a Pakistani to most Kiwis and that almost makes you an Arab."

"An Arab!" whooped Cliff, "a bloody Welsh Arab!" and he pretended to fall back against the wall with weakness.

And I felt Carole's fingers on mine. I felt them creep over my hand in the dark until she held it, then she pressed it gently.

"Right," I said to her, and to her alone, "a Welsh Arab it is then."

And so, with Pearl's help, I got into silk vest, arm bands, turban and pantaloons. Pearl never left my side, insisting, as Wardrobe

Mistress, that after all her work in making the costumes, she deserved her perks at the end of it. She stroked and patted me, pulled and adjusted me, always managing, despite the fact that she was at least six inches shorter than me, to get her bosoms in my face and her belly in my crotch. Arch stood and watched her whole performance, puffing furiously on his cigarette, making deep caverns in his cheeks at each drag, encouraging her to hurry and all the time making her more and more excited. And finally, I escaped onto the stage, mauled but fully garbed, to make my New Zealand stage debut: a Welsh genii, speaking like a Pakistani, doubling for a Kiwi, in pinned pantaloons, reading a blurred script behind fish-nets, silhouetted in purple lights.

It went to my head. Adrenalin pumping through my veins, sweating with excitement, I abandoned the invisible script and whenever the cave-bound, hapless Aladdin paused for breath, I rumbled out a deep, resonating "Yes, O Master" or "At your command, O Master", and, being a creative person, an occasional "Thank you, O Master", and ended up sounding like an Aboriginal didgeridoo played at the bottom of a well.

And then I heard a voice behind me, speaking in unison with my chanting, but instead of "Yes, O Master", it intoned "Yes, you bastard". Morrie, behind the backdrop, sniggering. He did it again, louder, more confident. I varied the lines but he synchronised perfectly. We were a duet. An obscene harmony.

Aladdin moved up close to the gauze, staring at me, puzzled.

This time, I said to myself, and I began to chant, "At your command ..." and then stopped abruptly, and Morrie's "... you bastard!" rang out, clear as a bell, to the back of the hall.

Chapter 15
Crisps, peanuts and cheerios

On Saturday afternoon Arch arrived with the drink for the Panto party. Arch had magnanimously offered the hostel as a venue for the celebration and so Haydn and I spent all afternoon vacuuming the carpets, washing dishes, stuffing under cushions, and spraying the toilet and bathroom with disinfectant and deodorant. We decorated the lounge with flowers – Haydn's touch – and then set out the crisps, peanuts and cheerios, uncorked the half g's, and sampled the bottle of Glenfiddich that Arch had brought along special.

Douglas was the first to arrive. And instead of going into his room for a quick prayer, he came into the lounge and sat on a stool next to our makeshift bar. One of the boys. He had a bottle of lemonade in one hand and a bottle opener and a glass in the other. Obviously raring to go. And within an hour he was. Haydn had convinced him that raspberry cordial added a touch of mystery to lemonade and in the process added more than a touch of vodka. Douglas went through a stage of grinning at everyone who came in, and for one terrible moment I thought he was going to burst into song but the vodka by this time had gone to his feet and Douglas embarked on a series of very ambitious stork movements with anyone who came near him. So no one did, and consequently, the party took the shape of women with their Pimms, talking clothes and babies, flattened against the wall, and the men at the other end with their whisky and beer, talking rugby and dirty jokes, pressed against the bar, leaving Douglas, who by now was in his African pink flamingo stage, in the middle. Someone had to do something about him, and someone did. Douglas did. He flaked out cold in the hearth. There was no fire so he was quite safe. We carried him into his room, lay him on the bed and crossed his arms over his chest. His Fellowship would have been proud.

Morrie and Nev struggled in with the barrel – no Nancy – and carried it into the kitchen. They set it on the bench with the tap over the sink, and Morrie asked for a hammer and a screwdriver – for the plug – to let the air in – only a little hole he said – piece of cake ... I retired hastily to the lounge.

Carole had arrived. With Cliff. She was breathless and excited, her face slightly flushed, as if she'd been hurrying. The record player was going and Arch was dancing with his wife Pat. Galloping Dutch polka steps. From Indonesia. To the Beatles. And on impulse, I asked Carole if she would like to dance. She turned to look at Cliff but Cliff had already gone. Probably got his head jammed under the keg by now, vying with Morrie and Nev. She turned back to face me, smiled, nodded, and held out her arms, old-fashioned style. I stepped inside her arms and slipped both hands down onto her hips. Not tightly. Just snugly, at arm's length. She checked, and dropped her hands to my hips. And we Latin-Americaned our way around the room. She hadn't been two minutes in the house and I had my arms around her waist, could feel her hips swelling under my fingers, could smell the woman smell of her, could look at her unashamedly and invite her, equally unashamedly, to look at me.

I saw Haydn watching us, peering over the rim of his glass, and then I saw him flinch involuntarily and edge further away from the doorway, and I knew Cliff must be there. I turned Carole so that her back was to the door and searched for him and found him immediately. Found his eyes. I smiled friendly, pleasant. He stood, unmoving, unsmiling.

I nodded my head to him slightly, saying hullo, I'm dancing

with your girl. Are you having a lovely time? He wasn't. I could tell.

The record track finished and Cliff immediately crossed to Carole's shoulder, touched her on the arm and moved to a stool at the bar and sat down. Just for a fleeting second, I thought I detected a look of anger or annoyance flash across her face but she smiled sweetly up at me, whispered, "Thank you Marc. I enjoyed that," and crossed to stand at Cliff's side.

I eased myself behind the bar, poured myself another beer and, noticing that Carole did not have a drink, I lifted an empty glass and asked, "What would you like to drink, Carole?"

Cliff got to his feet, reaching for the glass, "Don't worry, I'll get it."

"No worry," I said, leaning away from him, "I'm here now." I turned and looked directly at Carole. "What'll it be then, cariad?"

"Cariad?" she said, very slowly, stretching out the vowels.

"Yes, cariad. It means 'loved one.'"

"Oh, does it!" she cried, and she laughed out loud and long to hide her surprise. "Well," she said, "I'd better have a gin and lemon then please ... cariad."

Right under his nose. Right under his bloody nose!

But Cliff was no fool. They were gone from the bar as soon as I put her drink in front of her. With Morrie. With the boys. With the girls. Everywhere where I wasn't.

All night. Until the party started to break up. People were making the obvious signs of preparing to leave. Carole had picked up her plate and Morrie from the kitchen and they were hovering in the lounge doorway talking to Arch.

I pushed myself in and stood next to her. "Goodnight," I said.

"Goodnight," she replied softly.

"Goodnight, Morrie!" I called.

He ignored me. He was concentrating on lighting a cigarette.

He coughed on his first drag and then wheezed at Cliff, "Six in the morning then, Cliff."

"Six it is," agreed Cliff, "and don't forget the food. It could be a long day."

"And a little hip flask of something to warm the insides, eh?" laughed Morrie and he nudged Cliff in the stomach.

"No way," said Cliff, suddenly serious, "not with me anyway – drinking and pigs is just not on."

"Pigs?" I echoed.

"Yes, pigs," said Carole. "Dad's going pig-hunting with Cliff tomorrow. First time he's been since the War. Have you ever done it?"

"Me, pig hunting?" I laughed, "in Wales? The only pig I've ever grappled with has been in a pan with crackling and apple sauce."

"Bloody Poms!" laughed Cliff, and he rested his arm on Carole's shoulder.

I looked at his lips as he laughed. They were full lips – round, almost puffy, the lower one fatter than the upper one. It sagged in the middle so that his mouth always looked as if it was open, even when it was closed. I could see the spittle brimming behind, as he laughed, as he enjoyed himself. Nauseating.

"I'm not a Pom," I said quietly, "I'm Welsh."

"Welsh, Irish, bloody English – who cares?" and he was getting excited, the spittle brimming over, "... you're all Poms to me – pack of lily-white ..." and he turned to face Carole "... him pig-hunting? He'd sooner sing his songs and prance around on a stage in tights, am I right?" He dropped his arm from her shoulder and leaned towards me. "Listen, Taffy ... you prefer Taffy, do you – to Pom, I mean ...?"

I said nothing.

"... we're not into girls' games here mate – this is none of your dressing-up games here mate ... "and he leant even closer so that he was only inches from my face, "... have you ever seen a full-sized wild boar, have you? Have you ever seen a boar coming straight at you – all red eyes, tusks, and squealing like ..."

"Yes," I said.

He stopped dead, straightened up, and looked hard at me.

"Recently," I said.

"Recently?"

"Yes – so recently ... oh, seems like it was only seconds ago – and he was that far ..." and I held up my thumb and forefinger in front of me "... from my face."

There was silence for what seemed like a very long time indeed.

"When was that then?" asked Morrie.

Cliff didn't take his eyes off me. Carole gripped his arm and tried to turn him towards the door.

He didn't budge. He narrowed his eyes until he was almost squinting at me – and then he suddenly grinned, "Right, smart arse! Come and show us how it's done then – come and show us the Taffy way of sticking little piggies!"

"You've done some then, have you?" asked Morrie.

"No, not really Morrie. Oh yes, just the once maybe"

Cliff didn't laugh at this. Funny.

"There wouldn't be enough room for three, would there, dad?" suggested Carole, and she reached for Morrie's arm and tried to pull him towards the door.

"Tons of room in that Landrover of Cliff's!" Morrie cried, "... take three ... four, easy – plus the dogs." He turned to me, "No worries there – and I can show you what you need to know – used to hunt up north during the War – used to keep ourselves – pigs, rabbits, hares, pigeons – you name it, I've hunted it. Lived off the land we did – never had a ..."

"Come on Morrie ... Carole!" cried Cliff, "let's not waste any more time on this," and he stepped out the door, "let's get going."

Morrie then Carole moved towards the door.

"Okay!" I cried, "... seeing as you're insisting, Cliff – I'll come!" and I dropped my voice, "... see you at six, right?"

Carole stopped in the doorway and looked back at me. I knew she wanted to say something, to make it right, to make it all go away. But she didn't seem to know the words. She turned and followed the other two out.

Chapter 16
The pig hunt

"Get down, you silly bitch, or you'll get nothing."

Cliff opened the cage door and the bitch leapt out yelping.

She ran in a tight, low circle and then rushed back to him, jumping at his hands and face, licking and yelping at the same time.

"Siddown!" he snarled, and she belly-hugged the ground, tail sweeping back and forth, all eyes for him. He released the two other dogs. One was a young, lithe, black and white, the other a squat black bull mastiff. He fed each a small piece of gristly meat.

"They don't eat much," I ventured.

Cliff hadn't spoken to me since we'd got up. Just grunts and pointing. He stopped now and looked at me. Not my face. My kneecaps. He was telling me something. Then he turned his back on me without speaking and walked to the Landrover. The dogs followed him eagerly.

I got the message. It was going to be a game. All day. I went over to the ball. "They don't eat much, do they Morrie?" I said.

"No," he agreed, pensive, then yelled, "Hey Cliff! Not much tucker, eh?"

"That's just to whet their appetites, Morrie," he said. "They haven't been fed for two days, ready for the hunt. If I gave 'em a bellyful now, they'd be bloody useless."

And we had our rules.

"Right!" cried Morrie, "right! That's what I was thinking," and he took hold of my arm, confidential, "all piss 'n wind," he said. "Feed 'em now and they'll be all piss and wind."

And I laughed and slapped him on the shoulder and he grinned.

End of round one.

Cliff opened the back door of the 'Rover and the three dogs immediately leapt in. They seemed to know where they were going. We drove out of town. About five miles out, we turned into a pumice and dirt road. Great clouds of dust billowed up behind us. The road was fringed with low scrub, broom and fern. All covered in yellow dust. The setter and the black and white leapt up as soon as we hit the dirt road. They milled around one another and whined quietly. The mastiff hadn't moved. He lay on his side, as if asleep.

I caught Morrie's eye and nodded towards the mastiff. "He doesn't look very interested," I said.

"No," said Morrie, "doesn't look too healthy to me. He's not sick, is he Cliff?"

"No," snorted Cliff, "he's not sick. Don't underestimate that bugger. He'll move fast enough when he has to. It's the setter that worries me. Notice how thin she is?"

And we looked at her ribs and marvelled.

"Silly sod had a twenty-foot tapeworm in her," and he laughed uproariously. "She was lying on her belly and I noticed this white thing sticking out of her arse. So I put one foot on it and booted her with the other. Came out like a priest caught in a brothel, heh, heh, heh!" And he continued to bray at the memory of it as we sped along the narrow road. He took off his hat and wiped the sweat from his forehead. Wide-brimmed felt hat. Aussie outback style. Looked the part did Cliff – hat, bush shirt, stained, of course, army drills and heavy brown boots.

He turned off the road onto a track and stopped. He strapped a sheathed, bone-handled hunting knife to his belt and released the dogs. The black and white ran straight ahead down the track. The setter disappeared into the scrub to the right and the mastiff trotted a few paces ahead of us.

We walked on in silence for about half an hour. Safari style. Cliff in front, then Morrie, then me. I was excited – and the longer we walked, the longer the silence, the more excited I became. My mouth was dry. Everytime a branch cracked, I jumped. Elephant gun to my shoulder.

One of the dogs began barking.

"Anything?" whispered Morrie.

"No," said Cliff, "It's the setter. Silly bugger just barks. Setters are all like that when they're young. We may as well call them in," he added, "I'm not very confident here," and he whistled high and long, like a shepherd.

We squatted at the side of the track and waited.

"I noticed you didn't bring a gun, Cliff," I opened.

Cliff snorted violently and stood, facing up-track.

Morrie stood with him. "Cliff only carries a knife, right Cliff?"

"Too bloody right," laughed Cliff, "a man would have to be a cowboy to go after pigs with a gun." And they both laughed.

I thought about that. And an angry, red-eyed boar with blood-dripping tusks charged out of the undergrowth and gored and ripped the two of them into minute, unrecognisable little chunks.

"We may as well go back," said Cliff, "the dogs'll soon find us," and he set off back to the truck without waiting. The dogs arrived shortly after us.

We drove along the dirt road until it came to a wooden bridge over a gully. We turned right over the bridge onto a wide track and almost immediately Cliff yelled and slammed on the brakes. "Look! Look there!" he cried. "Fresh rootings." He leapt out of the truck and set the dogs loose.

The track we were on was cut into the side of a steeply graded hill. To our left the bush climbed out of sight and to the right the trees sloped down into the gully.

The black and white and the setter set off immediately up the slope into the trees. The mastiff stood on the road. Within seconds there was a crashing, yelping and squealing in the undergrowth, and before we could move, a large black boar rolled and fell down the bank onto the road not twenty paces in front of me.

The mastiff was moving. As the other two dogs tried to grip the pig by its head or throat, the mastiff, without hesitating, closed on the pig and clamped its teeth on the boar's genitals. The boar squealed and thrashed. The mastiff held on and kept low to the ground. The other two dogs seized their chance and sank their teeth into the ear nearest them then lay flat on either side of the boar's head. The boar was helpless.

I still hadn't moved. I stared at the animals in front of me. All four, pig and three dogs, were stretched out in perfect formation, all hugging the ground. The teamwork and the precision! Was it training or instinct?

Cliff had taken out his knife. He walked unhurriedly to the head of the pig. Stooping, he reached his left hand under the pig and gripped a rear leg. He heaved. The mastiff let go of its hold. With one fluid motion, Cliff turned the boar onto its back. As soon as it hit the ground the two front dogs regained their grip on the ears as the mastiff, which had moved around Cliff, once again sank its teeth into the boar's genitals. And Morrie yahooed and raced past me towards the pig.

For the first time I became aware of the din. The dogs were growling deep in their throats, Cliff was yelling encouragement to them, Morrie was playing cowboys and Indians, and the boar was venting scream after scream after scream. Each scream started low then escalated up through the scales, "Uh ... eee, uh ... eee, uh ... eee ..."

Cliff placed the tip of the knife at the side of the boar's breast bone, paused a moment, then plunged the knife in. I was not prepared for what happened next. A huge, fat, wet, red, glistening solid stream of blood shot from the boar's chest, arched over Cliff's shoulder and splattered onto the road. It was too unreal. It was too plastic. It was impossible. The boar died gurgling. The dogs continued to hang on.

"Fell into our laps!" Morrie was shouting, "fell into our bloody laps!"

I looked at Cliff. He was intent, focussed solely on the pig. He was sitting on the ground, his leg against the boar's gaping mouth. He looked down and inspected his knife, checking the edge of the blade. The screaming, the terror, the killing, the blood, were as nothing. He was seemingly unmoved. He wiped the edge of the blade on his pants and stood up. He ordered the dogs away and then knelt down close to the boar's genitals, as if he were going to pray. With great care he cut off the testicle sac. He held it up for Morrie to see. He held the sac in one hand and squeezed up from the bottom with the other – just like a tube of toothpaste. Then for the first time that morning he looked at me, full face. And grinned. He grinned at me, showing his teeth to the gums. His eyes kept flicking from me to the ball sac. He squeezed harder and slowly the testicles welled to the top. He stretched his hands towards me, asking me, telling me ... and then he tossed the lumps to the mastiff. They were gone in one gulp.

He split open the boar's stomach in one long cut and, humming quietly under his breath, he plunged his hands into the steaming cavity. He seemed to be searching for something. Then he lifted his hands out and brought the entrails with them. He carried them to the side of the road. "There's a shovel in the back," he said to Morrie. "Dig a hole would you, and bury this lot?"

I dug the hole of course and Morrie supervised. It seems there's only one way to dig a hole.

Chapter 17
Mates

Cliff pulled into Morrie's drive and drove onto the lawn in front of the house. He heaved the carcass off the bonnet onto the grass. The boar lay on its side, mouth open. A large blowfly was feasting on the dried blood that had oozed from a nostril. The boar looked so out of place there amongst the flowering shrubs, the rose bushes, and flat, recently mown grass.

Morrie ran up the verandah steps and, holding the front door wide, called for Nance and Carole to come and see. Carole appeared immediately in the doorway, ducking under his arm. She looked at the three of us – Cliff, me and the pig, and smiled, then she stepped warily down onto the grass and slowly circled the pig. She moved as if she expected it to come alive at any moment.

"It's ... it's so big," she whispered.

"Yes," I said, "it took three of the dogs ..."

"Only a young 'un," snapped Cliff, and he rolled the pig over with his boot to show her, "About two years old. Look at the tusks."

"But it must weigh ... nearly two hundred pounds!" laughed Carole.

"Nance!" cried Morrie down the hallway. He was agitated – wanting to be with us, with it, yet wanting Nance to be there to see.

"Not any more," said Cliff, "not with his guts out," and he splayed the boar's legs wide with the side of his boot.

Morrie couldn't bear it any longer. He scrambled down the steps and pushed between Carole and Cliff so that he was standing under Cliff's shoulder and with the toes of both feet resting on the boar's leg. "Big, eh?" he grinned at her, "this would be one of the biggest pigs to come out of that bush, eh Cliff?" and he peered up at him.

"You'd be right there, Morrie," said Cliff, his face blank, impassive. "Want it?"

"Want it?" repeated Morrie, not believing.

"Yeh, you may as well have it. You can shout me a beer some time."

"Are you sure?" urged Morrie.

"Too right," said Cliff, and he turned to Carole, "I thought we'd go to the Football Club tonight. There's a do on – nothing special – but it should be a good night. OK with you?"

"I'm ... I'm not ..." Carole stammered. She dropped her head, raised it quickly to glance at me, then looked back at him, "I hadn't intended ..."

"Of course, she will!" cried Morrie. "She'd love to go, eh Carole, wouldn't you?" and he stepped over the pig and put his arm around Carole's shoulder, "loves dancing, don't you love?" and he nodded his head at her, encouraging her, willing her. She nodded. "There!" he cried, "knew it. Knew she'd love to go – my God, what a pig! Just look at the size of it, Carole!"

I stared at the pig. I knew I should say something, do something, bite something. But I couldn't focus. I just stared at the pig.

"Right then," said Cliff, "I'll be back later. Get cleaned up a bit and pick you up at about seven. OK, Carole?"

"Yes," she said quietly, "seven'll be fine."

And as he roared down the drive Nancy appeared on the verandah and Morrie hurried to her. But she wouldn't budge. She wanted nothing to do with the pig. "I don't even want to look at it," she shrilled.

Morrie wheedled. I couldn't hear the words – just the wheedle.

"It's one thing going off playing hunting," she snapped, "but something else altogether bringing home a great smelly dead thing with you."

"Oh Nance!"

"Don't you 'Oh Nance' me," she warned. "What possessed you to ask for it in the first place?"

"I didn't ..."

"You did! You must have! And what are you going to do with it now, anyway? I'm not having it in my house, that's one thing you can be certain of," and she stepped back inside and slammed the door shut.

Morrie came down off the verandah and stood beside me. "Do me a favour, will you Marc? Pull it into the garage for me, eh? And you may as well start on it while I sort things out in there," and he jerked his head in the direction of the house. "I'll only be a minute." He hurried up the steps.

I looked at the pig. What the hell does 'start on it' mean? Cut it up, I suppose. But aren't you meant to skin them first? Carole was watching me. Not saying anything, just watching me. At least she was staying. At least she hadn't gone off to get ready. For him. She really wants to be with me – and the pig. She tried. She really tried. Accept it. Don't question it. I bent and took hold of the back legs and dragged the carcase over the lawn, across the drive and into the garage. Carole made little darting moves to help me as I struggled, but each time pulled her hands back so that she never actually touched the pig. The thought was there.

I knelt and ran my hand down the stiff black bristles on the pig's side. "Do you know if your father's got a sharp knife?" I asked, all business.

"Yes," said Carole, "I'm sure he has," and she crossed to the work bench. "He keeps them all so neat and tidy – yes, here's one," and she took a knife down from a hook above the bench top. "He uses it for fishing, I think," and she offered it to me, "will that be OK?"

"Fine," I said, "it'll do fine."

Where did I make the first cut? I remembered seeing someone skinning a rabbit once and he started at the knuckle of the leg. I pressed the blade against the skin just above the pig's ... er ... knuckle. Nothing happened. I strained. The blade bent and made a dent or furrow in the skin. I pressed the point of the knife into the dent and made a small hole. I widened the hole. The skin was about half an inch thick. I stood up.

Carole smiled encouragement at me. I smiled back and bent to the leg again. I tried extending the slit but the bristles were preventing me from making a clean cut, so, using the knife as a barber would, I tried to shave off the bristles near the cut. The first few bristles came away easily but then they simply bent with the strokes. The knife was blunt. I sharpened the knife and tried again. The same thing happened. The bristles were blunting the knife.

"Does your father have any razor blades?" I asked.

"I'll just go and get ... oh, hullo dad."

Morrie was standing in the doorway, lighting a cigarette. He dragged the first few puffs deep down into his lungs, squinted through the smoke at us and chuckled. And I knew in that instant that we were in the presence of an expert. It was the chuckle that gave it away. I was in the presence of one of those rare people who live in a perpetual state of amazement at the stupidity of every other human being. Each job they tackle results in awe-inspiring, unique engineering and scientific discoveries that no one else has thought of and which, if they had the time, they'd patent.

Morrie looked at the pig, the knife and at the small incision. He then looked long and hard at the two of us, shook his head, chuckled again and said, "Piece of cake." He took over. I knew he'd take over. If it was an argument, a children's game of hopscotch, a squeaking door, he would always take over. And I was delighted.

"You've got to burn the bristles off," he announced as if the fact were so obvious he didn't know why he had to say it. "Hories up north had the answer," he said. "Light a fire, skewer the sod on a spit and burn the buggers off. He dropped his cigarette on the floor and ground it out with his heel. "Pass me that bottle of meths from the shelf there Carole, will you?"

Morrie poured the meths liberally over the pig from snout to trotters. He used the whole bottle. He took out his box of matches. "Stand well clear now," he barked. Carole retired to the porch of the house. I got out of the garage. Morrie stood about three feet from the pig, leant forward, one leg extended out behind, the other arm stretched out in front. I stifled a laugh. He looked like an aged, calcified ballet dancer. He struck a match and threw it onto the carcase. It went out before it hit the meths. He inched forward, still pivotting on one leg. He struck another and threw. A sheet of blue flame engulfed the carcase, leapt to the ceiling rafters, bent on impact and curled two tongues of fire to the back and front of the garage. I staggered back then looked back quickly into the smoke and flame. Morrie hadn't moved. "Jesus!" he breathed, "Jesus!"

The meths fire quickly died out. I looked at the pig. It was now completely black and charred. So was the ceiling above it. But the bristles were still there, untouched.

Carole's head appeared around the garage door, "Everything

alright?"

"Yeh, yeh," said Morrie. He sucked in his breath hard, yah yahing his jaw to one side, as if he were trying to dislodge a piece of meat stuck between his teeth. "No problem. Make us a cup of tea love, will you?" He turned and looked me full in the face, "We didn't have enough meths," he said.

I felt a wave of panic. I looked at the shelves. "I don't think you've got any more meths, Morrie," I said. "Perhaps we should dig a pit ..."

"What about boiling?" asked Carole, still in the doorway.

"Boiling?" said Morrie.

"Yes, boiling," she said, a little annoyed, "pour hot water over the bristles and scrape them off. It works with chooks."

"Not the best way of doing it," said Morrie. "Not the Hori way of doing it. But if we haven't any more meths ..."

"We haven't," I said.

"... then she'll have to do. Boiling it is then. Better get some pans of water on then, hadn't you?"

Carole and I raced for the kitchen. Nancy was there.

"Hullo mum," said Carole, and she bent to the cupboards under the sink, "just getting a few pots for dad."

Nancy sniffed, walked out of the kitchen and went into a bedroom. She shut the door.

We got out two large saucepans, an old preserving pan, and, after a quick swill under the outside tap, a coal scuttle I found by the back door. We filled them with water and arranged them as best we could on the elements of the stove. And while we waited for them to boil Carole filled the electric jug and made tea. Cosy. We carried the cups out to the garage and listened to 'Life with the Hories up in the Hokianga in the Old Days' when Morrie had gone native and spent most of his time trapping crawlies by tying bits of meat to manuka branches set in streams, and drinking

Hori beer made from secret tribal recipes.

"Hories didn't give a damn," he said. "They'd laugh all day and drink and sing all night. Couldn't be serious. You'll never civilise them. In the blood."

When the water had boiled, we pulled the charred carcase to the front of the garage and draped it over the drain. Carole boiled, I fetched and carried, and Morrie poured and scraped with the knife. By the time we had used all the boiling water in the pans, the carpet in the hall was sodden, my hands were red and scalded, and Morrie had succeeded in removing the bristles from a six-inch square section of the pig's belly. About fifty-five bristles.

Morrie stopped and lit a cigarette and pondered the pig. "You fullas are obviously too slow with the water," he said. "It's gone cold by the time it gets here."

"Well, why don't you put it in the bath then," suggested Carole, "and pour water over it there?"

Morrie squinted at her. "Just coming to that," he said. "Right, you put some more water on Carole, and we'll get this thing in the bath."

And we dragged the charred, wet, bristled boar up the steps, into the hall, over the carpet, into the bathroom and into the bath.

And Cliff pushed his way into the already full bathroom. He stared disbelievingly at the pig. "Holy shit!" he breathed – and then he noticed Carole, "… oh, sorry Carole," he stumbled, "didn't see you there." He turned to Morrie, "How's it going then, Morrie?"

"Great Cliff, just great."

"No problems?"

"No problems, Cliff," laughed Morrie, "everything's fine. Just showing the youngsters here how to get the bristles off a pig. A bit of the old Kiwi know-how, eh?" He nudged Cliff and winked. The skin on top of his bald head wrinkled in waves.

"Yeh, teach them the tricks of the trade, eh," laughed Cliff. "Want me to get a hook for you, Morrie?"

"Hook?" said Morrie.

"You'd need a pretty hefty one to hold such a large pig, eh? Or have you got one already?"

"No, no ... we haven't got one yet," said Morrie. "I was just going to ... find the rafter in the ceiling first, I thought, to hang the hook from."

"Good thinking – I'll get some rope and a hook then. Where from? The garage?"

"Yeh, in the garage," muttered Morrie.

Carole left to get changed while I held Morrie steady, up on the edge of the bath. He tapped the ceiling in search of a rafter. Cliff was soon back with a six-inch-long, rusty hook and a coil of hemp rope. Morrie screwed the hook into the ceiling over the centre of the bath.

Cliff cut two holes in the skin of both rear legs of the pig and then fed the rope through the holes. And he and Morrie hauled the pig to the ceiling. Flakes of white ceiling paint floated down and lodged in the pig's bristles.

And the pots went back on the stove. Nancy came out of her bedroom and walked into the kitchen. She ignored everyone and crossed to the kitchen window. She picked up a glass from the sill. It contained dark leaves or seeds floating in a brown liquid. She tipped back her head and drank the liquid, leaving the seeds in a limp mass in the bottom of the glass. And she went into the toilet. No one had said a word. Carole seemed embarrassed for some reason and that made me uncomfortable. The toilet cistern flushed and she came out. She looked at us looking at her, stepped into the bathroom and slammed the door shut.

There was a thunderous crash and a scream. From the bathroom. Morrie was the first there, with the rest of us close behind. The pig was in the bath. So was most of the bathroom ceiling. Nancy was flattened against the wall behind the door. And she reminded me of the lamp-post outside our house after a snowstorm when I was a little boy. She was covered in white snow-plaster but only on those parts of her that stuck out or faced the sky – her hair, her nose, her shoulders, her little bosoms, and her feet. The rest of her was as clean as a whistle.

She picked her way carefully over the debris on the floor, walked past us as if we were not there and, still snow-covered, went back into her bedroom. There was a loud snap of a lock.

Morrie hesitated a second, then followed her and stood staring blankly at the locked door. He rattled the handle. "Nance!" he called, little boy's voice. He dropped to his knees and put his lips to the door crack, "Nance," he whispered.

Cliff coughed and dusted a large white flake off the shoulder of his jacket. "We'd better get moving, Carole," he said.

Carole knelt on the floor next to her father and held his shoulders. "Come on, dad," she urged, "don't worry about it. She'll be alright in the morning, you'll see." She paused. Morrie didn't move. "I'll stay if you want me to ... I don't mind. Would you like me to stay?"

"Nance!" pleaded Morrie.

Carole held him for a moment longer and then, with a shrug, released him and stood up. She turned and smiled at me. I smiled back at her but said nothing, could say nothing. And they left.

I got into the bath and levered the pig out onto the floor, then using the ropes around its rear legs, I dragged it down the hall, over the porch, across the drive and into the garage. I looked down at it. It had survived. Despite onslaughts of knife, meths, hot water and Morrie, it was unscathed. Victorious. So, I took the only solution left to an intelligent, well-educated, civilised human being. I took down an axe from the wall and chopped a leg off. A rear leg. Like one of those hams you see at Christmas. No trouble. I wiped it clean with a newspaper from a stack under the bench and carried it into the house, triumphant.

He wasn't there. The house was dark – I hadn't noticed the light going while I was working. "Morrie?" I called softly.

No answer.

I peered into the lounge. Empty. Kitchen the same. And then I heard the clink of glass on bottle. Coming from the bathroom. I searched for the light switch and flicked it on. He was sitting amongst the plaster and timber framing on the bathroom floor – with a glass and nearly empty bottle of whisky.

"Look!" I cried, excited, and I knelt down before him, offering the leg like a ritual sacrifice.

He looked at the meat for a long time. "She'll use this now," he said. "You mark my words! She'll use this as an excuse for months and bloody months!" He drained his glass. There was cigarette ash in the bottom. He lifted the bottle to the edge of the glass and poured. It spilled onto his legs. He giggled and wiped his trousers. With great care he turned the empty glass upside down and fitted it over the top of the bottle. Then he tipped the bottle over and the glass filled and overflowed. He righted the bottle and placed it carefully between his legs. It was empty. "Know what she'll say? She'll say, 'I'm not sleeping with a pig', she'll say, 'go and play with yourself'," and he started to laugh in little gasps, little explosions down his nose. "'Go and play with yourself' she'll say. Jesus!" He caught hold of my shirt front and pulled me down close. "Do you know ..." he said, serious, eyes moist, "I've never even seen her body? Can you believe it? – without her clothes on I mean – can you believe it?"

He waited for an answer. I shook my head.

"Never," he whispered, "never in all our married years have I seen ... she just ... oh Nance!" and he started to cry. He leaned forward so that his face was only an inch from mine. "I can't take it!" he shouted, "not night after night, not any more," and he clasped me by the arms and tried unsuccessfully to lever himself to his feet. He collapsed back against the wall and slid down to the floor, and came face to face with the leg. He stared at it as if he was seeing it for the first time. "It's that pig," he gasped, looking from me to the leg and then back again, "It's that bloody pig of yours!" he shouted, and he swung his fists at the leg, knocking it from my hands. It fell to the floor and rolled with the whisky glass in the plaster bits.

My pig? My bloody pig? I got to my feet.

Morrie struggled to his knees to follow me. "If it hadn't been ..." he gasped, "... for that bloody pig of yours and its bloody bristles, I wouldn't be in this mess now!" he cried. "I knew it! I knew it right from the start!"

"Right from the start!" I echoed, and I pulled him to his feet. "He should never have dropped the thing on you!"

"Right!"

"He kills the bloody pig in the first place – but then he dumps it on you and pisses off to some poncy dance!"

"Too bloody right!"

"And everything was going fine till he came back and poked his nose in, eh?"

"Yes!" breathed Morrie.

"You had it all worked out, didn't you Morrie? All the old know-how! All the old tricks!"

"All the old tricks," he repeated after me.

"And then Cliff smarms up and tells you – tells you of all people ..." I hooted my laughter up into the broken rafters, "...you were skinning pigs before he was born!"

"Before he was bloody born!" he screamed.

"And he has the nerve to tell you to hang the thing from the ceiling ... the bloody ceiling of all places – and now look what he's done!"

"The bastard!" hissed Morrie, "the jumped-up, know-all, interfering bastard ..."

And we were friends. As we scrambled around in the blood and snowflakes that Cliff had caused, as we looked for the whisky bottle, laughed because it was empty, gurgled over the fresh Jim Beam I got from the kitchen, we cursed his name and planned our revenge, until we were both totally pissed. And we were no longer friends. We were mates.

Chapter 18
With our feet dangling over the prow

As I reached the low water mark, I slipped off my jandals and walked bare-footed in the warm yielding mud. It oozed grey and plastic between my toes. Crabs reared up in front of me, guarding their holes, then, as my foot neared them, they bolted into the blackness. I stopped at the water's edge.

The channel was about thirty yards across, pale green at the edges, deep grass green in the middle. The water was flat, no waves, no ripples, just a thin wandering trail of white spume and an unnerving stretching at the edges as the incoming tide seeped its way over the mud.

I turned around. Morrie was reversing the car and trailer, snaking his way towards the water. I could see his head through the back window, twisting, straining, striving desperately to steer a straight path. Carole had her head out of the passenger side window. And it was like a silent movie. Her mouth was moving, opening and closing, obviously giving him directions, but I could hear none of the words, only the sound of the flickering machine. For Morrie was a weaver. First, swerve to the right, then to the left. Every ten yards or so he would stop, pull forward to straighten up and then begin his weaving again. He pulled up well short of the low watermark.

"That's close enough," he shouted.

I walked back to the trailer and began untying the boat.

"Salt rusts hell out of the car if you get too close," he said.

I undid the two thick hemp ropes at the back and attached the nylon ropes which criss-crossed over the top of the boat.

"Mudguards and bottom just fall off," he puffed, lighting up a cigarette.

I unhooked the elasticised bands from under the trailer and unwound the chain holding down the prow of the boat.

"Gets right into the metal. Rots it."

I tried to feed the women's stockings back through the rowlock holes but the reef knots had tightened during the short journey from the bach. I smiled at Carole and she darted forward and picked at the knots with her slim fingers and long nails until they were loose.

"And those sealing sprays they advertise wouldn't work. Bloody useless."

I collected up the hemp ropes, nylon ropes, elasticised bands, chains and women's stockings and dropped them into the boot of the car.

"Not with this salt, they wouldn't."

I took two firm hand-holds on the stern of the up-turned boat and nodded to Morrie, "You'd be right there, Morrie."

Carole moved to the front of the boat, then hesitated.

"Hold on," cried Morrie, "I'll give you a hand – got to be careful you do it right or she scratches." He dropped his cigarette into a puddle and gripped the front of the boat. We lifted it off.

We dragged the boat over the oozing mud to the water's edge. Morrie held the boat to make sure it didn't drift away, on the incoming tide, while Carole and I ferried the lines, nets, buckets, anchor, bait, oars, cutting boards, rod, tackle boxes and finally,

Morrie's pride and joy, his secondhand two horse power Seagull motor, across the mud. Morrie drove the car back across the flats – in a straight line this time – because he was going forward, and I held Carole's hand. Just like kids. It was lovely. Morrie parked the car on the grass verge and hurried back to us. I held the boat still while Carole waded through the water to the front of the boat, lifted one leg over the side, dried it with a towel, eased her weight into the boat, raised her other foot out of the water, dried it, and sat, content. Morrie climbed in over the stern, still in his sandshoes – they oozed water into the well of the boat.

And we were ready. I pushed the boat away from the shallows, stepped in over the side and, while Morrie talked to his Seagull, I rowed us out of the channel towards deeper water.

"Fuel tap on. Two and a half turns for the tank cap. Throttle on a quarter. Wind the cord nice and tight. Give 'er a good choke. Now we're set. Never fails. Most reliable motor on the market. So simple. Only two moving parts. Right, you beauty," and, kneeling on the bottom of the boat facing his beauty, he yanked hard on the starting cord. The drum turned, the motor tipped forward bringing the propellers up out of the water and Morrie sat back suddenly on his haunches. But the engine didn't fire.

"Not enough choke. Always does this when it's cold." He pumped the choke vigorously. Pancakes of slick yellow-green petrol spread outwards on the water beneath the motor. "Now we're right." He rewound the cord, braced himself and heaved. The knot on the end of the cord hit me just below the right eye. Morrie slammed back against my left rowing knee. The boat shuddered.

"Must be the fuel line," he said. His jaw and mouth were working hard, chewing, sucking, twitching.

I stopped rowing. We were half way to the wharf and in amongst the anchored keelers and houseboats. "I don't know much about boat engines, Morrie," I hesitated, "but what about looking at the spark plug?"

And I heard Carole draw in her breath sharply behind me.

"No, no need. Not that plug. She starts every time, that plug."

"She didn't ... it didn't start this time, Morrie."

"That's because it's not the plug. It'll be the fuel line for sure."

"No harm in looking at the plug, eh? What do you think?"

"Be a waste of time, but if it'll make you happy ..."

I rowed the boat into the shore. When we were beached, Morrie unscrewed the spark plug. It was covered in carbon.

"Sound as a bell," said Morrie, "I'll just give her a bit of a polish and then I'll get onto the fuel line." He scraped and brushed the points, dug out the carbon from the well of the plug and refitted it. Then he unscrewed the fuel line. A Shrove Tuesday of pancakes spread in the shallows below.

"There! See it?"

"What?"

"There. Look!"

He had a single grain of sand in the palm of his hand. "That's why she wouldn't start." He dropped the grain over the side and screwed the fuel line back on the carburettor. I pushed us off and started rowing again.

The motor fired first time.

"You beauty! You little beauty!" he yelled and scrambled back alongside the motor and gripped the steering arm with both hands. "Marvellous what one little grain of sand will do, isn't it, eh?" He looked up at me sharply.

"Yes, marvellous, Morrie. I wouldn't have believed it." I put the oars away, moved up to the prow of the boat, and sat, with Carole, feet dangling over the prow.

It was a beautiful day. The harbour was flat calm, and a light warm breeze, generated by our chugging forward motion, fanned our faces. Beautiful. We were passing an island of white, heaped cockle shells. Millions and millions of dead, dry, bleached cockle shells.

"I wonder if there are any live ones underneath?" I mouthed into Carole's ear, and I indicated the heaped mounds. "Fancy burrowing your life away, eating, sleeping and mating ... how do cockles mate?... and all the time with the dead weight of your aunts and uncles, grandmothers and grandfathers bearing down on you."

She laughed lightly, then leant her head against my shoulder.

On the other side of the boat, opposite Cockle Island, was the wharf, festooned with anglers. I waved to the perennially hopeful – little boys, little girls, after sprat and snapper and sharks and whales, but mostly sprat; grown men complete with tackle boxes, bait buckets, cane surf rods and towelling fish hats, impressing the little ones with their mighty casts and far splashes and their nonchalance. The little ones waved back.

Morrie lined up a cabbage tree with a cliff face on the distant hills ahead and the end of the wharf with the Four Square grocer sign on the shop behind, and we were on his "posie". He switched off the motor, and sat back, content.

"This is where the fish are," he said. "Big hole under here."

I looked over the side speculatively.

"Got to be dead right, otherwise wasting your time. Now, we'll just row up harbour a bit to the other side of the channel and put out the set line."

I fitted the oars and began rowing under his direction, tacking and veering as if we were an ocean-going yacht in a minefield. He dropped the sinkers overboard and while I rowed back across the channel, Morrie played out the twenty hooks and baits. He dropped the marker buoy overboard and I began tacking and veering again, back through the minefield, until we were, once again, smack on 'the posie'.

Morrie gave me a few tips – how much weight to put on, how to tie the hook, how to cut the bait, how to bait the hook, how to find the channel bottom, how to "feel" the line with your finger, how to recognise a bite, how to strike during a "run", how to haul them in. It seems there is only one way to do each of these things. And then we put our lines in the water. At least, Morrie and Carole did. I picked up one of the amazingly rectangular pieces of bait that Morrie had cut, and tried to put it on the hook. But it wouldn't do it. The silly bloody thing just kept bending and breaking. Obviously, the wrong kind of bait. I dropped it and picked up another.

And Carole stretched out her hand and took it from me. She leant close, "Now watch," she said, "flesh, skin, flesh … see?" And she'd done it. Just like that. God, I was impressed.

We didn't get a bite for over an hour. We had a few near misses though. At least Morrie did. He swore he could feel the fish sniffing at his bait, nudging it, turning it over. But they just weren't hungry. A slight breeze came up and we rocked gently up and down, swinging around on the anchor. And suddenly we were catching fish. One moment I was playing the game of fishing, holding a line from this world into that other world where fish live, and the next moment a live thing was tugging and heaving, jerking at my stomach, fighting, thrashing and lurching, from another world. And then it was staring at me, flashing red and blue and green and then red again, staring at me, gaping at me. Fish shouldn't have eyes, not live ones anyway. And they should die there, dead, like that, and lie still on the marble slab like a sausage or a leg of ham. But it wasn't doing that. It was gaping and heaving, red to blue to red, gaping and staring at me.

"Kill it!" yelled Morrie.

"Kill it?" I stared at him, aghast.

"Stick the bloody thing before it jags my veins." Bunches of blue-bagged veins disappearing into battered sandshoes.

"Kill it?" I repeated.

"Oh, for God's sake ..." he cursed and reached for my fish with one hand and grasped at the bait knife with the other. He still held his fishing line in the fingers of his knife-hand. "Put your foot on its head," he shouted.

"On its head?"

"Oh, for God's sake ..." and he placed one sand shoe on the fish. "You press here," he said, trying to control his temper, "through the backbone and you ... aaah!" he yelled, "I've got a bite!" and he dropped the knife and yanked hard on the line. "Got 'im!" he exulted, hauling on his line furiously.

My fish skittered off the cutting board into the water in the bottom of the boat. It buckled in a frenzy and sprayed water with its pounding tail. I trapped it between my jandaled feet and edged it out of the water towards the cutting board. I picked up the knife and placed it in the gap between my jandals, carefully manoeuvred the fish, my feet and the knife, so that I could hit the fatal spot. I closed my eyes and plunged. My nostrils filled with a nauseating, rotting stench and green and yellow tubes spilled upwards around the knife blade. Its guts. A stomach wound. The poor thing. I re-adjusted my feet and stabbed again. Eventually, it didn't move anymore. I removed my feet and looked at the carnage I had wrought. There was red, viscous blood everywhere, on the fish, on the boat, on the knife, on me and on Morrie.

"Got 'im!" I said, and I looked up at Carole. She had a strange look on her face. I think she was smiling but I'm not sure.

We caught eight more fish and I despatched my two with frightening efficiency. Then Morrie noticed that the breeze had blown us off the 'posie'. So we moved back onto the 'posie'. And from that moment we didn't get another bite. But Morrie was happy. We were on the right spot.

There was nothing on the first ten hooks on the set line. Most of the bait had gone too. "Crabs," said Morrie as he dropped the line between his legs into the bottom of the boat. He was standing in the prow of the boat hauling the line in while I rowed along its length. The eleventh hook produced a large fish that Carole identified as a Yellowtail and then the line got stuck. Morrie heaved and strained on the line, dipping the prow violently into the water, but he couldn't lift it off the bottom.

"Row us around a bit," he shouted, "come at it from different angles."

I frothed the water but the line wouldn't budge.

"Have to cut it," he said.

"You'll lose too much line and tackle," I said. "Let me have a go."

"You won't move it."

"Worth a try."

"No, you'll never lift it."

"But with you rowing the boat," I suggested, "and knowing the right angles to come at it ..."

"Might work ... might work. Change places then."

And we scuttled past one another. I took the strain and Morrie rowed along the line. It was a dead weight. The nylon cut deeply into my palms and fingers. I heaved backwards. The line lifted slightly for a second, then settled back again. Encouraged, I put all my weight into it, and the line started to come up, and once started, it moved heavily but steadily to the surface.

"It's coming," I yelled. "It's a fish. I can feel it."

"A fish?" shouted Morrie.

"Yes! It's trying to stay down but ... nearly got it ... yes ... here it is. My God, what's that?"

"What? What?"

"Huge. Black. Like a ... like a bird."

And it broke the surface two feet from the boat, just level with Morrie's head.

"Aiee ..." screamed Morrie and he leapt to his feet, swinging the oar up in front of him to ward it off. The boat rocked violently to the side, shipping water. "It's a stingray!" he cried, "a bloody stingray! Cut it off! Cut the line!"

"Cut it?"

"Yes, cut it! That thing can kill you with one flick of its tail!"

I released the strain on the line and it began to run out again. The ray sank beneath the water. I checked the run out. "We can't cut it," I said, "too much line and hooks and weights. And what about the fish that may be on?"

"Can't be helped. Have to cut it."

"What if we pull it into the shore?"

"Too dangerous."

"Not if we let the line out a bit and you started the motor."

"It wouldn't ..."

"That motor of yours would. It would take it, wouldn't it?"

"Course it would, but it's ..."

"Well, let's try it then. I'll hold the line up high while you start the motor."

And so, with great reluctance, he turned to his 'little beauty'. Every few seconds he whipped his head around, searching, making sure the stingray was still in the water, making sure it wasn't climbing into the boat behind him, tail in teeth, ready to cutlass him to the marrow. He started the motor and we planed the ray in to the shore. We hauled the line up onto the beach and thereby became the proud possessors of two snapper, one Yellowtail and a thirty-pound, live stingray.

"No trouble," wheezed Morrie, lighting up a cigarette, "no trouble at all to the little beauty. Knew she'd do it. Now we've got to go careful. See that tail there, and the barb on the end?"

I bent close over the ray and inspected its tail. And it did indeed have a tail to be reckoned with – a long thin. whip- like member with a spiked barb on the end. It looked even more like a bird on the mud than it did on the water.

"One touch of that," said Morrie, prodding the tail with the end of the oar, "and you're as dead as mutton." The tail sprang back into an arching curve as he removed the oar.

"Can you eat it?" I asked.

"Yeh," said Morrie, "the wings, anyway – haven't done it myself, but I've heard other fellas have."

"How do we get it back to the bach then?"

"We can't," broke in Carole, "not with that tail."

"She's right," said Morrie.

"But wouldn't Nancy like to see it?"

Morrie took a deep drag on his cigarette, then he chuckled. "We can't move it till we cut the tail off, and we can't cut the tail off till it's dead." He chuckled again. "So we'd better kill it, eh?"

"Kill it?" cried Carole.

"Well, it's going to die out here on the sand anyway – and I'm not carrying it back to the water," said Morrie.

"So, how do we kill it?" I asked

"No problem. Just hit it on the head. On the brain. Club it like they do game fish. Watch." And he raised the oar high in the air, paused a second and then brought it crashing down on the stingray's head. The oar shattered into pieces.

Chapter 19
Over a bucket of pipis

By eight o'clock the bach was full. They came out of the dark, carrying their bottles and their bowls of peanuts, shining gaudy in their beach shorts and flowered shirts and flimsy blouses that smelt musty when you got close, and they jammed into the din of the room.

Morrie sat in the corner, whisky bottle at his elbow, cigarette in his mouth and ukelele high up under his chin – the way George Formby used to hold his banjo, but with the strings tucked in tight to his right ear. He plucked a chord, made a whine like a car fading around a sharp bend, and started singing, strumming directly into his ear. We sang "You Are My Sunshine". In fact, I don't remember singing anything but "You Are My Sunshine" – but then perhaps it was just that all the songs simply sounded like "You Are My Sunshine".

The ladies went out the back door, clip-clopped in their clogs down the back steps, past the clothesline to the outside dunny where they stood in a row, waiting their turn, all talking, no one listening, and waving every now and then at the people back in the bach. The men went out the front door into the long grass that grew around the roadside power pole, and sprayed the moths in glistening arcs as they spiralled and fell from the streetlight above.

Morrie got onto the spoons. Two large, chrome-plated soup

spoons. Bending forward, his shining head close to the floor, stamping his foot in spasm knee-jerks and castaneting the spoons in a flamenco version of 'You Are My Sunshine'. The soup spoons sang against the backs of his hands, his neck, his puffed cheeks, his teeth, his bum, his neighbour's bum, in a clacking, squealing, lunging lewd harmony.

Carole bent low over the buckets of live shellfish, mainly pipis, her hair umbrellaring down over the water, shutting out the flamelight so that we could see: see the stretching, the easing out of their soft, pink and white feeding tubes, the flecked frilled mouths, pushing out and sucking in. That's what Fallopian Tubes must look like: wetly delicate, the unseen inner life jutting rudely through a crack in the hard shell. Hundreds of them, crowded on top of one another, each still blindly feeding, digesting, urinating, in a bucket. And they were going to roast them alive: drop them onto a searing hot tin sheet and sizzle them open so they could suck them down, blood, tubes, juices and all. I started to feel sick. Carole looked up into my eyes and held my gaze. She smiled uncertainly and then nodded, seeming to understand, to feel with me. She lifted her hands to her face and then plunged them into the blackness of the bucket. They came up again immediately, a pipi in each hand. She smashed the pipis together, splintering the shells and then, coaxing the moving, living flesh out with her lips and tongue, she chewed on the exposed meat.

She smiled at me across the bucket, her teeth flashing white as she chewed. She swallowed, ran her tongue along her lips, above and below, and then leaned across the bucket and kissed me. Mouth half open. Salt, wet and cold on the outside, warm, wet and yielding beyond. I felt suddenly giddy and unbalanced. Her tongue came hard and pointed into my mouth and I clamped my lips on it. She prodded forward, explored to the side, searching, arching. Then she flattened it, warm and fat, filling my mouth, my brain. I became aware of an overpowering, sweet sea tang. I could taste it. I could smell it. But I held on. We stayed joined, making love with our mouths for age-long seconds, flared by the fire, brushed by revellers, over a bucket of pipis. This was how I'd always thought it would be: total, knowing. With absolute certainty. None of your "Does she ...? Will she ...? Am I ...?" In those seconds, we made love more sensually, more completely, than in all the dreams of my young hunger life.

Slowly, lingeringly, she withdrew her spent tongue from my mouth and slid her lips to my ear, "Let's go," she whispered, "let's go for a swim."

"For a swim?"

She nodded her head slowly up and down, brushing her moist lips and tongue into and over my ear. Then she rose suddenly, took my hand and led me away from the fire to the corner of the bach. As we passed under the clothesline she deftly unpegged two beach towels, threw them over one shoulder and plunged into the long grass at the side of the bach. She was immediately swallowed up in the inky blackness in the shadow of the building. I stumbled blindly after her, trying to keep the fluorescent bob of her hair directly in front of me. She ignored the urinating men as she passed under the streetlight and headed unerringly for the path through the scrub beyond to the beach. It was black. I placed one foot tentatively in front of the other, expecting at each step to find myself plummetting into an unseen bottomless pit full of wetas and Huhu bugs.

She had undressed completely by the time I got there and, without waiting for me, she ran down the steeply shelving beach, headlong into the water. Her white, untanned bottom floated momentarily on the surface but then sank into the blackness.

I cursed myself for being so slow and tugged frantically at my clothes, trying all the while to keep my eyes fixed on the spot where I had last seen her. I dived into a breaking wave. The cold of the water took my breath away but then I was immediately lost in the quietness of it, the deep other-worldly silence, broken only by a soft bubbling sound set against a mouse-roar, far away. I hung beneath the surface, rolling with the swell, nude, gloriously bolshie, peeled back, swinging. I kicked my feet hard and broke the surface. And there was nothing but the tilting, rolling dark. She was nowhere to be seen. I turned a full circle in the water, thinking of the emptiness below me, empty but for the fish, gliding silent, sliding through the water. I drew my legs up sharply to my chest and peered down into the murk beneath me. How silly. How childish. Control yourself. I began taking deep regular breaths while all the time using my hands to turn in slow, searching circles. Something white flashed beneath me and then tried to close on my foot. I screamed and leapt convulsively sideways, thrashing at the water to get above the surface.

And she was laughing at me, great gulping shark laughs, at my efforts to get away. I turned to face her and she stopped laughing, treading water, only her sleek head above the surface, looking at me. We drifted towards one another. No apparent movement. Two disembodied heads being pulled together, as if on a string. I lifted my hands and gripped her shoulders. Her body was trembling rhythmically to the stroke of her treading feet. She lay her hands on my hips and pulled me in. I felt the hard points of her nipples against my chest and then the rub of her pumping knees. I lay my mouth on hers and drew her tight. We sank. Clasped together, one flesh, we sank into the bubbling, mouse-roaring dark. I dropped my hands to cup them over her buttocks. They were hard, tight, smooth as polished stone. I kneaded my fingers into the mounds of them. She pressed her pelvis hard against me, ran her hands up my chest, to my shoulders, and then, levering herself quickly upwards, was gone.

I caught up with her as she waded out of the shallows. She stopped and turned, took hold of my hand and kissed me lightly on the shoulder. Before I could respond, she began pulling me firmly up the beach towards our clothes.

She handed me a towel and then raised hers to her head and began towelling her hair dry, watching me all the time, studying me unashamedly, moving a little to the left so that she could get a better view. I lifted my towel to my hair and began rubbing slowly, trying all the time to drop my eyes from her face so that I could see. But I couldn't. Knowing that she was looking at me looking at her, I couldn't. I was vaguely aware of her body and could sense the lift and fall of her breasts in time to her rubbing but I couldn't look where I wanted to look. I couldn't take my eyes from her face.

"Turn around," she said.

I sighed deep inside myself and did as she asked. And she began to dry my back, rubbing the towel gently in circles over my skin, under my arms, over my buttocks, between my thighs, down my legs.

"Now me," she said.

I turned around and for the first time for a long time was able to look at her, albeit from the back but able to look freely, unheld. She had beautiful buttocks. They swelled out from the hollow of her back, round, slightly dimpled, full. Asking to be kissed, nuzzled, licked. I dried her back and shoulders very quickly and then dropped to my knees to dry her legs and those beautiful buttocks. I moved my mouth close and touched her with the tip of my tongue. I flattened it wet against the swell and lay my lips gently on her skin. It rose in stipples – in little hills that I drew into my mouth. It was soft and yielding, but beneath, it was hard, almost erect. I circled slowly, drawing in mouthful after mouthful, then she stooped suddenly and brought her head down level with mine. She opened her mouth and kissed me, holding on to me, sucking hard. Her eyes were open, staring at me. I leaned into her, pressing her backwards onto the sand. She resisted for a few seconds then yielded, and we fell, almost in slow motion. For an instant I felt the warmth and softness of her under me, then she twisted and rolled out. Her mouth was still on mine – working, probing, sucking like a leech. I moved my hand up to her breast and ran the tips of my fingers over her nipple. She caught my fingers in her hand and slowly pulled them up to her throat and held them there. My lips were going numb. I pulled my hand down to release her grip but it tightened, vice-like. I tilted my head back and ran my lips over her neck and into the fold of her shoulder. She closed her eyes. I lifted my leg and lay it over her thigh between her legs. She turned violently onto her side and clamped my leg tightly with her knees and feet.

I couldn't move. I was nude, erect, lying at night on a deserted beach with the woman I loved – who was nude, who was sucking me dry – but who had me hog-tied. My crotch started to sting with the saltwater, and somehow or other I'd managed to get sand under my testicles. With sharp little shells.

Perhaps she'll warm to it. Perhaps she'll suddenly open like a flower, wide petals, waxen. I returned her kisses and moved my hand down from her throat. She clamped it to her breast bone and brought up her other hand to hold it steady.

"Carole," I whispered.

"We ... we'd better be getting back," she said and immediately let my hand and leg go and sat up. She picked up her towel and tied it so they it hung from her breasts. She quickly pulled on her panties and stretched forward for her slacks.

I reached out and held her arm. "Carole," I said again, "what the hell are you playing at?"

"We should ... they'll be looking for us – wondering where

we are," she said. She didn't look at me. She was caught in a half-crouched position facing the sea.

"I don't give a damn about them," I cried, "I'm asking you what you're doing ... to me ... and to you."

She fell forward onto her knees and sat back on her heels, still facing the sea.

I moved in behind her and circled my arms around her waist. Gentle. Just touching. She leaned back against me and rested her head in the hollow of my neck. "Leave him," I said into her hair. She didn't move. "Break it now, Carole ..." I went on more urgently, "It's over. You're free of him!"

"Free? Free of him?" and she looked up at me, and when she spoke again, she spoke softly, almost in apology, "... you don't know what you're saying ..."

"Why? What do you mean?"

"Please! Can we go now? I don't want to talk about it," and she leant forward to get up.

"You don't want to talk about it," I said, my voice rising against all my efforts to stop it, "you don't want to talk about it ... and now you turn off the tap, right? You play me along until I'm dribbling like a schoolboy and then you put your goodies away and shut up shop!"

"I didn't promise anything ..."

"My arse you didn't," I laughed. "It's a little game, isn't it, Carole? Little game of dressing up and parties and holding hands and big kisses if I'm a good boy – and if I'm a very good boy ... is Cliff a good boy Carole? Is he, eh? Is that why you won't give him up, is it? Runs after you like a little Pekinese, does he ... all snuffles and tongue hanging out, right?"

"Yes, that's right," she said, and before I could move, she'd gathered the rest of her clothes in her arms and stepped past me into the dark.

I pulled on my trousers – I couldn't find my underpants – grabbed the rest of my clothes and hurried after her. All I could see was the lights of the bach. The ground before me was pitch. I caught up with her as she passed under the streetlight.

"Carole, please!" I pleaded, and I reached for her arm, "I'm sorry, Carole – I didn't mean any of it, believe me! I apologise ..."

She was crying. She was crying without a sound. I put my arm around her shoulders and walked her slowly down the side of the bach to the steps.

"Oho!" Morrie shouted, spit dribbling from his mouth. He was leaning over the back verandah, trying to balance his elbows on the balustrade, whisky bottle in one hand, his glass in the other. His elbows kept sliding forward so that his chest hit the balustrade. "Oho!" he cried again, "you and Marc been for a little swim, eh? Eh, Carole, eh?"

She nodded up at him and smiled.

"Hey Nance!" he cried, reeling around so that his back was against the balustrade, "Carole and Marc have been for a little dip in the sea. How about it, eh? How about you and me going for a swim and a cuddle, eh Nance?" he yelled and he poured himself another whisky, spilling it down the sides of his glass.

We reached the top of the steps. Cliff was standing in the doorway. Carole took a step back. I dropped my arm from her shoulders – then put it back again.

"Hullo Carole," he said.

"Hullo Cliff," she answered.

"Sorry I'm late," he went on, calm, measured, "I must have been out when you were sending out the invites to the beach – I only heard at the club tonight that you'd invited the genii here down with you."

"She didn't ..." I started.

"Shut up you!" he snarled, "I'm not talking to you!" and he

dropped his voice to a purr again, "Well, Carole? – you did intend asking me, didn't you?"

"I didn't ask anyone," said Carole, so quiet that she could barely be heard above the laughter of the people crowded around the pipi grill. "Dad invited Marc to the beach."

"Dad invited Marc ..." he repeated after her, mimicking her inflection. "Morrie!" he called.

"Yes?"

"Is it true? Did you ask this ... him ... to the beach?"

"I just told you he did!" snapped Carole.

"Who?" yelled Morrie, and he lurched forward from the balustrade until he was standing between us.

"Him!" spat Cliff, not looking at me.

"You mean Marc? Yes ... sure I did ... fishing partner is Marc ... hey!" and he rolled closer towards Cliff, "... you wouldn't believe the size of this bloody stingray we got today – you like stingray? You can have it if you like – got to be forty pounds ... got to be ... you wanna see it, eh? eh?"

Cliff brushed past him and stood square in front of Carole, "Not that it matters anyway, does it?" he said to her, confidential, "It's not the real issue here anyway, is it?" and he bent his head down close to her face. "You took me for a sucker, didn't you? You've lied to me all along – you lived with this bastard in Wales, right? – and you've been sleeping with him here since, right?"

"Wrong!" she cried, "that's just where you're wrong!"

"Aw, come on, Carole! Do you seriously expect me to believe that bullshit? Just look at you! Been for a little swim, eh? A skinny dip, eh? With our fishing friend here – and, you haven't even had the decency to get dressed!" and he yanked at her towel. It fell to her waist, exposing her breasts.

"Hey!" I cried, and I swivelled so Carole was behind me. "That's enough!"

"Enough? Too bloody right it's enough!" he shouted at me, inches from my face. "Carole is going to ..."

"Keep Carole out of this!" I yelled. He didn't move. He was breathing heavily straight into my face. "Can't you see she doesn't want to talk to you? She's had it. She's had you!"   And his reaction took me completely by surprise. He laughed. He laughed all over my mouth, nose, eyes. "How would you know what she thinks? You wouldn't even begin to understand her ..."

"I understand one thing," I said, quiet, slow. "She left you once before – to come to Wales – to come to me – and she'll do it again."

"That sure of her, are you?" and he was still laughing, still enjoying himself. "Well, you'll soon find out it isn't that simple ..."

"I'm going now," said Carole, behind me.

I turned.

"I've been listening to you ..." and she stopped. Her lips were trembling uncontrollably. She stared hard at my face as she fought for control, fought to stop herself from crying. "I've ... I've listened to the two of you talk about me, argue over me, decide what I'm thinking, what I'm doing, where I'm going, who I belong to ..."

"Hey Cliff!" yelled Morrie from the doorway. "Come on! Come and have a look at the bloody thing. You've never seen anything like it! Forty bloody pounds! It's in the trailer," and he staggered forward, grabbing Cliff's arm to steady himself and dropped the whisky bottle onto the deck. It smashed. "Jesus!" he cried, and he fell to his knees to try to save what he could. He grabbed at the largest piece and the blood ran from his fingers into the pools of whisky on the deck. He sat back on his haunches and looked at his hands. "Carole!" he cried. "Jesus! All that whisky ... Carole!"

And Carole let her clothes fall onto the deck at her feet and knelt to help him. She swept the pieces of glass together with her hands and the blood ran from her fingers and dripped into the pools of whisky on the deck.

"What ... what the hell are you doing, Carole?" cried Morrie. "Stop it for Christ's sake!" and he grabbed at her hands to hold them and toppled forward with the lunge and sprawled on top of her. And she cried into him. Into his face and neck. "Wassa ... wassamatta, Carole?" he mumbled. And she wrapped her arms around his neck and hugged him. "Come on," he said, "no crying – we're having a party! I'm having a party – everybody's happy!" and he tried to push her away to see her face but she held on to him tightly. He looked up at me. "Wassamatta with Carole?"

I shook my head.

"Wassamatta with her!" he yelled, and he unhooked her hands from his neck and heaved himself to his knees.

"She's upset, Morrie," I said quietly.

"Upset? Upset? I can see she's bloody upset, for Christ's sake!"

"She ... we've had an argument ... a fight over who ..."

"A fight?" he snarled, "a fight? With my little girl? Well sonny ... well sonny – let's see you have a little fight with me then, eh?" and he lurched to his feet, staggered back against the bach wall and then charged at me, his fists flailing.

Instinctively I ducked and twisted out of his path and he pitched head-first over the balustrade, turning over in the air and landing under the washing line.

Carole screamed and ran down the steps to him. She bent over his crumpled form and immediately started straining to lift him up out of the sand.

Cliff and I arrived at the same time and together lifted him and carried him up the steps and into the bach.

Nancy was clearing the table of glasses and empty bottles. "Still alive, is he?" she asked, matter of fact, emptying an overflowing ashtray into the kitchen tidy.

"He's got a bad gash on the top of his head," I said, and leaned Morrie towards her for her to see. "I'm very sorry, Mrs Meadows, it just happened so fast ..."

"Nothing to worry about. Safest place to hit him. Can't feel the pain anyway – he's anaesthetised. Put him on the bed over there."

"Mum!" cried Carole, "he could be badly hurt!"

"What him?" She stopped, dishcloth in hand, bent over the formica table, and looked side spy at Carole as if she were a small child. "Is he breathing?"

"Of course he is."

"Well then. That's all he ever does."

We lay him carefully on top of the bed. I put a pillow under his head.

"Look," went on Nancy, "the only thing that will hurt him tomorrow will be the thought of the whisky he spilt on the deck. Just let him sleep."

The party broke up rapidly. People melted into the night with their part-full bottles and empty peanut bowls. We tidied up until there was nothing more to tidy, and then I went down to my mattress in the boat pit and lay awake for the rest of the night, wondering where, worrying, wondering what – until near dawn when I must have fallen into a deep sleep because when I woke it was mid morning and Morrie was still alive, moaning and wheedling, lying in bed with a cup of tea, and Carole was gone, in the car, with Cliff.

Chapter 20
Holldrio!

"She's going to Auckland," confided Pearl and she rested her hand on my knee to show me she understood. Her breath was pure gin. She was drinking it neat, the way Russians drink vodka. She'd carried the bottle around with her ever since she'd arrived at the party, and simply kept topping up the glass.

I hadn't seen Carole for weeks. Not since the beach party. She hadn't turned up for the start of the school term and Dave McNeil wouldn't say why – just that she'd asked for leave, indefinite leave.

"Why's she going to Auckland?"

She sighed, took a deep breath and, obviously deciding I needed more comforting, she slid from her chair and sat on the floor between my feet, "Well, she's entering a contest."

"A contest?"

"Shshsh! I'm not supposed to tell anyone."

"But there's only you and me here. The others are all in the kitchen."

"Only you and me," she repeated, and she rose up then fell on my right leg, wrapping it tightly between her breasts.

"What ...?" I exclaimed.

"Shshsh!"

"What contest?" I whispered.

"The Miss Auckland thing." She whispered back at me.

"Miss Auckland contest?"

"Yes, beauty contest. You know – all falsies and lacquer with not a decent tit or bum between the lot of them!"

"What's that?" called Pat. Arch's wife. She stepped into the room and stood looking down at us. "Oh sorry," she said, "I didn't realise ... is this private or can I join in?"

I levered myself awkwardly to my feet bringing Pearl, who was still wrapped around my leg with me. My drink slopped onto the carpet. Pat was smiling at me, with that smile that had unnerved me ever since I'd first met her. She was built like a man – barrel chest, rounded sloping shoulders of a boxer, flat stomach, square hips and straight muscular legs. Not butch – just powerful, a man with melon tits and lipstick. And that smile. She was forty-odd, married with two children, but each time she smiled at me I felt her weigh my testicles in one hand, then in the other, and I was never sure if she found them wanting. "We were talking ..." I stammered.

"Oh yes."

"... about Carole, and this Miss Auckland thing."

"Shshsh!" hissed Pearl into my right leg.

"Oh, don't be silly, Pearl," scolded Pat, "everyone knows. Do you think you could keep a secret like that in a town this size? Well, especially with a mother like Carole's."

"What do you mean?" I sat down again and Pearl dropped back into her slot.

"Carole's mother was at the 'Flower Arranging For Novices' class, with her pine cones and thistle display – God, it was dreadful – she got second prize and hers was the only entry – and she just happened to let a few things slip." She stopped and smiled that smile at me again.

"About?"

"About you and Cliff and Carole and the beach thing. Oh, it was so erotic!" and she crossed her hands over her breasts and cupped them.

"And ...?"

"And ... she'll be staying up in Auckland with her grandmother – shopping, doing some modelling and ... entering, I suppose."

"When?"

"When what?"

"When's she going?"

"Today, tomorrow, I'm not sure – except it's soon, I do know that. Cliff's taking her up ..."

"Cliff!" I cried and stood up, bowling Pearl over onto her back. Miraculously she held on to her drink and bottle.

"Yes Cliff – of course Cliff! Who else were you expecting? God, she hasn't got a third man in tow, has she?"

"What?... no, no, not that I know of."

"I mean, it's always been Cliff, hasn't it? I don't know why you jumped ..."

"Nor me!" complained Pearl and she righted herself. "I wish you'd give me some warning when you're going to do something sudden like that."

"After all," continued Pat, "it was Cliff's idea that she enter in the first place."

"Cliff's idea?" I stared at her.

"Well, according to our budding lady florist – yes. All Cliff's idea. Carole wasn't interested at all it seems, but Cliff kept on and on until she agreed – well, that's Nancy's version anyway. She could have made it up, of course – the reluctant debutante and all that – but that'd be far too subtle for our Nance, for my money – no, it's open your mouth and let it all pour out with our Nance – no time for sub-plots or nuances, just ..."

And Pat's mouth continued to open and close but I couldn't make out a word. Why for Christ's sake? Why would Cliff want her to enter a beauty contest? Put her in the public eye – set her

up for hundreds, no thousands to look at, to admire, to gawp at –
especially the men, for God's sake! Why would he want all those
men to stare at her breasts, her arse, her mound – no, my arse,
my mound – how dare he! And the risk! Why would he want
to take the chance of losing her if she won – being chased by
every Tom … no, every Dick on the island, on both islands? Why?
Unless he's sure of her. Why is he so bloody sure? What's he got
to be so cocky about? – except that it's one certain way of getting
her away from me – breaking it – seeing lots of others, being seen
by lots of others. The devious bastard! He's more afraid of me
than of them! He must be … but why is she going along with it?
Does she want that? To be ogled at? Mentally stripped? Because
she'd be public property the moment she stepped out onto the
catwalk – "Here I am, boys!" … unless … unless she sees it as a
means of getting away from both of us! Well, she may get away
from him, but I can't be got away from! I'll die first! Christ! What
am I saying? Die first? Am I that far gone? Am I that obsessed?
I should go home – right now – fuck it, she's stuffing my life up!
I'll go home to Wales. Mam was right. She knew. Right from the
start. She knew me for what I was – no, for what I am – weak,
soft, vulnerable, living in a dream world – and that one day I'd
wake up. Like tonight. Like right now! I'll get pissed and piss off
home and forget her – that's what I'll do – get drunk … but I am
drunk – pissed – pissed to the eyeballs – with her! I reek of her –
the smell under her arms – I can smell it right now – her sweat –
her juices – they're in my head, in my veins. I'm drunk with her,
for Christ's sake! And I want to be! I don't want to be anything
else! I can make all the fucking promises I like – and it won't
make any difference. "I promise …" – like in Chapel each Tuesday
night at Band of Hope when I was seven or eight, standing and
chanting with all the others "I promise, with God's help, to
abstain from all intoxicating liquor and try to induce others to

do the same!" Well, dear God, by God, I promise now to abstain from all intoxicating liquor – intoxicating love – intoxicating lust – except one – and that one, dear God, I promise never, never to abstain from – but, by God, I'll certainly induce others to get the fuck out of it. Amen.

*

"YOU'LL LOSE HER for certain now – even if she doesn't win. You know that, don't you?"

I nodded dumbly, aware only of the ache of my bladder, holding on.

Pearl rested her head on my shoulder and nuzzled into my neck. "She'll never come back here – she won't spend a minute longer in this one-horse town than she has to. You know that, don't you?"

And she leaned against me, pressing against me, with her belly against my bladder, and I nearly lost it, right there in the hall. I half turned away. She kept talking to me, urgent, close, wetting my neck with her intensity, mouthing moist words while I waited, closed my eyes and concentrated. There was a clank, a rush of water and as I opened my eyes. The toilet door swung open. Haydn stood facing us, smiling inanely. I lurched forward and squeezed past him, groping for my zip. And the joy, the burning orgasm of pain rushed from me, pouring out of me.

"So you may as well forget her and think of me," said Pearl at my neck.

I turned to look at her, startled that she was still there, and sprayed the wall.

"Oh, you naughty boy!" she cried, and taking hold of me she steered it back into the pan. And kept her hand there, guiding the stream, squeezing it agonisingly off then, just as I was about to cry out, releasing her fingers and jetting it free. Playing, turning me off and on like a tap, fascinated, drawing it out.

"Which side?" she asked.

"Which side what?" I murmured.

"Which side do you tuck it?"

"Eh?"

"Most men tuck it to the left, I've noticed," and she folded me neatly inside the zip, holding the gap wide with her other hand, biting her protruding tongue in concentration. Then she straightened, zipped up the fly in one fluid, frightening movement, said, "There!" in obvious satisfaction and patted it in a motherly kind of way.

✳

"SHE'S LIKE MY Mam, you see. All love and soft and ... Oh Duw, I miss her!"

"Who? Who's he missing?" Pearl's voice, near my feet again.

"Carole," answered Pat, at my side, chest to chest, thigh to thigh, leg to leg.

"But he said his 'mam.'"

"Yes, his mother."

"But how ...?"

"And now she's going."

"I know," nodded Pat.

"His mother?"

"No, Carole."

"Oh, hell! I'm going to get another bottle," snorted Pearl and she gripped the arm of the sofa with both hands and heaved. Her body didn't respond, but then her buttocks quivered and rose slowly in a swaying motion until she was parallel to the floor. She stopped to regain her breath. It seemed to take a very long time. She heaved again and her buttocks rose up like a circus tent, a green tent with two camels in it. Her face was squashed against my hand and the sofa arm. And then the camels folded their legs and lay down again, groaning as camels do.

"Anyway," she said to my hand, "it's about time I drove you home."

"Drive me home?" I laughed, "You couldn't drive anyone home. You're as pissed as a newt."

"I am not!" shouted Pearl, and the camels bucked and reared. She thrust her face between my knees, "Pissed as a newt! A bloody newt? Anyway," she giggled, "how pissed can your newts get, eh? I bet I can get more pissed than any man or newt I know. Right Pat?"

"Right Pearl."

"Right. Now, where's my keys?" and she lumbered on all fours towards the kitchen door.

"You can't even stand up."

She turned her head to look at me, still on all fours. "I bloody well can. I can stand up more ... more ... more up than you bloody well can. Go on, stand up then, you bloody newt."

"Right then, I will then!" I cried and I heaved myself to my feet ... and the floor rose up sharply to meet me.

✳

I WAS DROWNING, sinking into an inky blackness, being borne gulping down to the oozing bottom by an enormous weight. I was smothering, gagging, my gaping mouth brimful with the dark – blind, sightless eyes drowning in flowing night pitch. I flailed my arms desperately to get to the surface and suddenly I broke clear, gasping at the night air. My hands came away from my face clutching Pearl's green dress. She was straddling me. In the back seat of her Ford Prefect car. Leaning up against the back of the front seats, her dress high up under her armpits, struggling with a fish. Trying to poke the fish into her little net. But it wouldn't go. It bent against her thighs, slipped soft and boneless between her fingers and flopped jelly-like on its side. Pearl started to swear at the fish. The fish lay limp and lifeless, exposed, out of its element. I willed it to jump, to flicker, but it merely gaped at me. I sank to the bottom again.

I woke to singing – an Alpine soprano trilling the joy of a spring morning in the mountains, all larks and swallows. I smiled to myself and opened my eyes – and immediately shut them again. Oh God! ... I remember! I remember! The larks turned to crows and the swallows cuckooed their spit at me.

"... the White Horse is calling to youuuuuuu..." O Duw, O Mam, O Nefoedd. I promise you God, I'll pray to you every day, I'll never drink again, never touch another woman. Depend on me God, if you'll just ...

Bacon, curling, coiling, smoking, burning.

"In Salzkammergut, Salzkammergut, come what may, Life's as bright and gay as can be."

I opened my eyes again and lifted my head. Soft, white puffballs popped silently in front of me, squirting a dry brown mist into the air. I closed my eyes. But the mist came inside, seeping, settling, filling up my eye sockets. I blinked furiously and forced my eyes to see, to focus. I was naked, except for my socks.

"... you can go a-yodelling. Holldrio!"

I slid off the bed onto the floor. There was one shoe. I crept to the end of the bed, hugging the ground, pulling myself along with my hands and found my shirt and a pair of stays. I inched to the doorway and keeping low, peered around the frame. Which was the worst angle I could have chosen. Pearl was wearing a diaphanous shortie nightie which just reached the humps of her camels. Within touching distance, and three feet above me. I edged back into the bedroom and, keeping as close to the ground as possible – it seemed right somehow – I put on as many of my clothes as I could find – one shoe, a shirt and a jersey. No pants. Which was not really enough. I had to have pants and shoes. I crawled to Pearl's wardrobe and prised open the door. It creaked. I knew it. I knew the damn thing would creak. I held still.

"Holldrio!"

It was full of skirts and dresses, smelling of must and mothballs, and pairs and pairs of high-heeled shoes. Not a single low-heeled shoe. I fingered along and found a pair of slacks – bright green – it must be Pearl's colour. I lay on my back and pulled and jerked them on. They bulged at the crutch, rode halfway up my calves, but they were on. Thank you, God, for camels. Mercifully the zip was on the side. I crawled to the window and looked out. Back garden. High fence. Thank you, God, again. I promise. I eased the catch open, swung the window out and dropped into a bed of chrysanthemums.

I remember very little about the journey home except for the sun and the scoria. The late morning sunburnt unmercifully bright and hot. Which was unreasonable in my view. I should have had an overcast sky or a light drizzle at least. I took my jersey off as soon as I was over the fence. And then I encountered the scoria. It is a mistaken belief that the Ministry of Works sprays tar and scoria on the roads for cars to run on. This isn't the real purpose. They do it to discourage pedestrians. The Ministry gums a tiny fraction to the roads and hides the rest – the millions of razor-sharp. granite-tipped, vicious little metal chips – in the grass, drains and front lawns for the unwary pedestrians. Because it's a well-known fact that pedestrians are unpatriotic. Not bloody Kiwis mate. Whingeing Poms, too lazy to afford a car. Keep the buggers off the roads. My shoeless foot was soon badly cut and bleeding. Proof for you. Soft, white, inferior Welsh foot. Bloody useless. I took off my shoe and put it on the damaged foot. Which was a mistake. It didn't fit of course and my newly exposed foot was soon as ripped and torn as its partner. I sat down in some long grass and inspected it. There were blue lumps in the pad and heel where the furtive little chips had insinuated themselves under the skin. Like the plague. And then I noticed the boys. Three little Maori boys sitting like pigeons on a front fence. Watching me. Saying nothing. Heads in their hands. I stood up. They didn't move. Their eyes seemed glued to my foot. I bent down and took off the shoe, tucked it under my arm and walked on in a purposeful hobble past them. They remained mute until I came right alongside and then the smallest one, four or five he must have been, intoned a deep, almost sad, "Hooray" at me, or maybe at my feet. And that decided me. I turned to face them. "Is your mother or father in?"

The smallest one nodded his head, just once.

"I wonder if you'd ask them if I could use your phone please," and all three suddenly galvanised into life, leapt to the ground and hared into the house.

The taxi sailed straight past us the first time. I saw the driver turn his head and look at me, at us, and then he drove on. One wild-looking Pakeha with green, shiny, short, bulging pants, no shoes, and his three little Maori friends. All in a row. And he said nothing when he pulled up on the second pass. He stared straight ahead through his windscreen. Funny bugger, I thought.

I lay back in the bath and tried to soak it out. Soak out the grit, the grime, and the memories, out. I scrubbed my feet. I lathered my skin. I shampooed every hair on my body. But then I'd close my eyes and Pearl would come sliding into the bath with me, rearing and pulling, plunging and squeezing ... and I'd shampoo all over again.

Still a virgin. By the Grace of God and drink.

Chapter 21
The talk

I waited outside the shop, just enough to the side so that I could look in and keep her in sight but still be sure she couldn't see me past the mannequins in the window.

In desperation, I'd finally rung her at home – and got Nancy. "No, she isn't in, I'm sorry, she's down town buying some clothes for her trip to Auckland, just something to travel up in really as she'd get a much better choice up in Auckland, wouldn't she? I mean, Flair Fashions is fine for Maranganui but when you want to look your best you really have to get the best, don't you? And it wasn't every day ..."

I'd been waiting outside the shop for nearly an hour. God knows how long she'd been in there before I arrived. For one outfit, for God's sake. How is it possible? Either they had too much to choose from or she was hiding. I'm sure I must look very suspicious out here – on the one spot – sneaking looks all the time into a women's clothes shop – if I were me watching me I'd call the police for certain – "Yes, there's a pervert outside Flair Fashions, officer, peering in at the women undressing, I'd say ..."

She's coming out – yes – now, wait ... wait – time it right ... "Hullo Carole."

She stopped as soon as she saw me and took a slight step backwards. Then she smiled a little smile at me, and looked down.

"So, you won then," I said.

Her head jerked up and she stared at my face. "Yes ... how did you ...?"

"Can we go somewhere ..." I cut in, "... to talk?"

"Talk?"

"Yes, I just wanted a chance to talk to ... talk with you before you left."

She looked down again and moved her right foot forward, scraping the ground in front of her, as if she were trying to rub something out. "Oh ..." she said quietly, still looking down, "I don't think this is the right place or time ..."

"Just five minutes, please Carole," and I stepped in closer to her.

She looked up at me again then glanced up and down the street. "Well, there isn't anywhere suitable really, is there? I mean, we can't just stand here in the street ..."

"There's a coffee bar in the next block ... yes? Just five minutes?"

She sat at the corner table while I ordered two coffees at the counter. I kept looking back at her to make sure she was still there, and each time she looked up at me and smiled the same little smile.

I lay her cup very carefully in front of her, concentrating on not spilling any, and sat down opposite her. She added some milk, took a small sip then folded her hands in her lap and looked straight at me.

"Do you remember the soup bones, Carole?" I said, quietly.

"Soup bones ...? Oh God!" and she laughed and lifted her hands to her mouth, "... your mother... your poor mother! How could I forget?"

"And you picking them up and dropping them in her lap!" I cried, remembering it, cherishing it.

"Oh – don't remind me! I was dreadful – simply dreadful!"

"You were lovely," I said, "and beautiful and kind and sensitive

... and you were about to seduce me."

She stared at me, not lowering her eyes this time. "That was a long time ago now."

"Yes, it was – but I'm no different, Carole." I waited for her to say something, to respond, but she continued to look me in the face, then she picked up her coffee cup and sipped from it, still looking at me over it.

"And now you're Miss Auckland," I said, "and off soon, tripping around the country."

"Yes," she said, as if it were a question.

"Why Carole? Why? I'd like to understand."

And she continued to stare at me over the cup, saying nothing.

I stared back and the seconds ticked away. You're going to blow it, boy. Smile, for God's sake! Laugh. Remember the good times again. Don't put any pressure on – no demands – no questions. Think – don't just emote, think! Lower the temperature, just keep her talking. It's the nearest you've been to her in weeks ...

"Do you love him?" I'd said it. I'd actually said it. It wasn't even in my head and yet I'd fucking well said it! Of all the stupid ... well, it's done now. Can't unsay it. After all the promises, all the swearing ...

"No," she said, "I don't love him."

Jesus! Sweet Jesus!

"I've never loved him."

Dear God, Brahma, Krishna, Mohammed, Yahwe, Zeus, Talfryn Rhys ... and any of you others out there ... thank you, thank you, thank you! "You've never loved ..."

"No, never – not that it makes any difference of course – Cliff will still be picking me up in a couple of minutes and taking me home." She put down her cup and sat up straight, "and, on Saturday, he'll drive me to Auckland and drop me off there, ready and eager to begin the Miss New Zealand grand tour!"

She doesn't love him. She never has loved him. Does he know? Has she told him? She doesn't love him! Is this the same girl who bought the Brogues for Shirt-out? Is this the same girl who cried when she saw him in his mother's white high-heel shoes? – who bought the playing cards? – who tricked me, who stripped me ..yes, God Almighty, it is the same girl! It's the same fantastic, unpredictable, loving, ruthless, glorious girl ...

"But I love you Carole," I whispered.

"I know," she said, gently, softly.

"And I'll never stop loving you – do you know that too? I will love you and only you until I die, do you know that? I have no choice."

"Of course you have a choice." she said, and she leant across the table and touched my hand.

"I don't!" and I was shouting, "I can't stop it – you're a drug – an obsession – believe me! I have no choice!" I leant across to her. "No matter what you do – no matter what it costs – no matter what it means for the rest of my life – no matter ... what – I will! Because I must!"

She was staring at me, wide-eyed. "That's crazy," she said.

"Yes."

"Mad."

"Yes."

"... and hopeless. It can't be ... I've told you."

"Yes."

She stood, picked up her bags and her outfit for Auckland and looked at me. "Goodbye, Marc," she said and she patted me on the arm.

"Goodbye, Carole."

ACT THREE

Auckland

Chapter 22
"You Are My Sunshine!"

The bus driver was an immensely fat Maori man in his late twenties or early thirties. He stood next to the rear door of the bus checking off the Monday morning mailbags, parcels, boxes, vegetable cartons and a long, sinister, black pipe with an 'Auckland Hospital Board' label dangling from it. He took my case in his ham of a right hand and, without looking, threw it on top of the pile. He propped the base of a clipboard against his chest, angling it so that he could read the list of names, licked a blue pencil stub tied to the clipboard and ticked me off the list. "Off to the Big Smoke eh?" he laughed. For some reason this was very funny. It threw his companion, a thin, greying Pakeha with yellow stained teeth and a peaked cap, into fits. He had to rest against the luggage door until he'd recovered.

"Yes," I said, a little uncertainly, "the Big Smoke it is," which threw peaked cap against the luggage door again – but he recovered much more quickly this time. It obviously depended on how you said it.

It took the three of us – the driver, me, the parcels and the groceries – four hours to get to the Big Smoke. We stopped at every settlement we came to on the way. No one got on. The driver threw more crates and packages onto the pile until they started falling out again. He went to the toilet in a lonely roadside hut marked 'Gents' and came out eating a meat pie. He must have taken it in with him.

When I closed my eyes tight and could hear only the scream of the engine and the rush of the wind, I remembered that first flashing night, years ago it seemed, when I'd raced through the blackness to a place called Maranganui, all hope, all expectancy, afraid and very much alone. What an incredibly stupid thing to do! To charge off like a risen Don Quixote, armed with a fishing rod, for twelve thousand miles, away from people who loved me, without question. And for what? For dreams. Different dreams. Better dreams. Dreams for going to sleep to. Dreams for waking up to. For Haydn and his green eggs and bread poultice, for Douglas and his pink flamingo dance. For Carole. For Carole. A wisp of a dream. You stretch out your hand and it evaporates in your fingers. So you stretch again. And again, and again, and again until you grasp it. And it's yours. To have and to hold. Forever.

The hotel looked expensive. Too expensive. But it was central, in Queen Street, and it was all that was available because of the school holidays. I unpacked my case, had a wash and went down to the dining room. Lunch had finished. I bought a packet of crisps in the Public Bar and ate them in the taxi.

I stopped the taxi at the entrance to the street, paid him, and got out. It was a tired street. Wilting pinks and faded blues. Bay windows fringed with lace half-curtains; black, cracked concrete drives inlaid with white cockle shells; painted porches hung with painted earthenware pots of geraniums; and tidy, trim, pocket-handkerchief front gardens with an occasional devil-may-care dash of begonias.

I knew I was in trouble. Serious trouble. My plan had been to secrete myself in a convenient copse of chestnut trees at the end of the long curving drive, and wait patiently behind a gnarled bole, hat pulled well down over my eyes, and then, at the right moment, as the carriage pulled up to the front door, step out in front of the horses and footmen, and be greeted with squeals of delight. And all would be forgiven. That had been the plan. But I knew that behind every twitching lace half-curtain in every house in the street hovered a wraith-like aunt or grandmother on the lookout for rapists, or murderers or Mormons or foreigners. I would be spotted, identified, and categorised within moments and the silent, deserted street would hum with the busy news. But perhaps that would be better. At least Carole would know I was there: cold, forlorn, probably starving, certainly sick and as romantic as buggery. Or should I just walk up to the door, knock her to the floor and drag her out by the hair to the nearest tram shelter. Not an easy decision. And that's you, Thomas, isn't it? All eager and puppy-eyed, rushing off to Auckland to win her back but without any real idea of what you were going to do when you got here. You expect her to melt in front of you like an ice-cream cornet, don't you? She's more than likely standing behind one of those lace curtains right now, laughing at you, thinking 'What a silly sod!'

Must be that house with the yellow bird-bath. A bloody yellow bird-bath! Yes, that's the one: number twenty-eight. She'll be in the kitchen: warm, smelling of lavender, wearing a pink and white checked pinafore, with her honey hair tied up in a knot, baking something spicy. Don't be a bloody fool! She's up here to preen and pirouette, all fluffed-up and back-combed for the bright lights. Baking something bloody spicy indeed!

I walked to the dairy at the far end of the street and bought a huge Sally Lunn and a paper. I'm sure the woman behind the counter gave me a queer look. I sat on the low garden wall opposite number twenty-eight and ate the Sally Lunn behind the paper. No one moved in the whole street. Then after about an hour a car pulled up at number twenty-four, and three very old district nurses got out. All in white – except for their weather-beaten faces – and carrying … no, they weren't district nurses, they were bowling ladies, and one, yes, one of them is going into number twenty-eight! She's going to ask if Carole can come out and play bowls! I folded my paper and stood ready. She went up to the front door, turned and looked at me … does she want me to come out and play too?… and then opened the door and went inside. So, Carole's granny is a bowler. Will that make a difference? Should I change my plan in light of this new information? What plan? And what if Carole can't play bowls? She had looked at me. She'll be describing me in detail to Carole right now. In a few minutes Carole will come to the door and… in a few seconds she'll throw it open … where the hell is she? Must be playing the waiting game. Keep me on edge. Make me hurt a little more. Come on Carole! You can overdo things you know. Well, right you are then. Two can play at that game.

I unfolded my paper and walked back up the street to the dairy. I'll have a milkshake. That'll show her. I'll wait till teatime and if she hasn't shown by then, well, serve her right. I returned to my wall and sat down again.

I sat down again. She might have come out while I was having my milkshake. Perhaps I should go across and check. Excuse me Carole, but did you just come out while I was having a milkshake? You didn't? Oh, sorry to have bothered you. No. Stick to your word. You said teatime, so teatime it's gonna be.

I had an early tea. Flounder in batter with chips. Just down the road at the intersection with the Great North Road. He didn't have any vinegar. Fancy a fish shop with no vinegar! Salt he had, pepper, tomato sauce, soy sauce, but no vinegar. The country'll never come to anything. And then there was no tea. Nothing but the ubiquitous coke. Fizzy rat's blood.

Right. Time's up. Coming, ready or not.

I rang the bell, and immediately a white face appeared behind the pebbled glass. Must have been waiting there behind the door. The door swung open and a little person stood looking at me. A little Nancy. Four foot nine if she was an inch. With stick-thin legs and big slippers, like Olive Oil.

"Yes, can I help you?"

"Good evening. My name's Marc Thomas. Mrs ... er?"

"Woollaston. Mrs Woollaston."

"Well, Mrs Woollaston, I wondered if I might have a word with Carole? Carole Meadows?"

"Oh, I'm sorry ..."

"It'll only be for a minute I assure you. I don't want to come in. Just a few words ..."

"But she's not here. You've just missed her."

"Missed her?"

"Yes, she's just gone. In a taxi. Funny you didn't see her."

"I've been down ... where has she gone, Mrs Woollaston?"

"To the T.V!" she cried, surprised that I didn't know, that everyone didn't know.

"The T.V? What do you mean 'The T.V', Mrs Woollaston?"

"The Quiz Show of course," she said, getting a little cross with me, "the one with thingamejig asking the questions."

"Oh."

"Yes, the Quiz Show. Our Carole's a celebrity, I think they called it. Oh, she did look lovely. Cream dress, satin. Matching shoes and handbag. Not too much make-up. Oh, she looked a picture – you should have seen her."

"Yes, I should have. Where is this quiz show, Mrs Woollaston?"

"At the T.V. place, you know – the place where they make them – with the cameras and that. Oh, I've never seen our Carole look more beautiful – and with her sash – she looked so tall! I've never seen our Carole look so tall. I was telling Arthur ..."

"Do you mean the TV studio, Mrs Woollaston?"

"No, Arthur – he's in there now – watching the set. But I told him, it'll be an hour or more yet."

"No, Mrs Woollaston, I meant is the show at the T.V. studio in town?"

"Yes, of course. I said it was – at that place down town. You know, they play music and you tell them what song it is. Though how they know the names of this pop stuff beats me. It all sounds the same, doesn't it?"

"Thank you Mrs Woollaston, you've been a great help," and I backed out of the porch.

"Oh, are you going? Wouldn't you like a cup of tea? Arthur could soon get one going, couldn't you Arthur? Carole will be very disappointed she missed you."

I stopped and came back to her. "Did Carole ... mention me? Did she say anything about me before she left?"

"Oh yes. We were looking at you earlier when you were sitting on the wall over there – must be very uncomfortable I said to her, sitting there all that time, with no one to talk to, and all that way from home, poor thing, I said to her ..."

"Yes, Mrs Woollaston ... and what did Carole say?"

She swallowed hard, then pressed her lips together tight. Her skin puckered, white and trembling. As if struck by God. I stared at her. She stared at me. She was obviously under great strain. Her button mouth ridged and twisted and then, all in a rush, she blurted, "Can't tell you made me promise not to say anything I'm sorry ..."

"Thank you," I yelled and ran. You fool. You bungling, flounder-eating fool. Of all the stupid ... at least she told her not to say anything ... that's something. I'll have to get a bus. I won't get a taxi out here. But where to? The driver'll know surely. Left here. Must be. Towards town. Bound to be a bus stop soon.

Damned dog. I hate wire-haired terriers. Sneaky. Always go for your heels. Bite and run. Yes, there's a bus stop. Thank God. Now!

I stopped dead and spun around, foot up. The terrier almost bent in two in his effort to avoid me but I caught him in the soft part of the belly with the point of my shoe. I felt it sink in. Warm. I'm sure I could feel the heat of him through my shoe. He wailed in surprise and fear, and then he was gone. And I felt a little better. I stood at the bus stop, waiting for a bus that might never come, and warmed myself with the memory of the feel of my foot in his groin. Now there's a nasty thing to do – a nasty way to think. Sick. I shouldn't have done that. I wouldn't have done that before ... before I came here ... before, before, before – there was no before! There is only now, and now isn't chocolates and flowers, pretty cards and being nice to wire-haired bloody terriers! Now is Carole, sole-thoughted, single-minded, one goal.

And a beautiful yellow bus came charging down the hill and stopped alongside me. I bounded up the steps and smiled my best smile. "Could you help me, please? I want the television studio in town."

"You mean where they make the programmes?" asked the driver.

"Yes, that's it!"

"Shortland Street, just off Queen Street."

"Marvellous. One to there, please."

"Sorry mate, we're going the other way. To Avondale. Not into town. You've got to cross over the road and go the opposite direction. Number seventeen."

It took me another frustrating hour to get there and then they wouldn't let me in. Seems it was by invitation only. So, I waited till the red light flashed on, indicating they were live, and then walked straight in. A startled usher, signalling frantically, raced on tiptoe to intercept me but I strode purposefully down the centre aisle and sat in the front row. Why do people always leave the front row empty? The usher retreated to the back. I smiled at him and my foot tingled warm again. It was a brainless show. A gushing M.C. dribbled joie-de-vivre all over the stage, the contestants and the four-piece band. He seemed to be in a hurry, packing as many of his teeth in the half-hour time slot as he could. The audience clapped everything, even his winks.

And she came on. For a moment she seemed dazzled by the lights but then she smiled, direct into the cameras. She ignored The Gush and smiled at the audience. And saw me. And stared at me. Her eyes flicked away and then she came back to me. The smile didn't waver. It was an Oscar performance. She was a natural. She took centre-stage, ignoring the footmarks I could see painted on the floor, and forced the cameras and The Gush to follow her, and finally, when she was ready, when the studio audience and the audience at home had received the full impact, she turned her attention to the little man at her side. I didn't hear what he was saying – something about Maranganui – I was watching her. Watching her chest swell and fall as she breathed deeply, saw the tiny beads of perspiration on her upper lip, caught in the fine blonde hairs, took in the curve and arch of her shining legs in those impossible high-heeled shoes.

The band started playing. My God! How is she going to name any of their silly songs? She's tone deaf. Can't even whistle. And the band played "You Are My Sunshine." I laughed out loud, and her eyes flicked to me again. But when the band finished the extract, she paused for one brilliant second, considered the matter and then, in deep, measured tones, named the song. The audience thundered their applause and I clapped louder and longer than anyone. She named two more ukelele-plucking, spoon-tapping bach songs and then missed the next.

"Oh, what a shame it's been marvellous having you along with us tonight and here's the lovely lady's £30 prize money now let's give our beautiful contestant a big hand for coming along to talk to us and wish her luck in bringing that little old title back here to Auckland where it belongs folks!"

She hesitated as she came opposite me outside the main door. I was sure she was going to say something, but The Gush took her arm and helped her into the waiting taxi. I tried to see if she turned her head to look at me as the taxi took off but it was too dark. And what now fychan? Grab a number seventeen bus and yell "Follow that cab"? What a farce.   Stuffed. By the time I get there she'll be tucked up in bed – and that's assuming there are any buses running at all at this hour. And what about tomorrow? Humpty Dumpty again? Till I fall off?

I must have impact. As she did tonight by God! The confidence! The panache! She took that show by the crutch. And that's what I've got to do – storm in, bugles blaring, and sweep her high into the saddle.

Of a number seventeen bus?

I walked to my hotel. The lift wasn't working so I had to climb the stairs to the fourth floor. Why am I buggering about? Thinking small. Thinking paperboy – when I should be thinking Beaverbrook or Onassis or ... now what would Rainier do? Buy an excursion ticket for two on the Monaco Public Transport system?

I lay down on my bed and closed my eyes. It had been quite a day.

No, the bugger'd throw his Grace into the back of a gold Rolls Royce or a diamond Mercedes, that's what he'd do.

And it hit me – where it should have hit me long, long before. That's exactly what Cliffie did. He bought her with a car! And it worked. So crass, so predictable. I've got more class than that, surely. More finesse. I could not be that amoral, manipulative, now could I?

Of course I could, and will.

Now, how much money can I scrape together? There's my

savings plus my double holiday pay – that makes just over £500 altogether. Not really enough. Now, I wonder ...?

I rang Haydn. He fussed and tut-tutted. Warned me against the dangers of impulsiveness and women, and then finally, with a long sigh, agreed to lend me £200. Enough. Enough for a twin-saddled, exhaust snorting dream of a stallion. Red of course. It had to be red.

I didn't sleep.

*

"AUSTIN HEALEY SIR. Six cylinder."

I slid my hand down her side.

"Only three years old."

I sank into her lap and stroked her leathers.

"One careful owner sir."

She was purring, vibrating under me.

"Dear old lady. Used it for shopping."

"What colour?"

"Red sir, with a black top."

"I'll take it."

"Pardon?"

"Look, I'll be there in five minutes. Don't sell it!" and I dropped the phone into its cradle. God is with me again with a Buy British stamp on his fiery forehead! God is British. God is a red, six-cylinder, two-seater British Austin Healey. Not too sure about the black top bit. But tops are off anyway, eh? I'll buy a ratting hat – one of those peaked ... the price ... I didn't ask the price! Oh God, don't do such things to me!

I slammed my room door shut. No keys. Still inside. No matter. They'll have spares. Lift occupied. Stairs again. She's mine. I've got to have her now. Perhaps they'll bargain. Perhaps they'll give me tick. No way. Bloody Kiwis don't bloody bargain. One price. Take it or leave it. Bloody uncivilised.

"£640 sir. On the road."

I could have kissed him – except he had a moustache. I bet God's got a moustache.

It took the whole morning for me to complete the transaction. Haydn couldn't deposit the money until the bank was open. The bank wouldn't authorise payment until his cheque had been cleared and the damned insurance company wanted verification of my character and identity. Of a Welshman! In the end they gave me a cover note until I got to their office in Maranganui.

I took the black top off the car and draped it over my case in the boot. I sank down behind the wheel and looked through the girder spokes down the length of her bonnet. She fired first time. Deep throaty rumble then a screaming snarl then a rumble again. Then a cough, two coughs – and she stopped. God! The choke. I still had the choke out full bore. I laughed carefree, man of the world, to the grinning salesman and got out and did a quick tyre inspection while she unflooded. We talked ratting hats and he offered me a cloth sun-visor with 'Monte's Mart' on the peak, but I declined. I eased her quietly, gently, past the ranks of pedestrian saloons and wagons in the parking lot – a bit like the queen inspecting the troops – and edged out into the traffic.

Hey look! It's me! Over here. Looking suave, nonchalant, debonair. Feast your eyes madame. Certainly madame. Wiggle your bum and you might earn a ride madame. Listen to that snarl, will you! Makes your genitals do a forward roll. Now cool. All cravat and hacking jacket. Pouting eyes. Bored. Yahoo! Wait till Carole slips her little satin bottom onto this. She'll laugh – with a little catch in her voice – untie her hair and let it stream in the wind – kiss my ear, my neck ... all the way to Wellington.

I turned into the street and moved slowly, majestically, along the length of the painted porches. She'll be watching now. Wondering. Marvelling. What lucky bugger owns that magnificent car? Must be rich, exciting.

I pulled up outside the house, got out, walked up the drive, saw the net curtains in the bay window to the left twitch – Mrs Woollaston, had to be – and knocked on the front door.

And to my surprise, Carole opened the door and stood there in front of me.

"It's you," she said.

"Yes, it's me," I said.

Her eyes flickered up and over my shoulder, at the car.

"Who ... why are you here, Marc?"

"I'm here to offer to drive Miss Auckland to Wellington – that is where the Miss New Zealand contest starts, isn't it?"

She nodded.

"As a chauffeur," I added quickly, "just a chaffeur – no hanky panky, no confessions, no dramas – purely professional service. When are you meant to be there?"

"Tonight. But Cliff's got a big rugby do on this evening – so he's leaving at dawn tomorrow to come and get me."

God is a Welshman. Has to be!

"From Maranganui? Poor Cliff! Well then, isn't that lucky? I can drive you down now, today, if that suits?"

Carole looked at me, then looked at the gleaming red beast behind me.

"Who does that car belong to, Marc?"

"The red one?"

She nodded.

"Me. Bought it this morning. Six-cylinder. One previous owner – dear old lady who used it on the weekends for shopping."

She laughed.

"Well, what do you think? ... I can put the top on to protect your hair, if you like."

"But Cliff's driving up ..."

"You could ring him and tell him you'd been offered a lift – which is true, isn't it? – to save him the double trip. He doesn't know I own a car, Carole – nobody does – except you and me."

∗

CAROLE USED THE phone in her Gran's sitting room.

"Cliff! Hi! I've got some good news!"

∗

WE WERE AWAY within the hour – all dressed and packed and booted. As I sped south, I kept my eyes fixed on the road ahead, not looking at my passenger, except for the odd sidelong glance, perhaps. Exactly the way a chauffeur should behave, of course. The car top was stowed in the boot and Carole's hair was streaming in the wind. And she was loving it. And I was loving it that she was loving it.

∗

WE GOT TO the lake town of Taupo in good time. I bought us a pie, a sandwich, and a bottle of Fanta each at a Dairy, and we ate and drank on the grass next to the lake. There was no rubbish bin nearby so, as a good chauffeur would, I stowed the empty bottles in a bag behind the seats, and took off again.

∗

WE STOPPED AGAIN soon after as we started to climb towards the mountains, as it was getting cold, so that I could fix the hood on the car, then drove on, snug as a bug in a rug. And we talked scenery and pies and the lake and what good time we were making and everything ... except us and where she was going and why she was going.

*

TAIHAPE WAS THE major toilet stop. His and hers in the main street, next to the railway line. Or was that Taumaranui? I was starting to lose track of all the little towns we passed through. Carole had gently coughed and pointed as we had approached the toilets. Beautifully done, I thought.

*

IT WAS STARTING to get dark by the time we reached Wellington. I drove into the centre of town, under Carole's directions, and we found the hotel almost immediately. Wellington, it seems, is not a big place, despite it being the capital of New Zealand. I pulled up in front of the Grand Hotel and switched off. We got out and stretched. I opened the boot, lifted out Carole's bags and suitcase, and deposited them on the sidewalk. A spendidly uniformed Hotel Attendant came out, picked up the baggage, and disappeared into the Hotel. We looked at one another.

"Thank you, Marc."

"My pleasure."

"Where will you stay tonight?"

"Oh, I'll find somewhere."

"Well ... I suppose it's goodbye again."

"Goodbye, Carole. I wish you luck."

There was another awkward moment as neither of us seemed to know what to do next – kiss or hug or ... I knew, of course, exactly what I wanted to do, but I had steeled myself to stick to the plan, to remain strong, friendly, but totally professional. So I just stood there.

Carole turned, gave me a little wave, and went inside.

Chapter 23
The Contestants

I slipped into the telephone booth, picked the receiver, dropped in the coins, and dialled the number written on a piece of paper.

"The Grand Hotel, Wellington. Can I help you?" said a female voice.

Button A. "Good evening. I wonder if I could ... do you have a Miss Carole Meadows staying at your hotel?"

"Carole Meadows?"

"Yes, she's one of the Miss New Zealand contestants ... Miss Auckland."

"Miss Auckland?"

There is a pause.

"... yes, yes, we do, sir. I'll put you through."

"No, no wait!" I gasped, "I don't actually wish to speak to her. I just want to send her some flowers. As a surprise. So, if you could give me her room number ..."

"Oh, that'll be fine sir. If you simply address the flowers to Miss Meadows, care of the hotel, we'll get them to her for you."

"Thank you. Good ... but I'd just like to make sure that Carole gets them, that I've addressed them accurately, so if you could just tell me the room ..."

"I'm sorry sir. It's management policy not to give the room numbers of the Miss New Zealand contestants to the general public. If you'll just send the flowers to the hotel, I can assure you ..."

Efficient bitch.

*

I HAD LITTLE spare money. Not for hotels anyway, so I pitched my tent in a park. Somewhere near the docks. I could hear the hoot and hiss of ships, the clang of shunting trains and the rhythmic shush-shush of heavy traffic. There were lights all around – shop signs, street lamps, ships' lanterns, webs of crane lights, flashing car headlights and a regular Guy Fawkes of twinking neon signs and symbols. And because of the lights I was all out at the eyes. I couldn't see the grass under my feet. I could feel it – soft, smooth. oily damp, giving slightly with a little sucking noise at each step but it was as if everything were invisible from the knees down. I felt the ground rise steeply to my right and I squatted on my knees to avoid the glare. There was a park bench to my left and then a flat piece of ground. I erected the tent by touch, pressing the steel pegs easily into the soft earth with my hands. I locked the car, took off my shoes and my ratting hat and climbed into my sleeping bag. Too dark to change. Too cold. Too buggered. Besides, I'd have to be up early in the morning before the park attendants came on. No watch. Have to be the birds then, or that damned traffic. Bound to wake me. If I ever get to sleep. I lay back in the dark of my tent and willed the traffic away. Dad used to say that you could wake yourself up at any hour you liked if you kept repeating the time you want, over and over, before you go to sleep. Body alarm, he called it. Six-thirty ... Six-thirty ... Six-thirty ...

And it worked. But how the collie could tell it was six-thirty beat me. It licked my arm and wagged its tail. I smiled at it, and immediately it leapt onto my face and licked my eyes and nostrils. "Good doggie. Lovely doggie. Get off doggie – GET OFF!" I could see the dark bulk of someone standing at the tent flap. Probably the doggie's owner. I rolled over my feet and poked my head out of the flap. The day was blinding. I blinked and pulled my head in again.

"Would you step outside, please sir?" Official voice. Important.

Shit. What have I done now? I crawled out of the flap and pulled the sleeping bag high up under my armpits.

Attendant's uniform. Faded, with shining buttons. "And what do you think you're doing here?"

"Doing? I'm sleeping – or at least I was before your doggie woke me up," and I nudged a laugh at him, inviting.

He didn't think it was funny. I could tell. He bent closer, and spat out each word with tin tacks sticking through, "It – is – not – my – doggie – er dog, sir! Do you realise where you are?"

"Yes, I know ... I know I shouldn't be here, but parks should be ..." and I looked around. The crowd was a surprise. Ten to twenty people were bunched in a picture frame gap in the hedge. Looking at me. Business men, shoppers, children on bikes, and a road sweeper. All quiet and still. Not wanting to miss anything. I pulled my sleeping bag higher. "Look, I'm very sorry," I said. "I didn't know where I was last night. I've never been to Wellington before." And then an inspiration, "I'm a Pom."

He nodded in acknowledgement of the confession.

"I'm very sorry – I'll pack up straightaway."

He nodded again.

"By the way," I said, "do you have the time?"

"9.15," he said.

Stupid bloody collie.

∗

THEY WERE SHOWING 'Shane' at the two o'clock session. I tucked my toilet bag under my jumper and wedged it firmly under my arm. Slight bulge. Like a shoulder holster. I sidled up to the cashier's cubicle. Here's looking at you baby. "Just one please." I waited in the foyer till the film started. When the bell went, I slipped into the Gents and sat on the toilet for a long time until I was sure it was safe. Then I ran the hot water into the hand basin and shaved. The hand towel looked dubious so I dried my hands and face on toilet paper. It was very difficult getting my head into the shallow hand basin to wash off the suds but even more difficult to dry my hair with those filmy rectangles that seemed to want to slide and glide over my glistening skull. The floor was littered with sodden tissue, the suds were stinging my eyes and the bell for Interval went. I swept the floor furiously with my hands, grabbed my belongings and locked myself in a toilet by jamming my foot under the door. I sat and waited. The door was rattled twice. Why do Kiwis have Intervals? And why so long? Five minutes would be enough surely? My hair was wringing wet and the soapy water was trickling down my shirt front and down my back. I ducked my head down low so that the water would run directly onto the floor, but I got giddy. You're not supposed to get giddy in that position. It's a time-tested cure for giddiness. "Stick 'is 'ead between 'is knees!" But it made my head swim so I stood up and dripped. I looked over the door at the clientele coming in and out. Funny lot they were too.

∗

I STOOD OUTSIDE the main entrance to the Grand Hotel and the side entrance to the Grand Hotel's Public Bar, and considered the options. I went into the Public Bar. It was ten to six and 'The Swill' was in full flood. The bartenders were furiously occupied with their spurting beer hoses and the bar manager was working the smoking till. I bought a beer and wandered down to the far end of the bar, next to the door that led into the hotel proper. I emptied my glass, placed it on the bar, then slipped through the door into the corridor. It was dark and narrow but there was a chink of light under the door to the right. I eased it open a few inches and screwed my head sideways to peer through. Kitchen. Neon lights, stainless steel and steam. Must be close to the dining room. I closed the door gently and tried the one beyond it. Subdued lighting. Tables. Muffled voices. I pushed it further open. Girls. Girls-barely-turned-women. Hair piled up on their heads like Spanish fans, black eyes, red-slashed mouths. The jackpot.

I pulled the door almost to and listened to the bird-twitter of them. Couldn't see Carole. But she must be there or coming there. Big matron voice calling for attention. I closed the door and stood for a quiet moment in the gloom of the corridor. Now what? I must see her. But even more important, she must see me. Wherever she goes. Wherever she looks. I must be there. In her reality. In her dream. Part of her dream. Like the night.

All I had to do now, was to get in.

Chapter 24
You must have a pen or a pencil

I walked into the kitchen and headed straight for the menu bench. There was a clipboard hanging on a nail above it. I unhooked it, hummed 'The White Cliffs of Dover' to myself – it was the only tune I could think of – and checked the items on the list. There was no pen or pencil. You must have a pen or pencil. The chef was looking at me quizically. I waved to him then smiled ruefully and said, "Some bugger's taken my pen again."

He nodded and shook his head, knowing what it's like, and pointed at a desk near the swing doors to the dining room. I crossed to the desk, took a pen from a drawer and looked through the oval door panes into the dining room. It looked like a doll's convention. They sat perched on the edge of their chairs, listening to Matron. She was talking and smiling, as only some women can do, smiling with the corners of the mouth and punctuating each word with a twitch lift of the lips. But the rest of her face was set, immobile, the eyes ice-cold. I didn't like her instantly. And I knew that, given the chance, given half a chance, she would detest me. An enemy, almost from instinct.

I swallowed hard but there was no spittle in my mouth. I worked my jaws in and out, pushed open the swing doors and strode in. Head down, mind you. Counting the chairs, napkins and side plates. Heads came around, fixed smiles smiled, and then dismissed me. Except for one smile. I could feel it following me. Glued to me. Sucking on to me. It was like a tickle between the legs. I wanted to laugh, to squirm, but I forced my tongue between my teeth and finger-counted the knives and forks on the corner table.

"... you will walk diagonally across the stage," Matron was saying, and back on, there was no smile at all in the voice, "... and stop mid-stage ..."

I turned to watch.

"... spin on the balls of your feet and then step off with your leading foot ..." and she executed one of those perfect, brittle, Parisian-model type turns, upper torso rigid, moving only, it seemed, from the knees down, but letting her hands fly with the swirl of her skirt, "... and then cross to the microphone. I will introduce you, giving your name, province and vital statistics ..." one of the girls giggled "... and then you will give your speech ..." She stopped and looked at me. I turned away and looked at the table again.

"Excuse me!"

I knew she was talking to me. I knew they were all staring at my back. What do I say? How do I get out? How did the old crow know? I picked up a knife and polished the blade furiously on my sleeve.

"Excuse me," she said, and she was at my side.

Shit. I sucked in my breath and nodded dumbly at her.

"What time will you be serving dinner? I need to know how much time my girls have got left before they get ready."

"Dinner madame? Certainly, madame." I scanned the list attached to the clipboard but my eyes wouldn't focus. 'Duck a l'orange', 'Coq au vin', 'Hogget with mint sauce', but no damned time. "Well, madame, I can assure you that we'll be offering you a full à la carte menu."

"Yes, but when?"

"Ah yes, well, any time madame – any time that suits you and your party. Could I suggest seven o'clock?"

"I'm afraid it'll have to be earlier than that. We have to be there by eight."

"Of course you do. Right, 6.30 it is then. I'll let the kitchen staff know." I nearly bowed but just caught myself at the last second and coughed into my hand. "Could I ask madame what time your party would be returning? The management wondered if the young ladies would like a hot drink or sandwiches made available to them in their rooms when they came in?"

"We'll be back by about 11 p.m., but I don't know if any of the girls would want anything at that hour."

I sneaked a look at Carole. She was staring at me with what I would best describe as disbelief on her face. Not horror, not disapproval, not delight – just gob-smacked disbelief. I took it as a positive.

"Perhaps I could ask each young lady quietly what she'd like, while you go on with your fascinating little demonstration, as long as you feel I wouldn't be disturbing you."

"No, of course you wouldn't. That'll be fine."

I exited into the kitchen and leant down low over the menu bench and took deep breaths. Now don't panic. Take it slowly and you're there. She can't expose you – not without causing herself a lot of embarrassment at the same time – and she won't want to do that on her first show evening, now will she? Definitely not. So smile. Keep smiling, and get another list and a pencil. The world's an oyster to a determined man with a sheet of paper and a pencil.

*

"THE MISS NEW Zealand party would like dinner at six- thirty," I said to the Chef, and I turned to go immediately before he had a chance to question me.

"Would they?" he said with heavy sarcasm, "well, that's considerate of them, because that's when we serve it anyway!"

I smiled at him and made a tick on my paper. "By the way," I added, "could the party have a list of what's available from Room Service for later on tonight?"

"Room Service? Crikey, they haven't had their dinner yet and they're worrying about bloody Room Service." He was obviously an Australian. "Pinned next to the phone," he added and turned back to his pastries.

*

MISS NIPPLES GIGGLED nervously when I asked her and looked around at the others for guidance. No tit at all, just nipples. Thin needle points that looked as if someone had sewn them on the outside of her dress. I'm sure she wanted something, but no one helped her, so she declined.

For Miss Mother Earth, pure fruit juice, natural, untouched by hand. She smelt of incense and hidden hair.

I can't remember what Miss Knockers wanted. I can't even remember if she spoke. She breathed a lot.

I felt for Miss Pudding. She was pretty the way some twelve-year-old girls are pretty – fresh, rosy-plump, but I'm sure her girdle was killing her. A spotted dick with round pink currants.

Miss 24 24 24 wanted hot buttered toast and coffee. Lovely smile. Granny's choice.

Miss Teeth, trying very hard, Miss Virgin, Miss French Tart, Miss Lick My Belly Button And I'm Yours.

And then Carole. Vintage Carole. Ding ding, seconds out, no butting or gouging and keep your punches up Carole.

"What have you got to offer?" she asked, sweet and innocent as a daisy ... or a snowdrop maybe.

I paused for what I thought was a tantalising moment, and then read her the list.

"Sorry," she beamed, and then in a clear, ringing voice, she said, "nothing you've got interests me."

To the bone. Cracked open. Sucking the marrow. And inside, I laughed. She didn't mean it in a nasty way, of course, but with all those others there, what else was a girl to say? And she'd smiled when she'd said it. A little lift of the lip. Just enough for me to see. No denunciation. No public shaming. No naming strangers present. Just a little quip between her and me. I understood completely.

I put a cross on my sheet of paper next to her name and stepped back against the wall, studying my list. And looked at her. She'd turned to face Matron again. "Nothing you've got interests me." I chuckled to myself. Oh, but it will, Carole. It will. I will do anything, lie anything, cheat anything – even me – cheat me – I've already done that. I've changed me – you've changed me. I've gone. Disappeared. Oblivious of everybody – except you and me. And I know you want me as much as I want you. You do! And is that so wrong? Is it? Yes, it fucking is! I'm going to hurt me – you – Cliff – God knows who else – and that's love! "She loves me – Yeh! Yeh! Yeh! She loves me – Yeh! Yeh! Yeh! Yehhhhh!" No – not the moaning Beatles bloody love – not the love Auntie May reads in her weekly "True Romance" fantasy – but the real love – the totally self-centred – no, two-centred – addiction that's mine and yours, Carole. You don't know it yet maybe, but you will. You won't be able to stop yourself pouring another glass of me and swallowing it and then pouring another and another until you're absolutely blind drunk full of me. That's love. That's my kind of love – and it'll be yours, Carole. It will, please ...

I mouthed a "Thank You" to Matron, and backed out into

the foyer. I crossed to the Reception desk. She looked up and smiled. Stick insect with lipstick.

"We'll be returning to the hotel fairly late this evening from the Town Hall and some of my girls ..."

"… your girls?"

"Yes, the Contestants – my girls in the Miss New Zealand competition – some of them have asked for a little something to eat and drink when they get in tonight so I thought I'd let you know early to avoid any hold-ups and, of course, to give you some advance warning."

"That's very thoughtful of you. What time do you expect them to arrive back at the hotel?"

"My best estimate – and I'm sorry, but it must remain an estimate only at this stage of the Tour – is between 11 and 11.15."

"That's good enough. And what would your girls …" she laughed indulgently at me, "… like at that hour?"

I passed my list across the desk to her and she copied down the names and their requests – and added the room number to each name. No Carole of course. Absolutely stupid me. Should have anticipated that. They were all in the twenties. Close together.

A light flashed on the telephone switchboard behind her and as she turned to deal with it, I called a hearty, "Thanks very much!" and climbed the stairs on the left to the bedrooms.

They were on the second floor. In sequence. I eliminated numbers 22 and 23 as I'd seen them on the stick-insect's list opposite Miss Pudding and Miss French Tart. I was banking on human nature to help me. An excited, nervous, trusting, hungry, young girl is not going to be so punctilious as to remember to lock her door every time she goes out. She's going to rush headlong, wide-eyed and breathless, hitching up her knickers as she runs, leaving the door … number 21 was unlocked. The handle turned easily and I pushed it open a foot and then immediately closed it again. I can't go on like this. What if someone is inside? What if someone comes down the corridor? I can't be the milkman or a Jehovah's Witness. Or can I? After all, how do they get those free Bibles in the rooms in the first place? No, that'd be Gideons. I'll have to be the Gideons then, won't it? Without Bibles.

And I noticed the large linen cupboard at the head of the stairs. Shelves and shelves of sheets and blankets, pillow cases and towels. Yes. I selected a pile of neatly folded bathroom towels and stacked them high in front of my face. Clever. Serve a double purpose. I craned my neck around the fluffy column and eased open the door of Number 21 for a second time. Case on bed. Clothes strewn everywhere. Make-up on dresser. Light on in bathroom. Light on in bathroom! I stood rock still and listened. There was no sound coming from the room. I crept heel and toe to the light. Nothing. Just left on. Lovely, excited little girls! There was a label on the suitcase on the bed. Not Carole's room, so I turned around, opened the door and edged the stack of towels into the corridor first and then peered around it. All clear. I walked blind past rooms 22 and 23 and knew I'd found it the moment I opened the door to number 24. The Miss Auckland sash was on the bed! It was a sign for me! Had to be.

I returned the towels to the linen cupboard, took out my sheet of paper and pencil and hurried back downstairs to the dining room. They were well into their tinned shrimps and limp lettuce cocktails when I got there. I supervised and fussed, straightened and tucked, fawned and toadied. A regular major domo. In the process I ordered, picked up and, in the gloom of the corridor, ate an extra coq-au-vin and an apple strudel. I was starving. Had to eat them with my fingers unfortunately, but when you're starving ...

Carole didn't look at me. She kept her head down throughout the meal and hurried out to her room and then the waiting bus without a sideways glance. I'd have done exactly the same in her position.

I sneaked back upstairs and let myself into her room, closed the door gently behind me and stood in the dark, listening. I could hear the faint surge of traffic, a boy's high-pitched voice crying somewhere far below, and my own breathing. I waited for it to become slow and regular. I followed each breath in and out, until I became giddy and had to lean against the door frame. The ceiling was flickering in a faint blue haze of reflected streetlight so that I wasn't sure if the dizzy spell had gone or not. I crossed to the windows and pulled the curtains closed. I felt my way to the bathroom door and turned on the light over the vanity.

I sat on the bed. Her sash was gone. Wearing it obviously. Over her shoulder, across her breasts, no, between her breasts, and down to her hips. I pulled her case towards me. Perfume. Sickly sweet. There were only underclothes in it. Dresses must be in the wardrobe. I lifted it onto the other bed, slipped off my shoes, pulled back the coverlet and sheets and climbed in. There was a slight body smell on the pillow. Her smell. I pulled the sheets over my head. It was stronger on the sheets. She lay here last night. Exactly as I am now. Her thighs where mine are. Her bottom, a little higher. I moved up the bed slightly and pressed my face into the pillow, and breathed deeply.

I woke some time later. Lost and startled by the strangeness of the room and by the light. And then I remembered. I had no idea of the time. I got out of bed and pulled back the curtains a fraction so that I could see the street. Plenty of traffic still on the road and streetlights full on. So can't be all that late. Better have a shower. Haven't had one since Auckland days ago. Can't count that headwash in the cinema.

I had nearly finished and was rinsing myself off in the tepid water when I heard her come into the bathroom. She turned on a tap into the washbasin, and then turned it off again.

"Sorry," she said.

By God, she's cool. In public she ignores me, and then in private accepts my presence in her bathroom with aplomb. She must have seen my clothes in the bedroom.

"Come on!" she called, "hurry up. I need a shower after that performance."

What an incredible girl! I think she'll always surprise me. And that's one of the things I love about her, isn't it? I turned the shower off and listened for her. She was running the water again, full bore. Well, if she insists on staying in the bathroom ... I stepped out of the shower and turned to face her. She was sitting on the toilet facing me. Urinating. Only it wasn't Carole. It was Miss Knockers. She gasped and stood up, still urinating. Her hands went to her mouth and then dropped, cupping her crotch. And still she urinated. The liquid welled and dribbled out between her fingers. Then she screamed.

I leapt. Straight through the doorway and into the bedroom. I grabbed my clothes in my arms, dropped a shoe, recovered it, and bolted into the corridor. She was screaming continuously now. Getting higher and higher. Oh God! Where? Which way? Someone is bound to come out any second. I ran to the head of the stairs. No. I can't. Not nude. Not soaking wet. Towels. I yanked open the linen cupboard door and heard the pounding of feet on the stairs below. I forced myself into the cupboard, lengthways, between two shelves, and twisting backwards, pulled the door closed behind me.

After about an hour I knew I had to move. Every limb was screaming. I was choking on the stink of soap and Naphthalene and I was as cold as a corpse. I had burrowed to the rear of the shelf when I'd first got in, pushing the sheets and towels to the front to screen me if someone opened the door. No one had. I'd heard shouting and running footsteps in the corridor outside, slamming of doors and then slowly, gradually, quiet. Quiet enough now to chance getting dressed. I forced the linen between the slats of my shelf onto the one below and, lying flat on my back, wriggled and twisted into my underpants, pants, socks and shoes. But I couldn't get my shirt, tie or jacket on. Not with only a fifteen-inch gap to the shelf above. So I pulled down some of the towels from the shelf above and wrapped myself to keep warm.

There must be two girls per room. Had to be. I know I had the right room. It was her sash, her case, her smell. So they must share. For protection. To stop men getting into their rooms. Sleeping in their sheets. Taking a shower. And looking at them urinating. Through their fingers. I started to giggle and had to bite on a towel to stop.

Poor girl. Poor little bugger. Perhaps I should go out now – covered up a bit of course – and say "Look, sorry! I wasn't flashing at you – I thought I was flashing at somebody else – well, not flashing really – just sharing, being friendly …" She'd have me locked up! Perhaps I can write to her later or send her a photo of the dressed me – the decent me – but the undressed me is decent! What did I do that was so wrong? She saw me nude. Is that so bad? My bits are no more ugly or naughty or huge or carnal or filthy than the next man's – tidier maybe – more … more in proportion for sure, than some of the things I used to see in the showers at school – I mean, some of those hairy sods … no, no, it's not what she saw of me – it's what I saw of her! Peeing. Is that so bad? We all pee. Or die. Archbishops pee. The Queen pees. Animals do it openly – in the street, in gardens – and that's it, isn't it! I made her into an animal. By looking at her peeing. But I didn't set out to look. I didn't know she was gushing away when I stepped out of the shower – I didn't even know it was her – and even if I did – is that so bad? Is it?

*

I WAITED TILL three or four o'clock in the morning before

I pushed open the door and lowered my crippled body to the floor. The corridor was still brightly lit. Very quietly, I finished dressing, then crept down the stairs. At the bottom, I stopped and peeped around the balustrade at the Reception desk. Empty. I took off my shoes to cross the tiled foyer floor to the front door, expecting at every step to trip some unseen alarm and let loose a host of clutching fiends and hellhounds on my quaking back. I snipped the catch and let myself out. And as I lay, sleepless, for what little was left of the night, in the car, I counted the day's achievements. I couldn't think of any.

Chapter 25
There was a bucket in the corner

The next morning I pulled in behind their bus and followed them up the coast road to New Plymouth. Tucked in close behind, like a well-trained puppy. Just outside Paekakariki, at the start of a long straight, I changed down into third and pulled out to pass. And we crept, my car and I, at a snail's pace along the whole length of the bus. Knowing they were staring at us. Knowing they'd be oohing and aahing. Inside themselves. Where the others couldn't see. I stayed parallel to the bus along the full length of the straight, and then roared away. Until the next corner and then I let them pass me. I repeated the manoeuvre once more before New Plymouth. Titillating them. Driving them mad with desire. Like one of those young bulls they use to tease cows into heat.

I shadowed them to their Show, from their Show, and into a coffee lounge afterwards. And all the time they pretended I wasn't there. I could tell. Carole must have put them up to it. They pretended to talk to one another, be engrossed in their coffee, have interesting things to look at.   But I knew. I knew that all the time they were acutely aware of me, but deliberately, consciously striving to show me that I wasn't there at all! I mean, it was obvious. They weren't looking at me so hard that it could only be premeditated. I'd catch most if not all of them not looking at me every time I glanced their way. Oh, it was well done.

Except for Carole herself. Too much for her to keep up right to the end. She made sure she was the last one out of the coffee lounge and as she drew level with me, she stopped, waited until the others were outside and then looked at me. "Your car needs a wash," she said brightly.

"I suppose it does," I said.

"Pity about the wings though, isn't it?"

"The wings? What wings?"

"The wings it hasn't got. We're flying to Christchurch tomorrow afternoon from Wellington. Bye, bye!" and she laughed. Not a big laugh. But not a snide laugh, either. It was a nice little laugh. A from-me-to-you laugh.

And she was gone. But she'd got her message through. She had tipped me the wink, given me the nod. She wants me to meet her in Christchurch! Clearly. Knows I'd need some warning to organise the ferry, and get there in time. You magnificently-devious, testicle-tumbling, glory-stroke of a girl. I'll be there. I'll be there!

I drove back to Wellington that same night, slept in the car outside the ferry building till dawn and was thus first in the queue for the morning car ferry to Picton.

*

THE SOFT MEMBRANES inside my nose were stinging, smarting from the overpowering stench of disinfectant and urine. I tried to sit up but scraped my head against the rough concrete, and with the sharp stab of pain I opened my eyes. There was a bucket in the corner. Galvanised iron with a heavy handle. There were white streaks of acid stain or mould down its sides. It was the only thing in the room apart from me. No furniture at all. No bed, no chair, no table, nothing. Just me lying on a concrete floor with a galvanised bucket. Everything was concrete grey – the floor, the walls and the ceiling. Rough, unpainted and damp-looking, three-inch drain in the floor, running from the end wall across the room and under the door, wooden door, thick, solid with some kind of black hole near the top centre. Difficult to see what it is. No windows. Just a light set into the ceiling with a grill hung under it. For protection? From what? From me? From the galvanised bucket?

The stabbing pain was inside, behind the eyes, running across my temples and down the sides of my neck. I braced my hands across the corner walls and levered myself to my feet. The bile rose in my throat, making me cough, dry and bitter. But I'm not going to use their bloody bucket. Hold on to it. Don't give them the satisfaction.

My feet were numb-cold. They were blue and white, with a tracery of darker blue veins, ridged and vivid. They must have taken my shoes and socks when they searched me. And my belt. Did they think I'd hang myself? From what? From the light grill?

Perhaps they were right. Perhaps I should. I blew it all in one glorious bout of bravado and beer and love and fun and vomit. It would probably have been alright if the audience hadn't laughed that first time. They didn't have to cheer and stamp. It only encouraged me. "Come on, Carole!" I'd yelled when she'd first come on stage, "give them everything you've got!" And they'd clapped and whistled. They shouldn't have done that. They must have seen I was pissed. I wouldn't have climbed onto the balcony if they hadn't clapped and whistled. And then Cliff probably wouldn't have seen me – until later anyway. She'd turned and pirouetted in her skin-tight, glittering ball gown, then smiled and wooed them at the silvery microphone. And we were a team. She smiled, I hipped, they hoorayed, and Cliff was staring at me from the front. Standing and staring.

Perhaps it would have been better if I'd been sick at that point. But some of the men around me coaxed me to the bar and shouted me a few more drinks while the floorshow was on. I know I shouldn't have, but the world was beautiful and fun and exciting, and they loved me. Then Carole came back in a swimsuit – and high, stiletto-heeled shoes. She looked stunning, almost wanton. The impossible shoes threw her pubes provocatively forward and tightened her buttocks so that they seemed as if they had a life of their own. And I remembered those buttocks, wet and glistening, dimpled, swelling under my towelled hands and, of all things, I started to sing. I sang an inspired version of an old rugby song an English friend of mine used to sing and I'd been singing earlier in the pub.

"Be I Hampshire, be I buggery,
I comes up from Fareham
Where all the girls wear calico pants
And I knows 'ow to tear 'em"

And that bloody audience! They went quiet, listening, and then encouraging me, willing me to sing it again.

Cliff was standing in front of me. Cliffie boy. Good old Cliffie boy. Steaming. White. So, I smiled.

"What the hell are you doing here?" He could barely get the words out, past his anger. I knew he was angry. I could just tell.

"And what the hell are you doing here?" I cried, and I nearly fell.

He stepped in closer. He was inches from my face. "I'm not playing bloody games, boy. What are you doing in Christchurch?"

"Doing? I'm doing what I've been doing all over the country, boy. I'm following Carole, boy. Wherever she goes, I go. Wherever she is, I am"

"You're what?" he snarled.

I stared at him. "Didn't you know?" I cried. "Didn't she tell you? Well, well ... what a naughty girl ... fancy not telling little Cliffie! Fancy not ... no – no, that's wrong – what a good girl! What a bloody fantastic girl! She didn't tell you! She kept it a secret – a beautiful secret – between just her and me! Now, isn't that lovely, eh Cliffie? It makes me want to cry – it makes me ..."

And then I vomited. I definitely remember vomitting. All over him.

∗

THE ROUND METAL flap over the peephole in the door slid back and an eye was framed for a second in the tunnel hole. Blue eye, red-rimmed. There was a jangle of heavy keys and the door swung inwards. He was fat, especially under the arms it seemed, from the way the creases radiated out from his armpits across his chest. "So you're awake," he boomed. "Right mate, out you come then."

I followed close behind him, treading carefully over the rough floor, avoiding the drain and then the larger drain which ran down the centre of the corridor outside my cell. For sluicing out, I suppose. We turned right at the end of the corridor into a large room with a counter at the far end. A man was sitting behind the counter but he was partly obscured by a heavy, portcullis grill. I went up close. He was a sergeant. Hunched over an open book. He was writing with great concentration. The tip of his pink tongue darted between his wet lips as he mouthed the words. "Name?" he muttered, without looking up.

"Marc Thomas. With a 'c' for Marc."

And he wrote my name at the top of the left-hand column in the book. Copper plate handwriting. In black ink.

"Occupation?"

"Er … teacher," I said, quiet.

He raised his head and looked at me for the first time. "Teacher," he repeated, still looking at me. I studied my blue toes. He sighed, and then with great deliberation, he asked me my date of birth, address and next-of-kin.

"I'm afraid my nearest relative is in Wales."

He looked up at me again and seemed to struggle with the concept. "It's someone to notify if you get killed or badly injured, and, as you're neither … yet," and he laughed deep, from the belly, and looked at the constable behind me who wheezed and rumbled with him, "… we'll leave it blank. Well, my son, you're being charged under Section 41 of The Police Offences Act 1927." He paused and looked at me.

I swallowed hard. "I am?"

"'Being found drunk in a public place'. You pleading guilty?"

"Guilty? Well yes, I suppose I am."

"That's alright then. Fined £4 and £1 costs, totalling £5. You willing to pay now?"

"Yes, oh yes, certainly I will, as soon as I get my things back."

"The constable will return your property to you shortly. And you can count your lucky stars you're not up on a 'Drunk and Disorderly' charge this morning – or worse. That'd mean court and a possible criminbal record, of course, and you wouldn't want that, would you, being a teacher?"

"No."

"Or worse …"

"Worse?"

"Yeh – bloke called Cliff Walker wanted to charge you with assault – but seeing as puking over someone technically isn't assault, we decided to let that one slide. So be thankful. Someone spoke up for you."

"Someone?"

"Yes, a young lady. She's waiting to see you now in the interview cell. So, get yourself dressed."

*

I SAT DOWN at the table opposite her. She was wearing a simple, white dress, spotless, unsophisticated. Her hair was parted in the centre and fell in long sweeps to her shoulders and then curved up at the ends, evenly, perfectly. I'd never seen her hair like that before. I stretched my hand across the table and with the tips of my fingers I touched the back of her hand. She started and pulled away slightly, then she inched her hand back across the table, until her fingers rested on mine.

Why are you here Carole, sitting on a chipped chair in a drab and dingy police cell that smells of sweat and urine? Because you're feeling sorry for me? Because you love me? Is that why you're here, Carole? If you are – I'm wide open. Walk in.

"Thank you, Carole."

"You don't need to thank me – I didn't really do anything."

"Thank you anyway ... where is Cliff?"

"He's gone back to Maranganui for a day or so – thinks you'll be out of the way for a while." Her lips trembled, and just for a fraction of a second, I thought she was going to smile, but she took a deep breath and went on, "... but he'll definitely be back for the final night at the Dunedin Town Hall."

The final night. Nearly over. What a stunning success! I was unshaven, haggard, unwashed, certainly smelling of booze and vomit, and now I was starting to cry. I could feel the tears well up in my eyes, brim and spill over, and there was nothing I could do to stop them. "I need you, Carole," I whispered.

She rose from her chair and moved around the table to my side. She lay her face down next to mine until I could feel her eyelashes brushing the skin of my forehead. "I know," she said, and she kissed each eye, gently, holding my face in her hands. I didn't move. It was the happiest moment I'd experienced for quite some time. I didn't ask any questions. No chat. No declarations. No nothing. Not even a 'Good luck in the Final'.

And she left.

The sergeant released me, in fact, he waved me off, with no record, just a warning not to do it again, "Count yourself lucky, boyo."

Oh, I did.

Chapter 26
In a wet, grey, plastic mac

When I was eighteen and in my first year at University, I fell in love with the woman who took us for poetry tutorials. She was a post-graduate student with a soft, singing voice, and simply being near her, listening to her, made me happy. It was infatuation, of course. It was lust, and it was secret. Because she wasn't aware of my feelings, and that made it even better. I nursed it and kept it privately warm without once taking it out to show her. In case she smiled understandingly, talked to me about it, and it softened and lay limp between us and died of the cold. One day, I copied out two lines from one of John Donne's 'Songs', and left them in her study cubicle in the library. Unsigned.

**"When thou sigh'st, thou sigh'st not wind, but
sigh'st my soul away,
When thou weep'st, unkindly kind, my life's blood
doth decay."**

And I retired to watch from a distance. She returned to her cubicle, lifted the paper, and read the lines, looked around, hoping to see, and then wistfully, lingeringly, as though she'd been cheated, she sat down. It was almost as if I'd caressed her, held her to me for a moment, kissed her mouth, her throat ... and it was enough. Consummated.

I sent the lines now to Carole by special delivery. And I was drunk with the thought of it. Of her reading them. Of her knowing it was me. Of her sitting in a public place, with strangers all around her, and my words drawing her away, sucking her into our private world. I waited in vain all day outside her hotel.

Early the next morning a bus pulled up outside the main entrance, the luggage compartment was piled high with suitcases, and the 'girls', in topcoats, hats and long gloves embarked. The Tour party was on the move again. To distant and, it seemed, colder climes. I followed closely, anxiously behind, and as the miles fell away, my fear grew. We were on our way to the airport. With no warning or word to me. Doesn't she care? Or is this her way of telling me she doesn't care? Or does she know I'll follow, that I'll be there, wherever it is? Regardless.

They boarded NAC Flight 158 to Benmore Hydro Dam and then, after a few minutes, came back out again and were arranged like a harvest festival fruit display, on the tarmac, up the boarding steps and into the plane, the chunkier pieces at the bottom. And all for one lonely, harassed, local photographer, in crumpled worsted suit, who had arrived late. They smiled and waved and stuck out their left knees the way Beauty Queens are meant to do and held on to their silly hats to spite the gusting wind and scudding rain. True pluck. Like the real Queen. I mean, the English/German Queen, of course. I waved back furiously from the terminal roof but they didn't seem to notice me. Then I got out my road map. One hundred and eighty miles to Benmore! What a ridiculous country. Fancy sticking a dam so bloody far away from civilisation, and then up a mountain! No idea.

I stopped at Timaru and bought two meat pies, a banana milkshake, a pint tin of water-based, white paint, and a real hair paintbrush. Just after midday I crested a brown, rolling hill and caught my first glimpse of Benmore. Not the smooth, shining-white, curve of concrete I'd been expecting, but a tin-roofed shanty town of construction huts and houses, set against a weeping earth scar of clay and rock spillings, mud tracks and slick wet terraces, and pipes, huge fat pork sausage pipes, open at both ends, as if someone had poked a giant finger through them.

I pulled off the road onto a grass verge, opened the paint tin with the tyre lever from the tool kit, took my shoes off so I wouldn't scratch the surface, then climbed onto the bonnet of the car. But my stockinged feet kept slipping off the waxed surface and so I took my socks off too.

I painted "I LOVE YOU CAROLE" in huge white letters, water-based of course, across and down the bonnet. It fitted snugly, with "CAROLE" stretching from one headlight to the other, as if it were made for it. I needed impact, real impact, and I think I got it. In fact, I thought it was beautiful. And persuasive. It convinced me anyway, and I'm pretty hard to win over at the best of times. I wondered if I should sign it but decided, in all humility, that she'd be bound to recognise the style.

I didn't register the first few drops. But as they grew larger and more frequent, I switched on my windscreen wipers and drove on resolutely, willing them to stop. It would only be a shower. Pity to have to put the hood up and spoil my entrance, but it looks as if I'm going to have to. Oh my God, the paint! I swerved off the road and forced the nose of the car through knee-high grass to get as far as possible under the overhanging branches of a large oak-type tree as I could. I stood up. The 'I' was safe. The paint seemed to have dried enough to have withstood the rain. The "LOVE" was streaked with tears, the "YOU" was crying openly, and 'CAROLE', my beautifully positioned "CAROLE" was a river of tears, a funeral of weeping. I yanked the hood out of the boot, pulled it open and hooked it into position with fumbling fingers, and then I leaned far out over the bonnet with my parka tented-out rigid over my arms and head, to keep the fat, wet branch-drops from raining 'CAROLE' away. I stood there stiff and aching until eventually the rain eased and then stopped.

I drove back out onto the road and inspected the damage. The message was still decipherable but it had taken on a sadder, more poignant look that was quite touching. I decided to leave it and trust to her sense of artistic licence.

They were standing inside a penstock pipe when I finally found them. Eleven girls looking about as silly as it would be possible to look – in their high heels, hats and gloves, crammed up the sides of a twenty-foot diameter, bolt-rusted concrete pipe, having their photographs taken again. What panache! What symbolism! What imagery! What crap!

Then they saw me, and they turned as one from the photographer and stared at the car. And I could see them reading, believing, not believing. And they turned to look at Carole. And my stomach began to drop away, began to yaw and plummet so that I felt I was going to be sick. I wanted to be sick. I deserved to be sick. She stared at me for what seemed like moments and then she rested her right hand on her neighbour's forearm and stepped carefully down from the pipe onto the slushy ground and picked her way over the ruts towards me. I wanted to run, to be a little boy again, to say, "I didn't mean it, Mam!" and she'd kiss me and it would be all better. But I stayed where I was and waited. She didn't raise her head from the rutted way until she was standing next to my door. I flinched. Then she circled around the front of the car to the passenger door, opened it, eased herself into the seat and said, "Drive."

"Drive? Drive where?"

"Anywhere. Just drive."

I stared at her. She was looking straight ahead through the

windscreen, not at me, not at the girls, not at anything.

"What are you ...?" I started.

"Drive!" she snapped, and I slammed into first gear and let out the clutch. We skidded and spun across the unsealed wet track and then, as the wheels gripped, accelerated back up the valley road. We drove in silence between raw, clay-banked road cuts and then mercifully came to a copse of dark trees. I slowed then pulled off the road into a siding and switched off the engine.

Carole sighed long and deep, still looking straight ahead through the windscreen. She hadn't looked at me once since getting in the car. And I didn't know what to say. What was there to say? I'm sorry I humiliated you? I didn't think? It was all completely my fault. My doing. So, take what's coming, absorb it. She could only spit at me, cry at me, and the spit and the tears would be more welcome than indifference. Let her. Roll with it. Because I need you, Carole. And that's how it has to be, isn't it? If I tell you enough, if I show you enough, then maybe, just maybe, you'll learn to love me – just like you'd love a helpless animal or a baby – yes, just like a new-born baby. Who can resist a ...?

"I can't take much more," she said. Her fingers were twisting in her lap.

She's going to cry. God make me strong – strong enough to cry too – and then I have a chance. "I'm sorry, Carole," I whispered.

"It's the hypocrisy of it that I can't stand," and she turned to face me. Her eyes had a wild look about them. "They use us, manipulate us. They tout us from one circus to another, and sell us to the public – the good Christian Kiwi girl that every mother would like her boy to marry. I marvel that they haven't asked us to cock a leg and prove we're all still sweet little virgins – not that they'd find many, thank God!" and she laughed, bright and shrill.

And I sang, in my ears, in my eyes, behind my eyes.

"You know," she said, suddenly earnest and evangelical, "they see us as bags of money, tied neatly at the neck with silk sashes. We smile and pirouette and flash our teeth and our boobs and our fannies, and they ... and they rake it in, hand over fist – "Would you like to see a little more, sir? A little more bum? Another pull on the udders perhaps? Certainly sir!" and she was trembling angry, crying angry, and I pulled her gently towards me, and she came until her head was nestled in my neck, and I was stroking her hair.

"They don't even like us," she said into my neck. "If they want a photograph on top of a hill and it's sleeting and blowing a gale then you stand and you smile. We can't drink or dance or go out unless they say so." She raised her head to look at me. Her eyes were almost touching mine and her mouth, her soft mouth – if I pushed out my tongue I would just touch it ...

"They humiliated me – dressed me down in front of all the others – made me feel like a naughty school kid – that day when I went to see you in ... the cell."

I wet my lips and rolled my tongue between. She watched it, then opened her mouth and slid to meet it, drawing my tongue in and swallowing. I drifted. I let myself float and sink in her mouth. And drown. She held me and then slowly, inch by drowning inch, she released me and pulled back her head so she could look. She brought her hands up and cupped my face. "What should I do?" she asked.

Care! Extreme care! Back away and do nothing. She smoulders. She burns. You so much as breathe a careless word and she'll flare and fire and maybe you'll go with it. Soft. "How do the others feel?" I said.

"I'm not sure. The same, I think, only they're too afraid or too keen to show it."

"What do you want to do?"

"Ah, that's just it. What I want to do is to go home ... just go home ... oh, I wish I'd never entered this thing in the first place!"

"Why did ...?" and I stopped. Too late, too late.

Her eyes widened and she looked at me hard, searching my face, and then she shrugged, "Oh, what does it matter why I entered? I did and that's all there is to it." There was a glow and a flicker and then she smiled ruefully, "I'll just have to make the best of it, won't I?"

I smiled back at her, "Yes, you will, cariad."

"Cariad! Yes ... well, cariad, do you think I should drop out?"

"I think that's something you've got to decide for yourself."

"That's no help! You're just avoiding the question."

"No, I'm not ... yes, I suppose I am. You'd never forgive me later if I persuaded you to drop out or stay in."

"Later?" she repeated, and she arched her eyebrows at me, then she smiled, "What are you going to do now?"

"Me? What I always do – what I must do – love you and be wherever you are."

She said nothing for a long time, then she looked up at me suddenly. "When ... when I was twelve, I had my first period," she said. She was looking directly at me – so direct that I couldn't drop my eyes. "I woke up in bed," she went on, "and there was blood everywhere – on my nightie, on the sheets – even down to the mattress. I washed everything. It was early on a Sunday morning and I was able to get it all out onto the line before mum and dad got up. Then I told mum. She didn't say anything. She just gave me a towel – a napkin – it must have been one of hers though I'd never seen her use one. Anyway, I wore it for five days till Wendy, my friend at school, told me I had to change them each day, but it was too late anyway by that time because it had stopped." She dropped her eyes to her hands, watched them work, watched them tear thin strips of paper that weren't there, long thin strips.

"Mum hadn't said a word to me. But it was dad," she said, very quietly, "I couldn't ... I didn't know what to do with the towels when I'd finished with them. Dad used to go through our rubbish – picking out the things to burn – he used to separate the rubbish into piles, inspecting each wrapping for tins or whatever ... so I put them in the bottom drawer of the dresser in my bedroom. For about a year. Wrapped in newspaper. Then got rid of them from the drawer whenever I had a chance – I'd burn them in the coal stove in the kitchen when dad was at golf – or I'd take them to school in my bag and drop them in the school incinerator – I was terrified someone was going to see me – then Wendy told me you could use things called tampons and flush them down the toilet – oh, the relief of it!" she cried. "Like waking up from a nightmare!" and she looked up at me, hesitantly, "do you understand?"

"Yes ... I think I understand."

"That's what I'm in now. I'm caught – and there's no way out! I can't stay – I hate it. I hate what I'm doing to myself. But if I walk out – just think of it! – Mum, dad, all my friends, the town – oh God! I couldn't bear it! I couldn't go back to that school, could I? I'd have to go ... somewhere ..."

"With me," I said.

She laughed. "You keep coming, don't you? No matter what happens, what I say, what I do, where I go – you keep coming ... because you love me."

"Yes."

"I know ... I know," she said, still not looking at me, "and, I know you'll find this difficult to believe after all that's happened, but ... I love you too. I did when I first met you ... and I've never stopped loving you since. Can you believe that? After all I've done to you? After all the pain I've caused ..." She turned to face me, "Don't say anything please ... please ... I know what I've just said

– I know what you must be feeling – because I feel it too … but I've got to get back …" and her eyes filled with tears, "I've just got to – or they won't give me a turn with the class ball at playtime!" and she laughed and cried at the same time.

I held her face in my hands and kissed her eyes, kissed her running tears, until my tears mingled with hers. The tears were of happiness … and I knew that everything had changed – and nothing had changed.

She lifted her head and looked straight at me, "Let's go," she whispered, "… now."

I did a Le Mans start – what else? – with screaming engine and spinning rear wheels – and the familiar horizon visible through the front windscreen disappeared from view. We found ourselves staring at the grey, overcast sky as the back of the car sank rapidly into the mud. I switched off the engine and, like an ancient arthritic, climbed out of the steeply inclined car. Both rear wheels were buried to the axle. I cursed them. I cursed the mud, and Benmore, and Monte's Mart … and then smiled as Carole's head peeped above the hood on the other side of the car, "No! Stay in," I said, "no need for you to get dirty. Soon have this fixed." Her head disappeared back inside.

I took off my jacket and tie and rolled my sleeves up. Which gave me time to think. Now, it should be easy, straightforward. All I have to do is dig it out a bit and get something solid under the wheels. I sat on my heels and began scooping out the mud from in front of one of the buried wheels. It'd be much easier if I could get down lower but that'd mean getting my trousers all muddy. I could take them off. I stopped and thought about that. It had its advantages. But I'd look right silly in shoes and socks and no pants. So I kneeled in the mud and scooped. The going was difficult to start with, because the soft surface mud kept seeping back into the hole and filling it up, but then I got down to the drier sub-surface and after about fifteen minutes had dug two sloping ramps each about three feet long in front of the rear wheels. There was no sign of Carole. I collected twigs and branches from the nearby trees and spread them under and in front of each rear wheel. When I was satisfied, I brushed myself down – which was a mistake – because all I did was to spread the mud in a bread poultice over my legs – and climbed into the driving seat. "Should be right now," I said cheerily and closed my eyes for an instant and in the blackness, I winged a fervent prayer into the void.

I switched on the engine, brought the revs up to a high, even pitch, slid the gear lever into first and slowly let out the clutch. The engine noise deepened, the wheels began a wet whistle and then bit on the branches and we jerked forward. For two feet, and then we began to sink again. I switched off immediately. It wasn't going to work. Branches weren't enough. I needed something more solid for the wheels to grip onto.

Carole was smiling uncertainly at me. The smile flickered like one of those old silent movies.

I reset the branches then got my sleeping bag out of the boot and lay it under one wheel and then my jumper and pyjamas under the other. I stuck my head through the side window into the car. "Carole, er, would you mind ... giving me a hand please?" Her expression didn't change, except I'm sure she went a little paler.

"If you could get out of the car and ... oh, take your topcoat and gloves off first, I think ..." She climbed out and lay her gloves then her coat on the seat. "And just ... push – just a little – it won't need much, but a push and a little lift perhaps at the start would help us get going. Do you mind?"

She shook her head slowly from side to side, the way children do when they're too frightened to speak.

"I'll put her into gear and when I yell, I'll let out the clutch and if you could lift and push on the bumper at that exact moment. What do you think?"

She nodded.

"Unless you want to do the driving and me the lifting?" I said.

She shook her head vehemently.

"Right then, good," and I got back in behind the wheel. I switched on again, put her in gear and looked through the mirror. Carole was bent over the rear bumper, straining forward. I brought up the revs, yelled, and let out the clutch with a jerk. The wheels spun. And then, the beauty! The little beauty leapt forward, skidded momentarily, and swept onto the road. I laughed and shouted in triumph.

Carole was still standing where I'd last seen her. But she had changed. She was covered in a wet, grey, plastic mac. From head to toe. Except for the pink holes of her mouth and eyes. Like a fresh-dipped, Grey and White Minstrel.

What could I say? Sorry? Naughty wheel for spraying little Carole? I kept on getting an image of Al Jolson down on one knee, his mouth wide open on mid 'Maaammy!', and I had to turn away in case she saw it too. I offered her the topcoat and gloves but she didn't want them. She just stood there, with her arms stretched out in front of her. I picked up my jumper and started wiping the excess off her face and hands and that seemed to bring her to. She took the jumper off me and began cleaning herself – the way a cat does, using the jumper like a paw and rubbing and smoothing the mud away. Then she put on her topcoat and said, "You'd better take me to the hotel." Just that. No tears. No recrimination. No anger. Just ... acceptance, and perhaps a smidgen of resignation.

*

MATRON WAS STANDING in the foyer of the hotel, hands on hips, pelvis thrust forward, waiting for us. We stopped in front of her. She looked Carole slowly up and down, ignored me, and then half-turned and pointed towards an open doorway behind her. "Step inside the manager's office, if you please. I'd like a word with you in private, my girl," and, without another glance, she strode into the office.

Carole followed her to the open doorway, then stopped and went no further. "I'm covered in mud," she said.

"That, my dear, is obvious, and I dread to think how you ... and this person ... got into such a state. However, that is not my immediate concern. Come in and sit down."

"I'm sorry," said Carole, "but I'm soaking wet, my clothes are filthy, I'm filthy, I'm freezing, and I have no intention of talking to anyone until I've had a shower, washed my hair, and changed my clothes."

"It appears you do not understand the situation, Miss Meadows," snapped Matron, and then she turned on her lip- smile again, "we need to discuss a few things ..." the corners of her mouth twitched, "... in particular, the terms of your continued presence in the Tour Party."

Why couldn't the silly woman see the smoke? It must have been stinging her eyes, choking her nostrils.

Carole turned away from the doorway and headed for the stairs. "I'll be in my room, if you want to talk to me later," she called, and then she turned to me, "come on up, Marc. You can have a shower too," and she smiled a twinkling smile, "you haven't had one for a while, have you?"

"That person ..." cried Matron, "is not to go to your room!"

Carole continued up the stairs as if Matron hadn't spoken, then stopped halfway and held out her hand towards me. I walked to her, took the proffered hand, and we went up the stairs.

We had no sooner stepped into the room when Matron burst in behind us. She stood in front of Carole, shaking from head to toe, and pointing her index finger at Carole's chest, and then she hissed, low and sharp, fighting for control, for calm, "I warn you, if you do not ask this ... intruder, to leave your room, and if you do not come down to my office immediately, I will recommend to the Tour

Promoter that you no longer be regarded a member of the Tour party and be sent home immediately."

And Carole started to sway slightly in front of her, as if to some unheard music. She let her topcoat fall from her shoulders, stepped out of her shoes and hooked her fingers in the top of her skirt, and worked it down over her hips. When it got to her feet, she stepped out of it, and whirled it, without taking her eyes from Matron's, onto the bed behind her. She unbuttoned her blouse and shrugged out of it in one movement. Matron started to back away but Carole followed her and, swaying in circular movements, she pulled her panties down, first one side, then the other, until they were at her knees, then she quickly whipped them off and threw them towards Matron. They floated to the carpet. But Matron had already turned to go. Carole quickly stepped past her and stood between her and the door, "That's what I think of your Tour," she cried, "and your Promoter, and you. I'm out – and I wish to God I'd never been in."

"That's not your decision to make!" snapped Matron.

"Oh yes, it is! I resign. Effective immediately," and she reached behind her to undo her bra.

Matron pushed past her, and without another word left the room.

Carole watched her go, her hands still bent behind her. Then she looked at me. Looking at her. She followed my eyes down, and laughed, light, happy, and finished taking off her bra. Then, very deliberately, she looked down at me. I didn't need to look. She turned and walked to the shower. "You'd better have a shower too," she said. She reached in and turned the water on. She picked up a towel and wrapped it around her waist, then seemed to change her mind, undid it and dropped it to the floor. She stepped into the shower cubicle and pulled the curtain across behind her, but immediately poked her head back out, "After me," she said, "when it's cooled down a little perhaps."

Chapter 27
No choice

It took me all morning to remove my poem from the bonnet of the car. I'd wanted to keep it permanently – as a public testimony, as an avowal, as a pledge – but Carole had just said "Off", so off it came. With buckets of soapy water, a tin of lacquer thinners, hours of gentle rubbing and a procession of motel onlookers who all wanted to know why.

*

I KNEW THERE was something badly wrong the moment I opened the door. Carole was sitting on the bed facing me, the half-packed suitcase she'd been filling when I'd left, still gaping open next to her. Her face was grey. She opened her mouth to say something then darted her eyes across to the window. Cliff was sitting on the sill, leaning against the architrave. Relaxed. At home. As if he'd been there for a long time. And he loved my entry. He grinned at me and hugged himself around the shoulders, rocking slightly back and forth. I crossed to the bed and sat alongside Carole and pulled her to me. He tutted loudly and seemed amused, shaking his head in wonderment. No one said anything. Incredibly, we all three sat there looking at one another, waiting for something to happen. I had no idea what had been going on before I arrived, but he seemed full of himself, confident, dangerously at ease – as if he knew something that I didn't know or that Carole didn't know – or perhaps that she did know. And that seed of a doubt in the back of my mind started to swell and grow. He shouldn't be so smug, so superior. He must know what's happened, what Carole had done. Nancy, or more likely Morrie, must have rung him immediately Carole was off the phone – otherwise he wouldn't be here now. So why be so bloody cocky?

I could wait no longer. "Well, well," I said, and I smiled my best smile at him, "... if it isn't good old Cliff! Fancy seeing you here then. Passing through were you, and decided to drop in? Morrie or Nancy must have told you where we were, presumably. Now, isn't that nice of Cliff, eh Carole? Looking up old friends like that," and I cuddled her to me, both arms around her shoulders.

I thought his control wavered just a fraction, but then he gave a little laugh and muttered the words, "old friends", almost to himself, laughed again and shook his head.

And the burgeoning seed split and sent out shoots.

I went on, relentless, "You may as well stay and have lunch with us ... before you go on to wherever it is you're going – don't you think, Carole? – I mean, we've got time, haven't we?... for old friends anyway ... before we start the drive up to Picton." I turned to face him squarely, "Sort of holiday – you know the kind of thing – a kind of pre-honeymoon honeymoon."

"Stop it, Marc!" whispered Carole, "please stop."

But I had to push him ... I had to know ... had to find out what hold he had on her – had always had on her. "You know the kind of thing I mean, don't you, Cliffie? – night here, night there, indulging ourselves a little – you must have done the same kind of thing yourself some time ..."

"Marc!" screamed Carole.

"Oh, let him be!" cried Cliff, and he got up off the window sill and took a step towards me. "Let the silly bastard prattle on ... he'll change his tune soon enough."

"Oh, you've got something to tell me! Isn't that exciting! Well, fire away!" and I sat down, waiting.

He moved past me to look at Carole directly. "You have told him, Carole, haven't you?

"Told me what?"

He ignored me. He kept staring at Carole, bobbing his head up and down, in encouragement. She didn't move. He stopped bobbing. "No ...?" he exclaimed, astonished, "... I can't believe it. Do you mean he doesn't know anything at all?"

"Carole?" I whispered, and I crossed to her.

She looked up at me. Her face had collapsed. She looked lost, beaten.

"Oh, go on, Carole!" he cried. "Don't be shy! Tell him!" And then without waiting for her, he stepped back and looked me straight in the eye and announced brightly, with relish, "Looks like it's going to have to be me! You see, our dear, sweet Carole here is the mother of a healthy, bouncing baby ... my baby."

There was a sharp intake of breath from Carole beside me.

I didn't take my eyes off him.

"Didn't know that, did you?" he laughed, "... not many people do – nobody at school, nobody in Maranganui – not even Nancy and Morrie, hard as it is to believe, and ... you can bet your bottom dollar nobody here on this Miss New Zealand thing ... oh no ... and do you know why?" and he squatted down on his haunches so he could be at the same level as me, so I could see, so he could see, "... because your lovely, sweet, innocent little Carole ran away so that she could have it on the quiet somewhere – so no one would see her get big and fat and pregnant. And I was the one who had to fix it for her, of course. Good old Cliff. Not good enough to marry – oh no – not good enough to acknowledge as the father – but good enough to find somewhere for her to hide." He leaned in close to me and whispered confidentially, "She stayed with my sister in Melbourne. For the whole pregnancy. And at nine o'clock in the morning, February 6th last year, she had a baby girl – sorry, we had a baby girl. And then ... and then," he stood up, "she gave it away."

"I did not give her away!" cried Carole, spinning around to face him.

"Left it," he said, smiling at me, "walked away and didn't look back ... Penny her name is ... and she had her first birthday ..."

"Stop it!" she screamed, and she was on her feet, facing him, daring him to say another word. Then she turned to me and shook her head violently from side to side. She was crying, she was crying so hard that she couldn't speak, couldn't say what she desperately needed to say. "She wanted Penny," she gasped, and she stopped and closed her eyes, breathing quickly, "... Marilyn, his sister, wanted her right from the moment she knew ... I was pregnant. She and Dave couldn't have children, could never have children, so she asked me – pleaded with me to carry it full term – not to have an abortion ... so I did." She sat down again on the bed, not looking at either of us. "I saw her only the once – when they brought her to me after the birth. Then Marilyn and Dave took her." She looked up at me sharply, "I'm not blaming them ... that's what I agreed ... and they said it'd be better if I didn't ... see her too much. So, I left," and she started crying again, in herself, without a sound.

I stretched out my arms and pulled her into me. I pulled her in so tight that her crying racked through me, making me cry with her. I lifted my hands to her face and eased her away from my shoulder. I kissed her eyes, her nose, her cheeks, her mouth. "And is that it?" I said to her softly, gently. "Is that why, all along...?"

She didn't answer. She just looked at me.

I released her and turned to face Cliff, "Is that it?"

"What do you mean?" he demanded.

"Is there anything else I should know?"

He stared, not comprehending.

"I mean, you've told me that Carole's had a baby – and she gave it to someone who desperately wanted it. What's so terrible about that? And the fact that it was your baby, that you were the father – well, biologically speaking anyway – was an accident, a miserable, regrettable accident."

"Keep your smart-arsed opinions to yourself!" he snarled. "No one is interested ..."

"Oh, but that's where you're wrong!" I shouted back at him, "it's your opinions that aren't wanted – you lost your right to have an opinion when you let Carole carry a child – your child – for nine months on her own, give birth to it in another country, go through the agony of adopting it out – and where were you? Where were you, eh? I'll bet you were sitting on your fat arse back in your little home town rugby club swigging beers with the boys, right?"

Jackpot! His mouth was working furiously but he said nothing – could say nothing. He started to move slowly towards me.

"And all you've done since, is to throw the blame onto Carole, heap the guilt ... no, no ... worse than that – you've used the baby – you've used your knowledge of the baby as a weapon against her, as blackmail, to threaten her ... to hold her!" I cried. "Oh, my God! Now I understand so much ... now I understand why you wanted her to enter this ... this bloody Tour in the first place – why you pushed so hard. It didn't make any sense – but it makes complete sense, doesn't it Cliff? Oh yes – complete sense to you, you cunning bastard – because you knew they'd throw her out if they found out about the child – they'd disqualify her, humiliate her. But that wouldn't happen, would it Cliff? – because you had complete control, didn't you? – because only you could expose her – only you knew! Jesus!"

He made a sudden move towards me. I circled around the bed away from him, determined to say it, to get it all out, to exorcise it once and for all. "Well, we're not interested in your opinions, Cliffie!" I yelled. "You're finished. You've blown it. Carole's not frightened of you any more – because you've used your trump card! You've used it! You've told me, and – listen to this, Cliffie – I love her all the more for it! All the more! Do you hear me? Now, what more can you do to her? It's over, Cliffie! You're over, Cliffie!"

His face was fused with blood. The veins in his neck were swollen and corded. There was one large blue knot at the side which was pulsing ominously as if it were about to rupture. Then he charged straight at me, blind, massive, and I backed away as he came.

My mind told me he would be like a crazed animal, easy to outwit, to dodge, to play with. But somewhere deep in my stomach, I also knew that he wouldn't stop until he had blood, that he would die in his fury, senselessly, brutally, like the crazed animal that he was.

I waited until he was almost on me and then I stepped quickly to the left and flicked his shoulder to help him on his way as he blundered past. He struck the wall, turned, winded, and then lowered his head to his chest and charged again. I didn't need to feint this time as he wasn't even looking. I sat down suddenly on the bed and as he lurched past, flaying his arms, I threw out my leg and he crashed headlong into the dressing table, shattering the glass. He came up streaming blood from his forehead and cheekbones, and he was crying. And I knew it was not from the pain of his cuts or the fall, but from inside – from his anger, his frustration, his humiliation.

And Carole knew it too. I heard her cry out, and in that cry, I heard her anguish, her hurt – she must have cared for him once ... when he needed her ... when he was vulnerable ... and I instantly knew what I had to do. For her, for him, but most of all, for me. I had no choice.

As he surged towards me again, I swayed away to the right and then just as he came up to me, I swayed back into his path. And my head exploded in shards of white and orange glass. The top of his skull smashed into my throat, driving the air from my lungs. I knew I was falling, but all my thought, all my energy went into my need to breathe, to force some air through my paralysed throat into my lungs. I was drowning numb, and then I started coughing, and with the coughing came the pain. Pain that came in waves from my back, from my spine, that made me gasp in fear, and then, with each successive wave, it began to subside, to fall away.

I opened my eyes. I was on the floor, on my back. I couldn't see Cliff but I knew he'd be coming. This is what he must have hoped for, dreamed of. And he came. I heard him first, panting and wheezing above me and then he dropped on me, fell on me the way boys do when they're fighting, all arms and legs and excitement, wallowing, pig-happy. He hit me with his fists and his elbows. He hit me in the face, on the shoulders, on the chest. He slapped me and missed me, hitting the floor with flat thwacks, even hitting himself in his excitement. And I took it all. I rolled with the blows, timing them, anticipating them, counting them, and the pain seemed to blur, seemed to melt into me. I pressed my chin into my chest to protect my throbbing throat and let him gorge himself. Then suddenly he stopped, and was still. I opened my eyes and looked at him. He was sitting astride my stomach, his face only inches from mine, staring at me. Then he heaved himself to his feet and stood over me.

"Get up, you bastard!" he panted, his voice coming in fits and starts as he gasped for breath, "get up and fight me," and he dropped his hands low in an ape-stance and waited.

I gathered my legs under me, turned over onto my side and levered myself to my feet with my arms. He brought his bunched fists up in front of his chest and crouched. I dropped my hands to my sides and straightened my back, then my neck. He feinted at me. I didn't move. He lunged forward and swung a wild, haymaker of a right hand. I saw it coming and closed my eyes. It burst into my face below my left eye and I felt the skin split and tear open, and then my legs gave way under me. And I heard Carole's voice shouting my name, and crying.

The waves didn't climb so high this time.

Cliff was screaming at me. I could hear the sounds but I couldn't make out the words.

He wants me to stand again. I don't know if my legs will hold me. If I get on my knees first, it'll be easier.

He didn't wait this time but caught me as I got to my knees. On the mouth and nose.

I don't think it's broken. Doesn't feel like it's broken.

What does a broken nose feel like anyway? Never had one.

He's yelling again. And screaming. He's kicking me. My God, he's kicking me! The stupid bastard's kicking me. I've won, Cliffie boy! Hands down. It's a rout. Don't stop! Keep kicking. Both feet, boyo, both feet!

She's mine now. Wedded. One flesh. One body. She can feel the kicks. I know she can.

And I smelt her scent, her yeast body smell, wrapping me round. She was crying and swaying, hugging my head to her breasts. Nursing me. Suckling me.

"Cariad," she whispered.

Chapter 28
Plastic strands

The midwife arrived at 6.28am. I had the door open before the echo of her knock had faded from the hall. I'd been waiting behind it, not knowing if I should go out and meet her on the street to hurry her along, or wait in the flat with Carole. Carole had won. She'd grabbed my hand during her last contraction. That had settled it.

I ushered Megan in and showed her into the main bedroom. She smiled, called out, "Hi Carole!" as she walked past the bedroom door and took her stuff into the kitchen. "Right," she said, "now why don't you put the kettle on while I have a little chat with Carole?"

"I want to be there, Megan, as you know, throughout – and Carole wants it that way too, if that's OK."

"So you've said, and that's fine by me as long as you stay out of the way and let Carole and me do our jobs. Agreed?"

"Agreed. I'll put the kettle on then. I've boiled lots of water already, just in case."

"That's nice," she said, and she disappeared into the main bedroom.

I quickly filled the jug, switched on the element, and followed her into the bedroom.

Carole was sitting up in bed, Megan standing next to her, holding her hand, "... and how many minutes are we down to now then?" she asked.

"Five minutes," said Carole, "and regular – which is why Marc rang you – as you suggested."

"I certainly did – so, well done! I rang Doctor Richards before I left, and he said he's on his way. So, let's get ready for him, shall we?"

And so it began. Only Doctor Richards didn't arrive till after it was all over. There's men, for you.

Nancy wasn't there either, of course, nor Morrie. They were back in New Zealand. Thinking of us, of Carole, they said, in Wales. Didn't want to fuss or make more work for us, said Nancy. And we were perfectly happy with that. Well, I was happy with the midwife and her reassurances that everything was perfectly normal and home births in Britain were best if things were normal ... but, deep down, I think Carole might really have wanted to be in a Nursing Home in New Zealand, and have her mother there – though she never said a word of this. We'd escaped New Zealand for Wales and both been teaching, me for nine months, Carole for eight. She'd insisted. And when Carole insists ...

But this was a different Carole now. She was staring at Megan, not saying anything, just staring.

I stood in the corner, as out of the way as I could be, and watched her. I knew she was scared. Very scared.

Megan unpacked her things and laid them on the bedside table and the floor but kept glancing back at Carole as she worked. When she was done, she moved up close to Carole and lay her hands on her shoulders, and massaged gently.

"You're very tense, Carole," she said. "Are you feeling light-headed at all? Pins and needles in the fingers?"

"Yes, both" said Carole, very quiet, as if she didn't want to admit it.

"Thought so," said Megan, "you're pulling your shoulders up towards your ears, and the muscles in your neck and shoulders feel very tight to me, so we'll work on that, shall we?"

She sat next to Carole on the bed and took her hands in hers. "You're breathing in short, sharp gasps, Carole, so let's change that – now, breathe in, through the nose ... and hold it ... and out, through the mouth, slowly – a long breath ... and again ... in, through the nose ... and out ..."

And Carole followed her instructions, breathing in through her nose – and then gasped as a contraction hit her, and she continued to gasp, with her mouth wide open, through the spasm.

Megan glanced at her watch and then stood, calmly watching Carole panic. Because that is what she was doing, I could see it clearly. The moment the contraction had started, her shoulders had lifted and the panting got more and more rapid.

When the contractions had subsided, Megan turned and looked squarely at me. She smiled, then, still looking at me, said, "I've got an idea, Carole. Why don't we use Mr Useless here to help a little? Seeing he's doing nothing at the moment, and seeing he's so keen to be here ... do you trust him?"

And despite herself, Carole laughed – a short, strangled laugh – but a laugh nonetheless.

"Would you join us please, Marc, next to Carole?"

I quickly moved to the side of the bed, close to Carole.

"Now, take her hand, and breathe in, through your nose ... and hold ... and out, through the mouth ... slowly."

And I did as I was told.

"... and again – in ... hold ... and out ... brilliant! But Carole – sorry to have to tell you this – but you're going to have to open your eyes, and look at Marc ..."

Carole's eyes popped open and she stared at me.

"That's better," said Megan. "Now, breathe with him ... at the same time ... in ..."

Carole stared at me fixedly and followed me ... in ... out ... in ... out ...

"Yes," said Megan." "He's quite good at it, really, isn't he? For a man anyway ... now, in Marc ... and out – blow softly into her face ... yes ... now keep going like that please."

I was concentrating so hard, so focussed, so regular, and slow, in ... and out, and blowing gently into Carole's face ... that I started to get giddy. The room went fuzzy, and moved just a little, like a shimmer.

And Megan stared at me and laughed out loud. "He's swooning, Carole! Swaying! You wouldn't believe it," and she laughed again. "Now, relax, both of you. Re ... and in ... laaax, and out, re ... and in ..."

The giddiness slowly faded, and the room stood still. I hadn't realised breathing was so complicated and so difficult – dangerous even.

We kept the duet going from that moment on – until the next contraction, and this time it was much better – Carole didn't immediately lurch into panic breathing, she stayed with me, taking long, slow, measured breaths. The pain was probably no better, no less – how would I know? How could any man know? But I felt better anyway, and a little proud of myself, if I have to admit it.

But then the real pain began, and Carole rolled her eyes to the ceiling, flushed red in the face and neck, and started to push.

"Don't push!" cried Megan, her head somewhere down between Carole's legs, "it's not dilated enough! It's too early, Carole. I'm sorry, but we have a fair way to go yet."

Each time she'd get a contraction, Carole closed her eyes, and moaned. Not a cry. Not a scream. More a deep, subliminal, maybe primordial sound, a sound I'd never heard before. I'd thought all mothers, giving birth, cried and screamed. De rigueur. Not Carole. She pushed and she heaved with a strength I would not have believed, and moaned.

For hours.

She strained so much that soon, both eyes were bloodshot.

And she started to get desperate.

It grew and it grew.

In her, and in me.

"Megan," I finally blurted out loud, "is there nothing you can do?".

Carole opened her eyes and stared at Megan. She said nothing. No words. But her face ...

"Actually, yes, there is," said Megan. "Countries with high standards in birth care – Canada, Sweden, Australia, and here in the UK – use a blend of fifty per cent oxygen and fifty per cent nitrous oxide to treat pain in labour."

"Nitrous oxide?" breathed Carole.

"Isn't that the gas dentists use?" I said.

"Not in quite the same dosages," said Megan, "but basically, yes, laughing gas."

"Laughing gas?" This from Carole.

"How does it work here?" I asked.

"In much the same way – Carole might still feel some pain – but she won't be as upset or as anxious about it. It doesn't put you to sleep – you're aware of everything that's going on."

"And it's safe ...?"

"Yes, completely, as far as we know. I use it quite often, and it helps."

"Side-effects?" I wasn't letting go.

"None, it seems – apart from making the mother feel more at ease and talkative perhaps – but don't count on side-splitting laughter."

"Carole?"

Carole looked at me, took a long breath, then nodded.

"Right you are then," said Megan. "I'll get the canisters. They're in the car – I didn't presume to bring them in when I arrived. Only be a few ticks ..." and she left.

And Carole and I breathed and breathed together.

*

"NOW, IT'S SELF-ADMINISTERING – you decide if you want it, when you want it." Megan held the mask up for Carole to see. "You simply place it over your mouth and nose, and breathe normally. Want to try?"

Carole reached her hand out tentatively and took the mask from Megan, placed it over her face, and held it there.

And within ten to fifteen seconds, I swear, I noticed a softening, a softening of her forehead, her jaw, her shoulders.

"And when you've had enough," continued Meagan, "just drop it on the bed. For some women, it's enough sometimes just to know it's there."

Carole didn't drop it. She held it in place, and kept it there until the next contraction came. When it was over, she lifted it up, held it a little distance from her face, looked at it and smiled, and said, "Mum never talked about me being born. Never mentioned it. It was like I was delivered in a van from a shop one morning." And she put the mask back on her face and took a long, slow breath.

A few minutes and a few contractions later, she opened her eyes again, took off the mask and said, as if there been no interruptionat all, " ... and sex was off the agenda for mum, as soon as I was born ... and for dad, of course ... twenty three years ago ... poor dad ... he was always complaining about it, without mentioning the word 'sex', of course ... twenty three years!" and she started to laugh, "so, when I ..." and she stopped mid sentence, and clamped the mask back on as a contraction started.

"You're doing great!" said Megan when the contractions had subsided, "but when the next one comes, I want you to push, push gently, to start with, yes?"

Carole nodded and lay the mask on the bed. "So, when I got pregnant ... the first time, I mean ... not with Marc ... with ..." and she took a deep breath, "... it was a surprise ... a complete surprise ... I didn't connect ... I know that sounds silly, unbelievable, but it's true ... I didn't connect," and she hid behind the mask again. As was her way.

✳

AT THE END, there was a problem. Megan decided that Carole needed help as the baby's head was too big for the opening, so the opening had to be enlarged by cutting slightly. The perineum. I wasn't a hundred per cent sure what the perineum was, but clearly, she did, and that's all that mattered really. She'd told me what she intended to do and told me she wanted me to help her. Was I up to it?

Yes, I was up to it.

When she cut, the pressure from the baby to come out might propel it out quickly, she said, and she wanted me to catch the baby if that happened.

And that is exactly what did happen. Megan cut, Carole pushed, the head emerged, and the baby, our baby, shot out into my hands.

It lay in my hands. Pink and blue and grey. With streaks of bright red blood. I held my breath at the wonder of it. At the sheer, mind-boggling beauty of it. At my daughter, our daughter.

Tears rolled down my face, and Carole immediately assumed something was wrong, and breathed, "No!" and I shouted, "Yes! It's a girl and she's absolutely beautiful and she's perfect!"

Megan lifted our daughter up out of my hands and lay her on Carole's stomach. Carole looked down at her, and then she cried too, cried with joy, with happiness.

What a pair!

Then I saw the umbilical cord. And I did not believe. It was like a cable, an electric cable, made in a factory, bought in an electric shop, with different coloured, plastic strands. The twisted strands or tubes were white and muted blues.

All made inside a woman's body, of a woman's blood, and nutrients, and life. It didn't seem real. It didn't seem possible. But it was.

And so, Helen was born. Sister to Penny.

Mount Snowdon, Wales

Mount Ngauruhoe, New Zealand